The **1066** to Hastings

The **1066** to **H**astings

being superfluous

Chronicles of **B**rother **H**ermitage

by

Howard of **W**arwick

From the Scriptorium of
The Funny Book Company

The Funny Book Company

Published by The Funny Book Company
Dalton House, 60 Windsor Ave, London SW19 2RR
www.funnybookcompany.com

Cover design by Double Dagger.

Explore the whole sorry business and join the mailing list at
Howardofwarwick.com

Another funny book from The Funny Book Company
Greedy *by Ainsworth Pennington*

With incandescent thanks to
Susan Fanning
Karen Nevard-Downs
Lydia Reed
Claire Ward
Mary

The 1066 to Hastings

Contents

The 1066 to Hastings

Caput I

Descended Upon

The people of Derby came out of their various houses, hovels, taverns and other people's houses to watch as the procession went by. It was usually a saint's day when there was so much activity in the street. Folk were worried that they'd forgotten one and that the priest would punish them; again.

They knew that Saint Everilda was coming up. Or was she the one they'd just done? It was hard to keep track sometimes. Perhaps this was Saint Alkelda.

They enjoyed Saint Alkelda's day, when the ladies of the town could re-enact the saint's strangling by Viking women. There was always a healthy competition about which of the women folk would play the Vikings and which the saint. As enthusiasm for the part frequently got out of hand, the competition was usually around not playing Alkelda. With no one putting themselves forward, the Viking women had to spend the day strangling one another.

'Where's the relic?' One small boy called out in disappointment.

Some of the adults now noticed that there was no relic being carried high, so this couldn't be a saint's procession.

Saints had to have relics, otherwise what was the point? It was the highlight of the day, seeing a box with a finger in it, or even a whole arm sometimes.

Of course, they didn't actually have any decent relics in the church of Derby, they had to rely on visiting bits and pieces. On very special days, some really important relic would be taken around the country for everyone to see and marvel at; and pay a coin to get close to.

The priest at Derby did his best, but following a stick that once poked the body of a dead ass that might have carried a saint's luggage wasn't the same at all.

Satisfied that this was not a saint's parade, the locals speculated about what on earth was going on.

There was a cart in the middle of the road flanked on each side by half a dozen men in uniform of some sort. They marched like soldiers but hadn't killed anyone yet, so perhaps they weren't. It was a grand cart as well, more like a small hut on wheels, solidly built and obviously well maintained. Whoever was inside this thing must be someone of great import.

The small boy wondered if it might be a living saint, hence the absence of relics. While this was an admirable piece of thinking, his elders and betters pointed out that all saints had to be dead, didn't they? And a cart like this would be no use to a dead saint, would it?

Most remarkable of all was the fact that the thing was being pulled by horses; two of them. The people of Derby hadn't see two horses at the same time for as long as they could remember.

Old Jeb reckoned he had seen two horses go by once, but most agreed that he'd seen one and then saw it coming back again.

The main vehicle was followed by a gathering of men and women, all of whom walked with upright demeanour, ignoring the common folk of Derby completely.

'They must be Normans,' someone said to widespread agreement.

There really wasn't anyone who would be parading anywhere these days if they weren't Norman.

As this clearly wasn't a church procession, it had to be a noble of some sort. And everyone knew that the only nobles still standing were Norman. The fact that they hadn't been nobles when they arrived at Hastings was irrelevant. Now they were, having very effectively separated the previous nobles from their nobility; and from their heads, in many cases.

'They don't look like Normans,' an observant woman pointed out, sounding quite bitter about the fact. This was Margery, whose skill as a Viking strangler was so renowned that the sheriff had banned her from three years of Alkelda days, a punishment about which she still nursed resentment.

Mistress Wenna had nursed a bruised throat for three weeks and hadn't been able to talk for a month.

But it was true, those marching along the street of Derby did not look like Normans. For one thing, the men did not have the ridiculous Norman haircuts that looked as if the owners had gathered the local population of hedgehogs and persuaded them to stand still in the middle of their heads.

They also lacked the horrible helmets, hideous swords and the long shields that could knock a man senseless on their own.

For another, they displayed completely the wrong attitude for Normans. These folk were marching along in silence, ignoring anything around them. They weren't threatening the locals with death or stealing anything they could get their hands on.

No one had been punched, kicked, robbed or simply taken away for some awful purpose, never to be seen again. Definitely not Normans, then.

But who else could they be? Someone suggested Scots, but as no one had ever seen a Scot, they didn't know what signs to look for. These people had one head, two legs and two arms, Scots were bound to have more of one or the other, so probably not Scots either.

The word "Spaniard" was whispered about, to much alarm and trepidation. A worried pall fell over the crowd as they gaped in wonder, until it was noted that these people were walking and everyone knew that Spaniards could fly.

Every known nation of the world was now thrown into the mix and dismissed just as quickly. French was only another name for Norman, apparently, so that didn't count.

The Welsh would have brought a dragon with them, the Cornish were all pixies and the Irish could appear and re-appear at will, so why would they have a cart at all?

Eventually, having no more names to come up with, someone shrugged and said, Saxons?

That really did throw a silence across the street. The crowd considered the passing horde with new eyes, eyes that found recognition after what felt like years of hardship under their cruel new rulers.

Saxons. Yes, these were Saxons. Saxon nobles marching up a street in their own land. Armed and mighty, well, unarmed but still quite mighty. With two horses and a cart. Joy of joys.

Word of the identification spread and the crowd was soon cheering the return of the Saxons. Perhaps King Harold was in the cart, having been not killed at all. The Normans had been lying all this time, they hadn't won the battle near Hastings; typical bloody Normans.

Wild speculation soon became fact as it was reported categorically that Harold had been raised from the dead by Saint Alkelda and now had the miraculous power to strangle a Norman with a single glance. That would stop them bothering humble folk.

Old Jeb disappointed everyone by reminding them that the Saxon nobles had been just as good at stealing and threatening with death.

Ah, but they were our own Saxon nobles, was the reply. It was perfectly right and proper to be robbed by your own people. Having some foreigner come over here and do it was simply not on.

The people in the procession did not react to the cheers and encouragement of the crowd, but simply continued on their way.

'Where they going then?' a voice called out.

'To get rid of William,' the reply came, to more wild cheering.

'Put Harold Godwinson back on the throne,' another cried.

This got a cheer that was a little bit more muted, as people started to recall what the Godwinsons had really been like.

'Where's the headman?' Ern, the landlord of the tavern asked. 'He should be dealing with things like this.'

Someone found the headman, loitering towards the back of the crowd and pushed him forward.

'There you go,' Ern encouraged. 'Find out who they are what they're up to.'

'They're nearly gone now,' the headman said, sounding as if he wished they'd called him earlier.

'Well run then,' Ern suggested, sounding as if the headman

had been hiding at the back on purpose.

By the time the headman had made it into the street, the last stragglers of the procession were passing by. These were the humblest looking servants, maybe even slaves; the ones who probably weren't allowed to walk with the main contingent as they made it look bad. By their appearance, their main employment would be cleaning things; things which were disgustingly dirty to begin with.

'Where you off to then?' the headman enquired.

One of the most revolting of the men or women, it was hard to tell which was which, sniffed revoltingly and looked surprised to be spoken to.

'Just passing though, is it?'

The man looked around to check that it was him being spoken to. 'How would I know?' he said in the sort of voice that belonged to someone who had to do horrible things for his living.

'You're in the gathering.'

'You don't think they tell the likes of me where we're going or what we're doing, do you? All I have to do is clean it up afterwards.'

'Where have you come from, then?'

The man nodded his head back down the road. 'That way,' he explained.

'Oy,' a voice called from further up the road. 'What are you doing talking to him?'

A very smart looking fellow strode back from the main body of the train. He looked ready to issue instruction to all and sundry.

The headman held his ground.

'I am the headman of Derby and I want to know what's going on.'

'And you talk to the likes of him about it, do you?'

'I don't know what the likes of him is, do I?'

'You can smell what the likes of him is.'

'Perhaps someone who isn't the likes of him would care to explain then?'

'Certainly not. And stop obstructing our passage.'

'I'm not obstructing anything. It's you obstructing my street.'

'Well, we'll be off your street just as soon as we can. Wouldn't want to loiter here.' The man looked up and down the street of Derby and clearly did not like what he saw.

'That's good then. Pass along quickly now.'

'We shall pass along as quickly as we please.'

'Are you Saxons?' The small boy had wandered over and was gazing up at the smart dressed one.

'Of course.' The man had more time for a small boy than he did for the headman.

'Cor. We thought all the Saxons was dead.'

'All dead? You're a Saxon and you're not dead.'

'All the important ones, I mean.'

'No, no. There are plenty of important Saxons still alive.'

'What you doing here then?'

'We have come to meet someone very special.'

'What? You couldn't tell me that?' the headman complained.

'You didn't ask respectfully.'

'Who you come to meet then?' the boy enquired.

'The new king's own high appointee.'

'That what who?'

'King William? You've heard of him?'

'We've all heard of him. You haven't got strangling Harold in your carriage then?'

'Strangling Harold?' the man looked a bit lost now and seemed to be regretting that he'd stopped to talk to anyone at all.

'King Harold. Come back from the dead to get rid of the Normans.'

'Oh, I see. No, I'm afraid not.'

'Shame. I'd like to see Harold strangling some Normans.'

'You'd better be on your way then,' the headman instructed. 'There's no king's high pointers here.'

'This is Derby, you said so yourself.'

'Yes, it's Derby.'

'Then we have arrived. As it happens, you may give me directions to the one we seek. I imagine he resides in a manor house nearby.'

'Manor house? There ain't no manor house in these parts. Not anymore.'

'A castle then.'

'A castle? I don't know who you're looking for, but I think you might have the wrong Derby.'

'The man we seek must be a significant personage in these parts.'

'If you told me who you was seeking, I might be able to help.'

The man looked a bit doubtful about whether he wanted to share this information with the headman. Or with anyone else for that matter. 'There is the question of confidentiality.'

'Not very confidential, you lot marching down the street with a cart and two horses, is it? And the whole town gathered to watch you go by.'

The man took the headman by the elbow and steered him away from the boy. 'We seek,' he looked up and down the street to check no one was in earshot. He even dropped his voice to a whisper 'We seek the King's Investigator.'

'Ha,' the headman shouted his amusement.

'Quietly.'

'Quietly? There's no point you being quiet about the King's Investigator. We all know him and where he is.'

The man looked a bit disappointed by this. 'Well, I suppose he must be a most influential figure in the town. Just direct me to his dwelling.'

'Direct you to his dwelling? Oh, yes, I can do that.' The headman smirked as he said this. 'Well, I can tell you where he lives.'

'Good.' The smart Saxon was showing growing signs of impatience with this impudent headman.

'And he's called Brother Hermitage.'

'Who is?'

'The King's Investigator. Young fellow. And his name is Brother Hermitage.'

'Odd name for a monk.' The man appeared to be quite surprised by this.

'Well, he looks like one and he talks like one, but you can make your own mind up.'

'I see. I suppose he must be a learned fellow. That would make some sense.'

'Oh yes, definitely learned. Not sure what he's learned about but there's lots of learning in there. None of it's much use to anyone, but he seems happy enough.'

'And where is his home? In a holy community nearby? A monastery?'

'Not exactly.'

'Not exactly? What does that mean?'

'I suppose I should say exactly not. He lives somewhere that is exactly not a monastery. Har har.' The headman was enjoying his moment.

'Tell me, or I shall ask some of the guards to come and help you out.'

'Wat the Weaver,' the headman said and burst out laughing for real.

'Wat the Weaver?' The man went rather pale and looked quite offended at the same time. 'What does Wat the, erm, that man have to do with anything?'

'You've heard of him then?'

'I may have come across the name.'

'Seen any of his works?'

'How dare you? Certainly not. I wouldn't dream of even glancing at anything of that nature.'

'No, of course you wouldn't. There's lots would though.'

'I can imagine.'

'I'm sure you can. Well, that's where the King's Investigator lives. So if you want Brother Hermitage, you'll have to speak to Wat the Weaver.'

The Saxon was having trouble taking this in. 'The King's Investigator, King William's own investigator, lives with Wat the erm...,'

'Weaver. That's it. The one who did all those naughty tapestries of people without their clothes on. That's the one.'

The smart Saxon man's mouth was hanging open now, which gave the headman another good laugh.

'And young Cwen,' he added to the obvious confusion.

'Cwen?'

'She's a weaver too; she makes sure we're very clear on that. They all work together.'

'Wat the Weaver, a woman, and the King's Investigator? I don't believe it.'

'You don't have to. Just knock on the door and you'll see for yourself. Mind you, Wat doesn't do the rude ones anymore. It's all pious now, apparently. I blame Hermitage. He ruined a perfectly good weaver.'

The man now looked as if he was wondering whether this was all some sort of trick.

'You got a murder, then?' the headman asked.

'A murder?' The Saxon didn't seem too surprised by this suggestion.

'Yes. That's what Hermitage does, murders. Well, he works out who did them, he doesn't do them himself. Mind you, if he wanted to, he could probably do a good one. What with him knowing all the ins and outs.'

'A murder? Erm, there is a matter we want him to look into.'

'He's just the man then. Never fails, they say.'

'Do they?'

'But you just get along to the workshop of Wat the Weaver and ask for Brother Hermitage. He's so clever, he's probably expecting you.'

'Yes.' The man now appeared to be deep in his own thoughts. He looked towards the cart that was still rumbling slowly up the road and was obviously wondering how on earth he was going to explain that they had to go and see Wat the Weaver.

Caput II

Quick; One Tapestry for The Rich People

'Hello.' Wat the Weaver looked out of his single upper storey window onto the road outside his workshop. 'Customers.' He rubbed his hands as if he could already feel their silver between his fingers. 'And good ones, by the look of them. They've even got horses. Two of them, can you believe? Don't let Mrs Grod out of the kitchen to see them; we'll be eating the things for weeks.'

Brother Hermitage didn't even put his book down to go and look. But then he seldom put his book down at all. It was a volume from the library of Colesvain in Lincoln that had been his reward for helping catalogue that place, and deal with the murder, or course.[1] But then everything he did seemed to necessitate dealing with a murder. He often suspected that if a murder came to his door, it would be hiding another murder behind its back.

Still, the book was his most prized possession, even if it did have a rather morbid provenance. It was pretty much his only possession, apart from the habit he stood up in; that and a slim volume of prayers that he had carried for many years. He knew that pride was a sin, but he felt very pleased that he only owned three things in the world, and two of them were books.

Cwen was down in the workshop directing and assisting the apprentices, so she would have to be summoned to help deal with the customers. The apprentices would doubtless be

---

[1] *The Hermes Parchment* - a tale of literature and death.

grateful for a bit of respite from direction and assistance, both being largely indistinguishable from her shouting at them.

'They look a bit Saxon,' Wat commented with some suspicion. Just like the people of Derby, he was surprised to see this many well-equipped Saxons gathered in one place at all. The Norman conquerors didn't like gatherings of any sort, reasoning that the people involved were probably gathered to do some harm to a Norman or two. They were usually right.

That this many people could travel the country freely could only mean one of two things. First, they were no harm to anyone; or second, they were friends of the Normans.

Wat did notice that for all their organisation and well-presented turn-out, there wasn't a single weapon in sight. None of the marching men carried swords, the horses weren't hung with axes and lumps of metal on sticks and no one carried a shield. Harmless then.

Which probably also meant that they didn't have much money. A serious Saxon household like this one would have been first in line when the Normans arrived to steal everything.

The entourage drew to a halt at Wat's gate and one of the men walked over to the cart and opened the door set in its side. As he did so, he drew a simple set of steps from under the cart and put them down so that whoever was inside could descend with ease.

'Definitely harmless,' Wat said out loud as he saw a very well-dressed woman descend from the cart and look around her as if she'd never been outside before.

She had the look of someone who was used to being in charge, so the Norman conquest must have been a real disappointment. She also had the years on her face that said she had been running things for quite some time before the

Normans even thought of turning up.

The man with the steps bowed at her and nodded his head towards the workshop. He leaned forward and whispered some words into her ear.

The woman immediately took a step back and gave him a very puzzled look. She then turned her puzzled look towards the workshop.

'She's been told where she is,' Wat said with a smirk. 'Doubtless, she's another Saxon who's decided she needs a great big pious tapestry, just to show the Normans what a God-fearing and church-loving sort she is. Exactly like good King William.'

Hermitage let go a small "tut" at this. Wat was now making a very good living from selling great big pious tapestries that could be displayed as a sign to the Normans; a sign that said, "please don't slaughter us, we're God-fearing".

The man was now offering some sort of explanation to the woman, but it required quite a bit of gesticulation and shrugging of shoulders to prevent her simply getting back in the cart and driving away again.

Eventually, it became clear that the man was going to do the actual walking up the path and knocking on the door; and the talking to Wat the Weaver, probably.

Wat smiled to himself and shook his head. He'd likely sold one of his old works to someone in this household, whoever they were. They looked just the sort to shout out how disgusting Wat the Weaver and his works were, while whispering that they'd take half a dozen.

The woman now climbed back into her cart, but it didn't move off. Instead, the man straightened his uniform took a deep breath and walked up the path.

'I'll go down.' Wat turned to Hermitage. 'Can you go and

get Cwen?'

Hermitage reluctantly closed his book, but still didn't put it down. Instead, he clutched it to his breast and stood to do as he was asked.

'And tell her to be nice. You never know, these might be rich people.'

Hermitage shook his head sadly as Wat's greed paraded naked in the room.

'Hurry,' Wat urged, as Hermitage wandered towards the rickety steps and took them at a slow and safe pace. 'We don't want to keep the rich people waiting.' As he said this, he even tried to tidy the unruly mop of black hair that followed its own inclinations on top of his head.

Hermitage may have managed to move Wat away from his old tapestries, drenched as they were in the sin of lust, but he clearly had his work cut out if he was going to make any inroads against avarice.

He did pick up his pace as he walked through the corridors that led to the back of the workshop, and the large room where the apprentices worked at their tapestry. He didn't want to leave Wat on his own with visitors for too long; goodness knew what he'd agree to once he saw their money.

Old Hartle, the weaving master, was ostensibly in charge of the apprentices but Cwen had taken it upon herself to teach them the finer points of her art. Hartle didn't object to this, and in fact they made a good team. Hartle was calm and sanguine and instructed by giving gentle direction and encouragement. When that didn't work, Cwen took over. The apprentices quickly learned to follow Hartle's guidance speedily, that way they could avoid one of Cwen's lessons: the ones that always left bruises.

Hermitage had even overheard one or two of them referring

to the pair as "good weaver, bad weaver." If Cwen ever found out she was called "bad weaver", she really would dole out some lessons.

There was no doubting that she was a very fine weaver indeed. Even in Wat's opinion, her delicate hands and skilful eye meant that she would one day be his equal. According to Cwen, that day was several years ago.

'Ah, Hermitage.' Cwen looked up from a loom she was working on, the rest of the apprentices all having their heads down, trying to avoid her gaze. 'Don't tell me, Wat the Weaver has forgotten the way to his own workshop and sent you to look for it.'

Cwen's pretty constant complaint that Wat didn't actually do any weaving at all anymore, was met with the similarly persistent reply that the whole idea of owning a workshop was so that he didn't have to do any work.

'Some people have arrived and he asked me to come and get you.'

'People?'

'Rich Saxons, apparently.'

'There aren't any rich Saxons anymore.'

'I haven't seen them. He was going to meet them at the front door.'

Cwen stood from her seat at the loom and stretched herself. 'And he sent word that I should be nice.'

Hermitage just shrugged at that.

'Come on then, let's go and have a look at some rich Saxons. They could be the last ones we ever see.'

Hermitage was sure that he heard a huge sigh come from the apprentices as Cwen left.

Back at the front door there was no sign of any visitors. The cart still sat out on the path, and quite a large number of people was gathered around it. Most of them had found somewhere to sit, resting legs after what might have been a long journey.

'Must be upstairs,' Cwen nodded towards the single room on the upper storey; the room Wat kept for receiving his customers.

He said it was so that they could be welcomed in comfort, away from the noise and bustle of the workshop. Cwen suspected it was so that the apprentices never got to see who the customers were. That way they couldn't go behind Wat's back and undercut him.

Cwen led the way, and before they reached the top of the stairs, Hermitage could hear Wat's voice.

'This is awful,' he was saying.

'I know,' a male voice replied.

Hermitage and Cwen emerged into the room and the uniformed Saxon man who was sitting in a chair opposite Wat, turned his head.

Obviously, there was no feature that said this man was a Saxon, but there were many that said he wasn't Norman, so what else would he be? He had normal hair no weapons and his accent was not Norman. Hermitage accepted that he was a Saxon, and one in a uniform at that. It was puzzling that he was allowed to walk around Norman England dressed like that.

'Brother Hermitage?' the man asked.

Hermitage nodded acknowledgement. There had obviously been some small talk while Wat was waiting for Cwen.

'And mistress Cwen the weaver.' The man gave a short nod.

'That's right,' Cwen said. 'Cwen the Weaver. Just so.'

Hermitage turned to go and leave them to their discussions.

'You'd better stay, Hermitage,' Wat said.

'Really?' Hermitage couldn't think why they'd need him. Unless, of course, this was a commission for a big pious tapestry and they would want his advice on the degree of piety.

'This is Renweard,' Wat introduced the man.

'Master Renweard,' Hermitage nodded again.

'He's with the household of Lady Gudmund.'

'Gudmund?' Hermitage didn't know the name, but it had a very Norse ring to it. It explained why these people looked more Saxon than Norman. The family could have been here for generations.

'The rest of them are waiting outside.'

'I see.' Hermitage didn't, but it seemed polite not to ask.

Wat took a deep breath. 'And they're looking for you.'

'Me?' For a moment Hermitage thought this must be a mistake. Why on earth would anyone come to a weaver's workshop looking for a monk? It was only a moment though, he soon realised why they had come for him. 'Oh, no,' he sighed.

'I know,' Wat agreed. 'That's why I said this was awful. There's been a murder.'

Hermitage dropped himself onto a spare chair. 'A murder,' his voice trembled slightly, even though he'd dealt with more of the things that he cared to think about. 'That's terrible.'

'It is.' Wat nodded. 'They don't want to buy a tapestry at all.'

Hermitage gave Wat a fierce look, which had no effect at all. 'Who has been taken?' he asked.

Renweard stood. 'You are the Brother Hermitage who is the King's Investigator?'

'Yes, that's me,' Hermitage admitted.

'We have heard of your prowess at dealing with matters

18

such as this. Now that I know you are here, perhaps we can go and discuss the matter with Lady Gudmund?'

'She can come in here,' Wat said.

'Oh, I don't think so.' Renweard said this as if his mistress had just been invited for a tour of the local privies.

'Can't be seen coming into the workshop of Wat the Weaver, eh?' Wat said with some bitterness.

'I'm glad you understand.'

'Ha,' Cwen smirked.

'Lady Gudmund's carriage is spacious,' Renweard said.

Wat got up and went over to the window to look. 'Not for all of us, it isn't.'

'All of us?' Renweard was confused. 'Only Lady Gudmund and Brother Hermitage need meet. And Mistress Gudmund, the daughter of the house, has accompanied us.'

'Ah, but that's not how it works.' Wat managed some condescension. 'Investigation is a complicated business. It needs Hermitage, me and Cwen.'

'Really?' Renweard now seemed to be thinking that investigation was a bit more unpleasant than he'd been led to believe.

'That is right, I'm afraid,' Hermitage said. 'The three of us look into these things together. We each have our own talents, it seems.'

'As we've only said to Lord Le Pedvin in this very room,' Wat added. 'You do know Le Pedvin? Good friend of the king? Who we also have to meet quite regularly.'

'Wat the Weaver meets the king?' Renweard was clearly having trouble believing this.

'He certainly does.'

'And does he know what you do? Or what you used to do, rather?'

'We're usually too busy talking about investigating a murder for the king to worry about tapestry.'

Hermitage thought this was a generous interpretation of their meetings with William. They all knew that if the king ever did find out what sort of thing Wat had produced, it would not end well.

Renweard seemed persuaded by this name-dropping. Perhaps the Lady Gudmund could be persuaded to set foot in the workshop after all.

Still looking thoughtful and quite reluctant, he went over to the window and opened the small pane that swung back. He waved a gloved hand at someone down by the carriage.

The signal was acknowledged and the carriage door was opened once more.

Those in the room all gathered by the window to get a look at this Lady Gudmund as she emerged.

Hermitage saw a rather stout and powerful looking woman who was very well dressed and clearly commanded all those about her.

Several people leapt into action as the lady stepped down to the ground. They bustled about doing nothing that looked particularly useful, but the lady appeared used to having them about.

Before she moved up the path, she turned back to the door of the carriage and beckoned that someone else should follow. Another attendant stepped to the door and held a hand up to help the next person out.

A much younger woman appeared now, blinking from the darkness of the carriage and looking around to see where they were. This must be the Mistress Gudmund Renweard had mentioned.

She too appeared to be very well dressed and unused to

being out in the country. Doubtless her time was spent in whatever great house they had come from.

This lady brushed and straightened her fine skirts and ran a hand over a fall of long blonde hair that framed a very fair young face.

There was a loud "clack" in the room. Hermitage turned to see that Cwen had slapped Wat's jaw shut from where he had obviously been gaping at Mistress Gudmund.

She was now simply pointing a finger at Wat, but lined up behind it was one of her very demanding looks.

Wat swallowed and gave a rather weak smile.

'Whoever is dead,' Cwen said in a rather stilted manner, 'you and I might be investigating it on our own, Hermitage.'

Caput III

Her Ladyship

The arrival of the Queen of Gudmund, for that's what it felt like, was quite an affair.

More men in uniform busied themselves preparing the way for their mistress. This mostly involved entering the workshop, examining it in some detail and sniffing their disappointment.

One even said, 'Is this the best you can offer?' And Wat had to be restrained from showing him the best view of the privy.

They even sent a man with a broom to sweep Wat's hallway while another closed the door to the kitchen, presumably so that Lady Gudmund didn't have to see anything like work going on.

'Where will you receive her Ladyship?' One rather officious woman asked. She too looked at the workshop as if she'd never been anywhere quite so nasty.

'I thought about the garden gate,' Wat said. 'After all I haven't actually invited her to visit.'

The woman simply looked confused at this. 'What's up there?' she asked, looking at the stairs.

'The top of the stairs,' Wat explained helpfully.

'Hm.' The woman made to explore herself, before Wat took her by the elbow and turned her around towards the door.

'Thank you,' he said brightly. 'Do come again when you're passing, but I don't think we'll be in.' He then shooed the others in his workshop to the door and shut it on some very puzzled faces.

'Coming in here treating my workshop as if it wasn't good enough,' he explained to Cwen and Hermitage as they stood and watched.

'You've shut out the lovely Mistress Gudmund,' Cwen said sweetly.

'It's them who's come looking for us, not the other way round,' Wat grumbled.

There was a knock on the door.

'Could you see who that is, Hermitage?'

Hermitage was very confused as he thought they all knew perfectly well who it was. Nevertheless, he went to the door and opened it.

'What's going on?' the officious woman asked.

Hermitage turned back for some explanation from Wat as to what was going on.

Wat stepped forward now. 'Can I help you?'

'Can you help me? Lady Gudmund is come to see you.'

'Does she have an appointment?'

'A what?'

'It's a word we picked up from a largely mad person who lived in some woods. Apparently, it means an arrangement to see someone.'[2]

'Lady Gudmund wishes to see you.' The woman clearly thought that would be all anyone needed.

'How lovely for her.'

'So you must prepare.'

Wat looked as if he was thinking about this. 'No, don't think so. Now, if you were the king, or Lord Le Pedvin, that would be different. We are his servants. We are not Lady Gudmund's.' He made this last point very clear. 'Whoever she

---

[2] The Hermes Parchment introduced the world to the concept

is,' he added as a final insult.

The woman at the door simply gaped at this unbelievable behaviour.

'What's going on here?' A very commanding voice demanded.

'Oh,' the woman at the door let a little squeak out. 'Your Ladyship. Erm, that is, this weaver fellow is being very difficult.' As she finished her sentence she seemed to recover her natural arrogance.

'Well, of course he is. A carriage full of people has turned up without notice.'

A large hand was placed on the shoulder of the officious one, and it pushed her gently to one side.

What could only be Lady Gudmund stood in her place.

Hermitage instantly determined that her voice had been commanding because the rest of her was as well.

She was not overly large but was just that little bit bigger than everyone else to make people notice. She seemed tall and broad, although the drapery of clothing that swathed her might account for some of that. Close up, she looked at least fifty, but a very fit and healthy fifty, having clearly lived a comfortable life. Her hair was loose, but cut quite short, as if she had instructed it to keep out of her way.

All in all, the impression of command was oozing from everything about the woman. Her expression was quite blank at the moment, giving nothing away, which would make those encountering her very wary indeed.

It was the sort of expression a lot of nobles carried. King William himself was very good at it. And there was absolutely no telling whether it was going to lead to great reward, or a speedy death.

'Wat the Weaver eh?' Lady Gudmund said, and then she

winked.

Hermitage had never seen a noble wink before. And the smile that broadened Lady Gudmund's mouth had a hint of something a bit rude about it.

Wat was obviously taken aback by this. 'Erm, yes.'

'May I come in?' Lady Gudmund asked nicely, giving her officious woman a sideways glance of disappointment.

'Of course, of course. More than welcome.' Wat looked to the awkward woman as well. 'You only had to ask.'

'I do apologise for my people,' the lady said as she stepped over the threshold. 'They get all sorts of ideas about what's proper and what isn't. Some of them seem to think they're more noble than I am. But they can't get it right.'

Lady Gudmund stopped before she walked forward and looked around the hall.

Hermitage thought that perhaps she was going to cast some criticism on the place after all.

'The workshop of Wat the Weaver.' She seemed impressed for some reason. 'If anyone told me I'd one day be standing in this place, I'd have slapped them in the vitals.'

'Erm, I see.' Wat appeared to be having some difficulty dealing with Lady Gudmund.

'My dear departed husband had quite a collection, you know.'

'Did he?' For once, Wat seemed to be quite embarrassed by his own past.

'Oh yes. Kept them hidden away of course, or so he thought. Ha, ha. I particularly liked the one with the three maids dealing with a fellow in a peculiarly harsh manner, if you take my meaning?'

'Ah, that one.' Wat frowned. 'Lord Gudmund? I'm not sure I recall the name.'

'Well, he wouldn't have given his real name, would he? Not for something like that.'

'I suppose not.'

'And who is this charming young lady?'

Cwen gave her genuine smile to Lady Gudmund. She clearly liked the woman. 'I am Cwen, the weaver.'

'A weaver eh?' Lady Gudmund clearly appreciated that a woman was not supposed to be a weaver. 'Good for you, my dear.'

Cwen smiled even more.

'And have you ever produced anything as downright filthy as Master Wat here?'

'I used to make the works of Briston the Weaver,' Cwen said, sounding quite proud of the fact.

'Oh ho, did you indeed? Lord Gudmund had a couple of those as well. Very fine work. Yours?'

'Most likely.'

'Well done.' Lady Gudmund congratulated Cwen on producing tapestries that Hermitage knew were positively anatomical in their detail.

'And this is my daughter.' Lady Gudmund turned and beckoned that the young woman in her shadow should step forward.

'Mother.' The young Lady Gudmund, who must not yet be out of her teenage years, said this single word in the manner of many a child; it conveyed embarrassment, annoyance and a deep wish to be somewhere else; and that this person who claimed to be their parent, was not.

Mistress Gudmund nodded her head to acknowledge them all, and then brushed the long blonde hair from the side of her head.

Hermitage thought he heard Wat sigh.

26

'Ow,' he said.

'Pardon?' Lady Gudmund asked.

'Oh, nothing, nothing. Just a little irritation I have.' Wat took half a step away from Cwen. 'Do come to the upstairs chamber.' He held an arm out to bid them go up.

'Upstairs, eh?' Lady Gudmund seemed impressed.

'Hermitage, do you think you could get one of the apprentices to bring wine?'

'Of course,' Hermitage smiled, and then wondered why he'd been asked to do it when it was him that Lady Gudmund had come to see.

He shook his head that it didn't really matter, as he watched Wat follow Mistress Gudmund up the stairs; follow her quite closely it seemed, probably to save her if she fell.

Hermitage delivered his message to the apprentices, every one of whom said that they were apprentices in a weaving workshop not a wine merchant's.

He felt positively ashamed when he said that he would just have to get Hartle to do it. He knew very well that an instruction from Hartle would be obeyed, and one of the apprentices reluctantly set about the task.

By the time Hermitage got back to the upper chamber, everyone had found chairs. Lady Gudmund took the prime position by the fireplace, as well as the largest and most comfortable chair.

Renweard had re-joined them and was sitting at his mistress's side. Next to him was young Lady Gudmund and next to her was Cwen. It looked as if Cwen's chair had been squeezed in between Wat and the young woman, and every now and again she would jostle it sideways to make Wat move further away.

Hermitage took the remaining seat, which faced everyone

else and was obviously the focus of attention.

'Brother Hermitage.' Lady Gudmund nodded her head politely.

Hermitage stood again and bowed. 'My Lady,' he said, thinking it was proper.

'Oh, no need for all that. We are here to see you, Brother, and to crave your assistance.'

Hermitage sat again.

'We are told that you are the King's Investigator.' She made the title sound very grand indeed.

Hermitage just nodded his acknowledgement. He didn't like to say the words out loud as he still thought of it as a temporary appointment that would go away one day.

'And what does that mean, exactly?' Lady Gudmund sounded genuinely interested. 'From the Latin, *vestigo vestigare?*'

'Just so,' Hermitage was delighted to hear that. 'The role of the investigator is to track the wrong doer. In essence, find out who did it.'

'Excellent.' Lady Gudmund turned her head to Renweard. 'This sounds like just what we need.'

'And King William appointed you?'

'He did. And before him King Harold.'

'King Harold.' Now Lady Gudmund sounded really impressed.

'I managed to resolve an issue concerning the death of a monk at the monastery of De'Ath's Dingle.'[3]

'Good God.' The Lady couldn't stop the expletive. 'De'Ath's Dingle? Really?'

'There was a bit of, erm, unpleasantness there.'

'Only a bit? If what we have heard of the place is true it is

---

[3] *The Heretics of De'Ath* - where it all began; who knew it would never end?

the repository for all the world's unpleasantness.'

Hermitage couldn't disagree with that. 'King Harold arrived there and appointed me his investigator. King William continued with the role after we discovered what happened when one of his men was killed.'[4]

'And you have continued ever since.'

'Yes, I have rather.' Hermitage felt quite miserable about that. Being an ordinary monk in a monastery had never gone terribly well for him, but investigating murders was simply ridiculous.

Lady Gudmund took a moment to consider all of this. 'Then you are the man for us.'

Hermitage gave a humble shrug to indicate that he would do what he could.

'My husband, Lord Gudmund, has been killed.' She was quite matter-of-fact about this, as if slightly irritated that her instruction to her husband to stay alive had not been obeyed. Mistress Gudmund did give a single stifled sob.

'I am sorry.'

'Just so. And we come to you, the King's Investigator, to see if you would be willing and able to discover what happened to him.'

Hermitage had never been willing to investigate anything, and he even doubted that he was able. All that happened was he ended up figuring out who did it. But apart from figuring out who did it, he couldn't immediately think what else there was to an investigation.

'When did this happen?'

'Some while ago now; we are not sure exactly when as he was away from home at the time. We have been fretting about it and demanding answers, but no one has helped at all. It was

---

[4] *The Garderobe of Death* - titles were simple in those days.

only when we heard of the King's Investigator, that we thought there may be some hope of discovering what the awful truth may be.'

'Do you know how he died?'

'We do not. All we had was word that he had been taken from us.'

'I see.' These people didn't know when this man had died, or how. Hermitage wasn't sure what he was going to be able to do. There was usually a body for him to look at at least. Had the man been stabbed, or struck with a sword or even poisoned perhaps? Maybe he'd just died. If he was of an age with Lady Gudmund, that was a strong possibility.

'Do you know where he was? You say he was away from home?' Hermitage had no idea how knowing where someone died would help, but there was nothing else to go on at the moment.

'In the south.'

'The south.' Well, that wasn't much help either, there was a lot of south. 'And what took him there?'

'Harold,' Lady Gudmund said.

'Harold?'

'King Harold?' Wat asked.

'That's right.'

'Your husband went south with King Harold?'

'As you say.'

'When was this? I mean, what year?'

Hermitage couldn't believe that this murder, if it was a murder, would be so long ago that you needed to ask which year.

'The year of our Lord ten sixty-six.'

Wat ran a hand over his face and looked around the room. The expression on his face was saying that surely he wasn't the only person to come to a rapid and quite obvious answer. 'Can I just get this straight, then? In my own mind. Your husband, the Saxon Lord Gudmund, went south with Harold in ten sixty-six and didn't come back.'

'There you have it.' Lady Gudmund seemed delighted that they were making some progress.

'Do you think he could have gone anywhere near, oh, I don't know, Hastings, at all?'

'Hastings?'

'It's in the south, and there was a bit of a commotion there. Saxons versus Normans. The Saxons lost? Ring any bells?'

'Of course, we know of Hastings, Master Wat.' Lady Gudmund was getting a bit commanding once more.

'And the victory of the Normans involved killing quite a lot of Saxons in battle.'

'We have heard that this was the case.'

'Saxons under the command of Harold, who went there from the north. Which necessitated a journey to the south. Just like the one your husband took.'

Wat gave Hermitage a rather hopeless glance. It didn't really take the skills of an investigator to work out what probably happened to Lord Gudmund.

'As Harold travelled south from the battle with the Danes at Stamford Bridge, he gathered Saxons to join him in battle against the Normans.'

The Gudmund party nodded that this seemed to be a sound strategy.

'And what happened at Hastings, when the Saxons met the Normans, was that most of the Saxon nobles got killed,' Wat went on. 'William not being in the mood for hostage taking, apparently. Better to get rid of all the nobles and replace them with Normans, which he has done with some success.'

31

'He has.'

'So,' Wat was now looking rather desperate and quite surprised that no one was leaping to the conclusion ahead of him. 'The chances are that your husband, who went south with Harold about this time, wound up in the battle.'

Lady Gudmund nodded as if she hadn't considered this until now.

'The one where all the Saxon nobles got killed.' He paused but still no one spoke up. 'Let me think,' he mused. 'How does Hermitage put it?'

Hermitage had no idea how he put it, or even what it was. He was certainly no expert on battles.

'Something like this.' Wat cleared his throat. 'Saxon nobles went to Hastings and got killed in battle by the Normans. Your husband was a Saxon noble who went to Hastings. Therefore, your husband got killed in battle by the Normans. There we are.' He rubbed his hands that this was all nicely settled.

Hermitage nodded and smiled at Wat's excellent construction of an argument. The weaver was picking up something from his time with a monk.

Wat continued. 'And now you would like Hermitage to investigate which particular Norman killed your husband at the Battle of Hastings? Out of the ten thousand who were there at the time.'

Hermitage baulked at that idea. Who would he ask, William? It was bad enough that the Normans had slaughtered widely in the heat of a pitched battle. He'd be very surprised to find that they had kept any proper records at all.

'You have narrowed it down already,' Lady Gudmund commended them.

'But.' Wat seemed lost for words. 'It was a battle. That's what battles do, kill people? No one gets accused of murder for killing people in a battle. How would that work? It could be that he was killed by William himself.'

Hermitage definitely wasn't going to investigate that.

Lady Gudmund was softly shaking her head. 'My husband was a great man, and of advancing years. He was never a warrior and would not be in the thick of battle.'

'They didn't come much greater than Harold and look what they say happened to him.'

'Someone murdered Lord Gudmund,' Lady Gudmund insisted.

'I'm sure they did,' Wat agreed. 'But even if we could find out which Norman did it, they'd probably boast about the fact.'

Wat had clearly given up on this request from Lady Gudmund as an utterly hopeless and pointless task. 'It'd be a complete waste of our time and effort,' he went on. 'We've got tapestries to make, we can't go traipsing around the country looking for every Saxon who got killed at Hastings. I'm sorry,' he gave his conclusion. 'It simply can't be done.'

Hermitage felt huge relief at hearing this. It frequently occurred to him to turn down a request to investigate but when that request came direct from King William saying, "no thank you" was not an option.

Unfortunately, the next thing Lady Gudmund said threw all reason out of the window.

'I am prepared to pay handsomely.'

Caput IV

Interest of Conflicts

Pay? thought Hermitage. You don't pay for investigations.

'Pay?' Wat sounded a bit less sure about that conclusion.

'Of course. I wouldn't expect the investigator to do this for nothing.'

Hermitage wondered about mentioning this approach to King William; perhaps not.

As he opened his mouth to say that there would be no question of any payment being required, he noticed that Wat's face was contorted into a very strange expression.

It could be profound revelation that he had suddenly seen something that had escaped him until now, yet it seemed tinged with regret. Hermitage quickly concluded that this was regret that he might have charged for all of the investigations they had done to date.

'No,' Cwen said quite plainly, obviously interpreting Wat's response in the same manner. 'We cannot send William a bill.'

Never mind the question of not paying for an investigation at all, Hermitage was keen that they should all understand that there was no investigation to be done here. The death of a Saxon noble at the battle of Hastings should take all of half a moment to resolve. If investigations were paid for, this one wouldn't earn a quarter-penny with the wrong king stamped on it. Wat was studiously ignoring everyone in the room except the woman with the money. 'I'm sure we could look into what happened.'

'We could do what, exactly?' Cwen sounded more disappointed than anything. 'Confirm that there was a battle near Hastings and that quite a few Saxon nobles were killed? That won't take long.'

'The family want to know the truth, that's quite understandable.' Wat's voice was full of sympathy and fellow feeling.

Now Hermitage knew there was something wrong.

'You mean they're prepared to pay for the truth,' Cwen said.

Wat just shrugged as if there was nothing he could do about it and he would have to take their money; reluctantly of course.

Cwen narrowed her eyes. 'And who knows who else in the country would be willing to pay for an investigation, eh?'

Wat's eyes went in the opposite direction. Hermitage could tell that he was fighting an overwhelming urge to rub his hands together.

Renweard coughed and he was looking rather pale. 'What's this *we*? Surely Brother Hermitage is the investigator?'

Wat developed a quite horrible smile 'Not only does Brother Hermitage live in the workshop of Wat the Weaver, but we work together on the investigations.'

'Yes,' Renweard said with a little contempt, 'you explained that. What I mean is that if there is payment, it goes to the investigator. If he wishes to employ you, that's up to him.'

Wat was looking a little confused so Renweard spelled it out.

'We don't pay you as well as him.'

'That is a good point.' Cwen spoke with some cunning in her voice.

'Oh, yes?' What is?' Wat asked, although he was clearly worried about this development.

'That Brother Hermitage is the investigator.'

Hermitage nodded at this. He didn't usually like to acknowledge the fact, in the hope that ignoring it would make it go away. This time he almost felt the need to speak up, before Wat descended to a new depth of greed and self-interest.

'If there is any money to be paid, it would go to Hermitage.'

Wat moved his face from a scowl for Cwen to a smile for Hermitage.

'And he'd probably give it all away to the church.'

Now Wat's pallor turned to that of a light fog. He gripped the sides of his chair.

Hermitage hadn't thought of that. Here was a rich woman who was willing to pay him for his services. What an opportunity that would present to do good in the world. He would happily give up his own meagre possessions if charity demanded it so there was no question that he would keep the money for himself. He would give it as alms. Perhaps not to the priest of Derby, who seemed to be a very questionable fellow; one of the main questions being whether he was actually a real priest or not. No. He would help the poor. He even had one or two specific poor in mind.

Wat seemed to be able to read the thoughts in Hermitage's head as they passed by. 'We'd need to discuss this, obviously.'

'What you do with the money is neither here nor there,' Lady Gudmund spoke up. 'I am willing to pay for your time and your travel and such like. But there must be an investigation into my husband's death.'

Hermitage still thought that such an investigation would take absolutely no time at all, but if there was a chance to divert some of the Gudmund fortune to a worthy cause, perhaps it would be worthwhile. The prospect was actually quite exciting - if a bit worrying at the same time. He'd always felt that the support he could give to others was spiritual in nature. If it now came with a bag of coins, he suspected things might get complicated.

He looked to Cwen for some encouragement and she gave a non-committal look that said it might be worth a try, even if there were problems along the way. She also glanced towards Wat, making it quite clear where the main problems would come from.

They all seemed agreed to this now. Even if it was obvious that Wat agreed because he thought he would get some money, while Hermitage agreed because he would get some money that he could then give away.

Cwen now seemed amused by the whole situation and was probably agreeing so that she could watch what happened. 'If King William finds out that his investigator is being paid,' she said, 'he'll probably think the money is his.'

Wat and Hermitage both frowned at that idea. 'He's got more than enough already,' Wat said, to Hermitage's nodded agreement.

Lady Gudmund leaned forward to interrupt their discussion and get on with business. 'Where will you begin?' she asked.

'Begin?' Wat's concentration on the money had clearly taken his mind off what they were supposed to be doing.

'Your investigation,' she reminded him.

'Oh, that. Yes, begin. We will definitely begin.'

'Where?' Lady Gudmund was starting to sound a little annoyed.

Wat looked around the room as if they might start in the

fireplace.

'We will need to talk to those who saw him last,' Hermitage said, in a fit of investigation.

'Wouldn't that be the one who killed him?' Renweard asked with a frown.

'Well, yes, it would, but before that.'

'The one who saw him earlier than last?'

'Not exactly,' Hermitage was getting lost.

'We talk to anyone who saw him,' Cwen spoke up. 'Starting with you and working our way up until we find the one who saw him last.'

'What's the point of talking to us? We know he was alive when we saw him. It's what happened after that we want to find out about,' Lady Gudmund growled a bit. 'That's why we've come to you. Unless we've wasted our time, of course?'

'Yes, but you saw him.' Cwen persisted.

'But he wasn't dead then.'

'There you are.'

'There I am what?' Lady Gudmund even threw her hands in the air now. 'Is this really what an investigation is supposed to be?'

'Where did he go?' Cwen asked.

'Where did he go?' Lady Gudmund seemed puzzled by the question.

'I mean Hastings, obviously, but when he left you, what were the circumstances? Who was he with, how was he?'

'Alive. I don't think Harold would have taken him otherwise.'

'He went with Harold then?'

'We told you all this.' Renweard was now sharing his lady's irritation.

'He went with Harold, actually with Harold, in person?'

This just brought frowns that seemed to suggest the Gudmunds had really come to the wrong place and were now worried they wouldn't be able to get out.

Hermitage took up the question, which he saw was a good one. 'Did the king himself come to your manor, or was it some other noble who sent word?'

'Of course it wasn't Harold himself.' Renweard snorted at the idea.

'Aha.' Hermitage was pleased they'd got there in the end.

'The king couldn't go knocking on every door, could he? He needed to get to Hastings to deal with William.'

'Or not,' Wat added unhelpfully.

Hermitage scowled at him to be quiet. 'Which noble was it who came for your husband?'

Lady Gudmund looked to Renweard as if she didn't bother answering mundane questions herself.

'It was one of Earl Waltheof's men.'

'Did you know him?'

'Oh yes. It was Edgulf. He's a very good friend of the family.'

'Edgulf, eh?' Hermitage said, fascinated by a real piece of information.

'A man of Earl Waltheof,' Renweard specified, as if this was even more reason to be impressed. 'Did you know him?'

'Oh, no. But it's good to have a name.'

'If you say so.' Renweard seemed to have doubts that this investigation was turning out to be a good idea at all.

'This Edgulf came to the manor and told Lord Gudmund that the king wanted him.' Cwen checked.

'That's correct.'

'And when was this, exactly?' Hermitage asked.

Renweard looked at the ceiling as he marshalled his

thoughts. 'It would have been about noon, I think.'

That wasn't what Hermitage had meant at all, but he didn't like to appear ungrateful. 'Noon, I see. And what day?'

'What day?'

'Yes, what day was this?'

'Is that important?'

'It is, rather. We need to establish when Lord Gudmund might have arrived at Hastings. That will give us a good indication of what happened.'

Lady Gudmund and Renweard both appeared to be lost.

'Did he arrive before the battle had begun, or could he have been late?'

Renweard gave the shrug of a man who doesn't really know what's going on. 'It would have been around the middle of Winterfylleth, I suppose.'

'Winterfylleth.' Hermitage was intrigued to hear them use the old Saxon name for the month of October. Being a monk, immersed in the language of the Romans, he was entirely used to the calendar of Julius; he just assumed the rest of the world was as well. He supposed that the ordinary folk, out there in the country might still follow the old ways and old words, but these people were noble. Were they really *that* Saxon?

'We know that the battle took place towards the middle of the month. It is quite possible that Lord Gudmund didn't get there in time.' Hermitage realised there was one pretty basic fact still missing.

'Where is your manor, by the way?'

'Where is it?' Renweard now sounded quite offended by the question, as if everyone should know where the Gudmund manor was.

'Yes. Did he have far to go?'

'It is in the demesne of the Abbey of St Edmund, isn't it?'

'Is it?'

'Of course it is.'

Hermitage nodded that this was a start. Which particular abbey of Saint Edmund would narrow it down nicely, after all there was quite a lot of them.

'Bury Saint Edmunds,' Renweard explained impatiently.

'Of course.' Hermitage tried to sound as if he had known that all along. 'From there to Hastings would mean a journey into London and across the river.'

'We have rights to a ferry,' Lady Gudmund informed them.

Hermitage, Wat and Cwen exchanged glances of alarm at that. There was one ferryman they knew of only too well, More the Boatman.[5]

There must be hundreds of ferrymen in the country, dozens working on the River Thames alone. But the last they had seen of More he had been back plying his dubious trade on the River Thames.[6] Hermitage felt the weight of fate upon him as he saw the chances of More being involved in this somehow were horribly realistic.

'It wouldn't have taken him long to get there, then.' Cwen shook thoughts of More from her own head.

'Who did he take with him?' Hermitage asked. 'I assume it was not only him.'

'Of course not,' Renweard dismissed that nonsense. 'He had half a dozen housecarls with him.'

'Houscarls, eh?' Wat seemed to have emerged from his cash-soaked reverie. 'Must be a rough part of the world, Bury Saint Edmunds, if you've got housecarls in your service.'

---

[5] More the Boatman keeps popping up in Chronicles of Brother Hermitage. Perhaps he'll get his own Chronicles one day.

[6] He got in the way of *The Bayeux Embroidery*, if you want to look him up.

'Why so?'

'Harold's housecarls were his fighting men. Mercenaries, mostly.'

Renweard shook his head. 'A housecarl is simply a servant. Lord Gudmund just took the men of fighting age with him.'

Hermitage found that another interesting use of language. This family Gudmund seemed more Norse than Saxon.

'But not you,' Wat was asking the pointed question of Renweard, who did seem to be of perfect fighting age.

'I am Lady Gudmund's carl,' he explained simply. 'Someone had to stay to protect the family.'

'Quite.' Wat sounded a bit suspicious.

Hermitage summarised the information, mainly for his own benefit as he liked to have things in order. 'Around mid-October, Lord Gudmund was summoned by this Edgulf, and he then left with some housecarls, headed for Hastings.'

Nobody contradicted him.

'Did any of them come back?'

'Any of who?' Lady Gudmund asked.

'The housecarls? We know that Lord Gudmund didn't make it, and you have been told that he fell. Did any of your housecarls return alive?'

Lady Gudmund and Renweard looked at one another as if they hadn't thought of that.

'Someone must have brought word of Gudmund's death. Was that one of the housecarls?'

'No.' Renweard shook his head. 'That was Edgulf again.'

'He survived, then,' Wat said quietly.

'Would you know if any of the housecarls made it back?' Cwen asked.

'I suppose we could check,' Renweard suggested.

'That does seem like a good idea.' Cwen's irritation with

these people was growing steadily. 'See if any of those who went off with your dead master might still be around to tell you what happened?'

'Or if any of them have come back wearing his jewels,' Wat muttered so that the Gudmunds couldn't hear.

They looked as if talking to the housecarls was not the sort of thing nice people did.

Hermitage didn't like to ask the final question he had in his head, but then he never liked to ask any of the others either, so he just plunged in. 'Can you think of anyone who would wish Lord Gudmund harm?'

'Apart from all the Normans at the battle,' Wat added for clarity.

Lady Gudmund shook her head. 'Absolutely not. He was a dearly loved man and leader. There are none who would wish him dead.'

'But you still think someone murdered him,' Cwen spoke plainly. 'That's as much wishing someone harm as you can get

'We're back to an accident of battle then,' Hermitage concluded.

There didn't seem to be much more he could get from these people. Apart from the request to investigate the murder of a dead man, they didn't have much useful information at all. He could just give it up as a bad job and send them on their way, but then there would be no alms for the poor. The only other thing to do was find some information of his own.

He could only see one way forward. 'I think the best thing we can do is come back with you to Bury St Edmunds. We can see how much of Lord Gudmund's trail there is left to follow.'

Lady Gudmund seemed happy with this plan, as if it was what she'd been expecting all along. The others nodded their agreement, even young Lady Gudmund, who had remained silent all this time.

Renweard stood ready to move back down the stairs again.

Wat beckoned them all to go ahead, the smile on his face being the one usually reserved for people who were going to give him their money.

Lady Gudmund and Renweard went to the top of the stairs and started to move down. As Hermitage drew up to follow at the end of the train, the young Lady Gudmund paused and touched his arm. He looked up and smiled.

'Might I have a word with you in private, Brother?' she asked quietly.

Hermitage was a bit surprised by this approach but of course, acquiesced.

'Not you.' Cwen grabbed Wat by the arm and dragged him away from young Lady Gudmund, who he had looked only to keen to assist in any way he could. 'She said Brother. Are you a monk? No, you are not. And never likely to be one. Get down those stairs.' Cwen gave a healthy push to remind him of the right direction.

Wat gave young Lady Gudmund an apologetic smile as he disappeared from view. Strangely, Cwen's voice seemed to get louder the further away she went.

'What can I do for you?' Hermitage asked.

The young lady spoke very quietly but quickly, perhaps thinking that she might be interrupted at any moment.

'It's about my father, and something my mother said.'

'Something she said?'

The lady started at Hermitage's voice and beckoned him to be quiet. 'About no one wishing him harm.'

Hermitage whispered his reply. 'Ah, yes. You think that someone did wish him harm?'

She nodded.

'Anyone in particular?'

She answered as if her reply was should be obvious. 'Everyone.'

'Everyone?' Hermitage didn't understand.

'Everyone,' she confirmed. 'He was horrible.'

Caput V

To Bury or Not to Bury

Hermitage longed for the chance to talk privately with Wat and Cwen about what young Lady Gudmund had said. Unfortunately, the bustle of preparation for departure made this impossible. Perhaps, once they were underway, he would be able to have their ears.

With the entourage of the Gudmunds at their service, there was no need to wait for a new dawn before setting out. In these times of Norman rule it was pretty important for a Saxon not to be out after dark; or at least not to get caught. A large cart and an actual parade of people should be enough to ward off unwanted attention.

Hermitage had a reasonable idea where Bury actually was, but no firm understanding of the distance involved. It would be quite a pleasure to visit the place, apart from the dead man and the investigation of murder, obviously. Perhaps, once that was sorted out, he would be able to visit the monastery. The opportunity to see the shrine of Saint Edmund was quite humbling. He knew that Wat and Cwen would not be interested but they might find it inspirational; probably not, but he lived in hope.

As usual, Wat was ready to leave straight away, his pack always waiting, "just in case" a-s he always said, without explaining. Cwen let him carry all that was necessary, and Hermitage's few possessions were always on him. They stood at the door while the Gudmunds were escorted from the workshop by Renweard.

'We need to speak,' Hermitage hissed quietly when the chance presented itself.

Wat and Cwen frowned but nodded that they understood and would find a moment.

'How far is Bury?' Hermitage asked more brightly, as Renweard stood waiting for them to come along. 'Will it take long?'

'About a week,' Renweard replied without concern.

'A week!' Hermitage almost shouted with quite a bit of concern.

'Of course. It is over one hundred miles, and the cart does not travel quickly.'

'A week,' Hermitage repeated with a touch more calm.

'Assuming we have no mishaps on the way.'

'Mishaps.' Hermitage was already formulating quite a creative collection of mishaps that were even now preparing themselves for his passage. Being the King's Investigator, he reluctantly suspected murder would be amongst them. He hoped the people who lived on their route knew they were coming and were taking appropriate precautions; like getting out of the way.

The idea of a journey lasting a week was not in itself disturbing, it took that long to get to many places around the country. Twenty miles in one day was a good pace for anyone to keep up. There was something else about the time that bothered Hermitage, though.

'It took you a week to get here?' he asked. This did raise some questions in his mind. Why on earth would these people take a whole week to come and find him? And why would it be all of them? Surely people of the import of Lady Gudmund sent messengers about their business; they didn't go themselves. A lone man on a horse would have made the journey much quicker.

'We were about the country on other business,' Renweard explained. 'The Gudmund estates are wide.'

Hermitage thought they'd have to be pretty wide to reach a hundred miles.

'And to be honest..,' Renweard started but seemed a bit reluctant.

'Yes?'

'Well.' Renweard scratched his ear. 'We thought that the King's Investigator would be a, erm, slightly different; that is to say, in a somewhat different situation than the one we found.'

'Eh?'

'We thought you'd be a significant noble in the king's service,' Renweard blurted out.

'Ah.' Wat nodded knowingly. 'You thought this would be an opportunity to ingratiate yourselves with a servant of the king in all his finery.'

Cwen took up the tale. 'The last thing you expected was a humble monk living in the workshop of Wat the Weaver.'

'Not really the last thing.' Renweard nodded. 'Way, way beyond the last thing.'

'Right,' Wat smiled.

'I mean,' Renweard warmed to his explanation. 'The King's Investigator in a place like this.' He managed to get a tone of disgust into his voice.

'Yes, all right,' Wat said.

'With Wat the Weaver, for God's sake. I shall have to instruct the servants and slaves not to talk. We don't want this getting out.'

'I think you've made your point.' Wat was sounding somewhat irritated now.

'He is the King's Investigator, is he?' Renweard checked. 'We haven't been talking to the wrong monk all this time?'

'Definitely him, favourite investigator of King William. And definitely Wat the Weaver,' Wat almost growled.

'Does William know?' he tipped his head back towards the workshop. 'About the tapestries and all? I bet he doesn't.'

'Sounds like your master knew all about them,' Wat said pointedly.

'Not my master,' Renweard corrected. 'As I said, I am Lady Gudmund's.'

'Bit of a fine separation, isn't it?' Cwen asked. 'Strange way to run a family, one lot of servants for him and another lot for her. Didn't they get on?'

Now it was Renweard's turn to be defensive. 'The Gudmunds are a fine noble family. Their ways are not those of ordinary folk.' He made "ordinary folk" sound quite revolting and was perfectly clear that Wat and Cwen hadn't even made it as far as ordinary.

'It's a good job the ordinary folk aren't the ones getting killed in battle.' Wat's gaze at Renweard was quite explicit; if the man was doing his job properly, he'd have gone off and got killed in battle along with all the other Saxons.

Choosing to ignore them with studied contempt, Renweard led the way down the path towards the waiting cart.

The Ladies Gudmund were climbing into the wagon, assisted by two liveried servants.

Cwen was first to arrive at the door to the cart, only to see it shut in her face by a servant who appeared horrified at the idea that she would get in.

'We walk,' Renweard said, as if this should be blindingly obvious. 'It is not for the likes of us to travel with the Gudmunds.'

'Just sort out their murders for them,' Cwen spat the words.

They seemed to have no impact on Renweard, who simply gestured towards the back of the cart.

'I think Lady Gudmund was right,' she said loudly to Hermitage and Wat as they drew up. 'Her servants think they're more noble than she is.'

'What are you doing, Renweard?' Lady Gudmund's head appeared through the hole that constituted a window in the cart door.

'Simply organising the train, my Lady.'

'With the King's Investigator and his companions on the outside?'

'Quite so,' Renweard agreed that this was the proper arrangement.

'Quite wrong,' Lady Gudmund corrected. 'You would have the investigator report to King William that he was forced to walk at the side of our carriage?'

Poor Renweard looked torn in half. It was clear that the King's Investigator had turned out to be a huge disappointment, mainly due to his own pretensions. His voice was weak and almost broke with the horror of his words. 'Wat the Weaver?' he croaked.

'And mistress Cwen,' Lady Gudmund said. 'There is room for them all in here. We have a long journey ahead of us.'

It seemed to be as much as Renweard could do to keep standing. Cwen didn't help by turning her nose up at him and sniffing as the reluctant steward opened the cart door.

Wat stepped quickly forward, only to be dragged back harshly by Cwen. 'Manners,' she said as she climbed up into the carriage.

Wat went next and Hermitage followed. As he ducked his head into the space, he saw that although they would be sitting, the journey would not be a comfortable one.

There were two simple benches at either end of the carriage, facing backwards and forwards. Lady Gudmund sat facing the horses, and her daughter was opposite.

Cwen had already sat herself next to the young woman, almost pushing the poor girl into the side of the carriage. She smiled at Wat and patted the seat next to her, indicating that he was going to sit there; no discussion.

Hermitage climbed across the legs and found plenty of space next to Lady Gudmund.

'You will actually find this most tiresome,' Lady Gudmund informed them all. 'It will not be long at all before you need to get out and walk, just to stretch your legs.'

The door shut behind them and Renweard's grumbling voice could be heard moving away and shouting at people who hadn't done anything wrong.

'You really came all this way like this just to find me?' Hermitage asked. 'You could have just sent word.'

'We could,' Lady Gudmund admitted. 'But we didn't know what to make of the King's Investigator. These are troubled times for all of us, let alone Saxons of noble blood. It is best to keep on the right side of the Normans in all circumstances. For all we knew you were some great Norman noble.'

'Sorry,' Hermitage apologised.

'It is good that you are not, Brother.' Lady Gudmund smiled. 'A great Norman noble would doubtless have less than no interest at all in the death of my husband.'

There was a jerk as the whole world appeared to suddenly stumble forward down the road. Hermitage felt the hard bench of the carriage beneath him and thought that he would probably like to get out and walk quite soon.

There was certainly no chance in these cramped

surroundings for a confidential discussion with Wat and Cwen. In fact, the noise of cart's creaking woodwork and clattering wheels forced any discussion to be quite a loud one.

'So,' Hermitage began.

'Pardon?' Lady Gudmund called back.

'I said, so.'

'Did you?'

'Yes.'

'I see.'

'Your husband,' Hermitage raised his voice now and leaned over towards Lady Gudmund's ear to make himself heard.

'What about him?'

'I am still not entirely clear as to why you think his death may be suspicious.' There, that had made the problem clear. The background noise meant that Hermitage had had to be far blunter than was his custom; which was not to be blunt at all.

'Pardon?' Lady Gudmund said again. Perhaps she still hadn't heard him.

'What he means,' Wat said. 'Is why don't you think your husband was simply killed at Hastings along with all the other Saxons?'

Hermitage frowned. There was blunt and then there was rude. There was no need to put the two together.

'You said that he was elderly and would not get involved in the heat of battle,' Hermitage stepped in before Wat could say anything even more upsetting. "But King Harold sent for him. He must have thought there was some use in that.'

Lady Gudmund nodded that she understood. 'He was a great leader,' she almost shouted. 'He could inspire men with his oratory.'

Young Lady Gudmund seemed to develop a bit of a

coughing fit at that. She beckoned out of the window, as if explaining that some piece of dust had got into her throat.

'Doubtless, King Harold would want him to help rally the troops.'

'Sally the who?' Hermitage asked, Lady Gudmund's words having been drowned out by a shout from the cart man outside.

'Sally some hoops?' Lady Gudmund asked, looking very puzzled.

Hermitage was really not used to raising his voice at all. The words of a monk should be quiet and modest. Shouting out was absolutely forbidden except in some matter of urgency. He had also learned to keep his voice down in case the other brothers found out where he was and came to cause a matter of urgency.

'Lots of Saxons went to Hastings,' Wat almost bellowed into the space. 'Most of them wound up dead. King William decided that killing them all was for the best. Why would your husband be any different?'

'As I said,' Lady Gudmund could generate a good level of noise herself. 'He was an elderly man. He would simply direct the action of the battle in some part. He would not be there wielding a weapon.'

'Killing the person who is directing the battle could be quite a good thing,' Wat said. 'Kill the leader and the rest will fall into line. Ideally, try to shoot the king in the eye, that's always good for a quick victory.'

'This Edgulf?' Cwen now asked, her own piercing shriek managing to cut through the hubbub quite effectively. 'Did he say how Lord Gudmund had fallen. When? Where?'

'No,' Lady Gudmund shook her head. 'All he reported was that he had fallen.'

'Like we say,' Cwen reiterated Wat's point. 'A lot of Saxons fell that day. Most of the nobles of England, it seems. It would almost be a bit odd if your husband survived.'

Lady Gudmund shook her head gently. 'King William would not kill an elderly man.'

'Yes,' Wat said loudly and with some conviction. 'He would. He'd kill anyone; young, old, fit, infirm, they're all the same to him. And if he didn't do it himself, his man Le Pedvin would.'

Hermitage felt a shiver run through him at the mention of that name. If there was any one Norman who could be relied upon to kill old men, it would be Le Pedvin.

'And who's to say it was anyone important at all?' Wat carried on. 'Word is that after failing to spot an arrow coming his way, Harold himself was hacked to bits by the ordinary fighting men. Your husband could have gone the same way.'

Hermitage tutted as he considered that suggesting Lord Gudmund had been hacked to pieces really was going a bit far.

'Why don't you believe Edgulf?' Cwen asked. 'He says your husband fell. He could be telling the simple truth.'

'I will not believe it,' Lady Gudmund said quite fiercely.

'Why not?' Wat was demanding.

'Does it matter? You have your belief and I have mine. And mine is the one with the money. I want you to investigate, and I am paying you to do it. I am convinced my husband was murdered. He simply would not have succumbed to some accident of battle. Someone of ill intent approached him.'

'Or an intent of battle,' Wat said more quietly. 'Death being the object of the whole exercise.'

'I've told you my reasons. How many times do I have to repeat them? He was an old man. He would not have been in the thick of the fighting, so he would not have been killed in the natural order of things.'

'And we say that he may not have been given a choice,' Wat shouted.

'Then you had best find that out.' The lady had taken on her natural demeanour of instruction; instruction she did not expect to be questioned by anyone. 'It is what I am paying you for, after all. Why does it matter what I think? It's Lord Gudmund who has gone.'

'It matters because of the investigation,' Wat persisted. 'If you have another reason to believe your husband was murdered, we need to know it. How can we investigate otherwise? Did someone else tell you he did not simply fall? Have you had word?' Wat clicked his fingers. 'Has your husband sent word that he did not fall in battle?'

'Of course not,' Lady Gudmund dismissed that. 'Why on earth would I pay you to investigate his murder if he'd sent word that was still alive?' She gave Wat a rather worried glance. 'As I understood it, murder almost always requires a death of some sort.'

Hermitage could only agree with that.

Lady Gudmund's brow narrowed. 'You have done this sort of thing before, haven't you?'

'Oh yes,' Hermitage confirmed the fact. He could see why the lady might be doubting it just at the moment.

'Then there must be some other reason.' Wat counted out the steps on his fingers. 'King summons noble to battle. All nobles get summoned to battle. Battle gets lost. All nobles dead. Including king. Except one? Except Lord Gudmund?'

'There are plenty of others,' Lady Gudmund objected.

'Plenty?' Wat scoffed at this. 'Colesvain of Lincoln and Thorkill of Warwick. That's two. Hardly plenty.'

Lady Gudmund said nothing.

'And they only survived because they were on the side of the Normans to begin with.' Wat's eyes narrowed as he considered Lady Gudmund. 'It was Harold who summoned your husband, was it? You are sure about that.'

'Of course.'

'This Edgulf wasn't a touch more Norman by any chance?'

'No, he was not. He was a fine Saxon. How dare you suggest such a thing?'

'Only trying to work out why your Saxon noble, of all the Saxon nobles, is still up and walking about in the middle of the battle. And the only reason I can think of for a Norman not to kill a Saxon at Hastings, is that he wasn't actually fighting on the other side.'

Caput VI

Carted Off

Hermitage thought that really was the most awful suggestion. Poor Lady Gudmund had come to ask for help in finding out what happened to her husband, and here was Wat, accusing him of being a Norman.

He knew that he had trouble being suspicious about people generally, but surely this was going too far. It was one thing to struggle with suspicion about possible killers, but doubting the victim? Who on earth would think such things? And why would the poor lady seek aid if she knew her husband was a Norman sympathiser?

Unless, of course, she didn't know? Even so, why on earth would she think him still alive, but still ask for his murder to be investigated? Oh, this was all too confusing.

'It's a very good reason for not dying at Hastings,' Cwen now put in.

Her too? Was no one going to give the Gudmunds the consideration they deserved.

The frost from Lady Gudmund's look could have frozen the entire inside of the carriage. In a rare moment of perspicuity, Hermitage thought that perhaps they had better not pursue this line of thinking. Pursuing lines of thinking was his only strength, really, and it seemed a shame not to put it into practise here, but he could see that they weren't going to get anywhere.

'Perhaps we should step outside,' he suggested to Wat and Cwen.

Neither of them appeared to see the point in that.

'Then we can consider and discuss what we have discovered so far.'

Wat's expression made it quite clear that he thought they hadn't discovered anything.

'Away from the noise of the carriage,' Hermitage explained.

'That sounds like a very good idea.' The frost from her face had obviously found its way to Lady Gudmund's voice. She simply nodded her head towards the door, indicating that there was no need for the carriage to stop moving before they left.

Hermitage went first, suspecting that Wat and Cwen would simply sit there exchanging fierce looks with Lady Gudmund for the next week.

The movement of the horses was not much faster than walking pace anyway, and so Hermitage had no trouble making it to the ground without mishap even with his habit billowing about around him. He turned and held the door for the others to follow.

It only seemed sensible that Cwen should come next as she was closest to the door. Instead, she beckoned with a sharp nod that Wat could go first. With a sigh and a shake of the head, the gestures he usually employed when Cwen was being unnecessarily difficult about something, he stood and stooped before heading for the door. As he did so, the cart lurched and he staggered slightly, putting his hand out to steady himself.

The next thing Hermitage knew was that Wat had almost fallen on top of him, such was his leap from the carriage door.

'What did you do that for?' Wat demanded when Cwen landed behind him. 'I nearly fell.'

'You nearly did,' Cwen confirmed as she closed the door firmly behind them. 'Next time you fall, find something to steady yourself other than the knee of young Lady Gudmund.'

Wat looked to Hermitage as if pleading for support against this outrageous suggestion.

Hermitage hadn't a clue what was going on.

Cwen now pushed Wat quite firmly and they all moved to join the retainers and servants who were following the carriage.

Renweard gave them a very satisfied glance, as if content that they had been put in their place.

'What's to discuss then, Hermitage?' Wat asked quietly, seeming to almost ignore Cwen for some reason. 'We're no further forward at all. We say Gudmund could have died quite naturally, his wife says not. I'm not sure she's even going to believe us if we prove it.'

Hermitage found that hard to believe. If someone was given proof, they had to believe it. That was the whole point of proof. The world would be in a very sorry state if folk didn't believe proof. You'd have to call it something else.

'There is much,' he said. 'Not least what young Lady Gudmund told me.'

'And what did young Lady Gudmund tell you?' Cwen snapped the name out as if it was a nasty taste in her mouth.

'That her father was not liked. In fact, he was horrible.'

'Horrible?'

'The very word.'

'Not the shining knight beloved by all and leading his men to glory, then?' Wat said.

'It seems not.'

'In which case, motivations for murder could be numerous and widely shared. Makes you wonder if Lady Gudmund the elder is aware of his real reputation.'

'Hard not to be.' Cwen appeared to have calmed from her

annoyance at the young Lady Gudmund, who, as far as Hermitage could tell, hadn't actually done anything wrong. 'If the Lord of the manor is widely reviled, you'd think his wife would spot it.'

'In which case she's not being entirely honest with us.' Wat didn't sound surprised at this.

'Perhaps she's reviled as well,' Cwen suggested. 'Or do we even trust what the lovely Lady Gudmund says about her father?'

'Oh Lord.' Hermitage shook his head. Occasionally he thought he would get used to the dishonesty. After all, he dealt mainly with murderers who tended not to be trustworthy. But still it came as a disappointment. He was used to the main protagonists not being entirely honest, but if the people asking for help were hiding the truth where would it end?

'Let's talk to the staff.' Wat nodded towards the troop of people who were accompanying them.

'Are they likely to speak up against their master?' Hermitage wondered.

'They might now he's dead. Murdered or killed in battle, he's going to cause them a bit less trouble from now on.'

'Here's a likely lad.' Cwen nodded over towards a young fellow who looked like he had some wits about him. He was carrying a large pack on his back but did look up at his surroundings now and again. This made him stand out from his fellows who seemed to think the ground was the most fascinating thing for miles around.

With the thought that Lord Gudmund might be a harsh master, Hermitage saw that most of the members of this train did look rather downtrodden and hopeless. They carried the looks of servants who might not have known what their place was when they started work, but they did now. It wasn't a nice place, but they knew to stay in it. And they probably had regular reminders where it was.

The younger one Cwen had spotted might be new. He could be less in thrall to the Gudmunds than the others, which might make him more willing to speak out.

'Hello,' Cwen said plainly as they all sidled over to the lad.

'What?' The boy replied, as if he didn't understand the question; which wasn't a question anyway.

'I said, hello.'

'Oh, right. Yes, hello then.' The boy was clearly having an experience that was well outside of his expectations.

'What are you doing?' Renweard's voice arrived just before the man himself.

'Investigating,' Wat said. 'You know, like your mistress instructed us to do.'

'I know that very well indeed. And what are you doing investigating with him?' Renweard didn't even give the boy a name.

'Oh, we have to investigate all over the place. People, places, you'd be surprised the sort of investigations we get up to.' Wat turned to Hermitage. 'Wouldn't Renweard here be surprised at the sort of investigations we get up to?'

'Erm, probably.' Hermitage had no idea what would constitute a surprise for Renweard so didn't really know why he was being asked.

'The thing is,' Wat put his arm around Renweard's shoulder and gently steered him away. 'When we talk to people, we tend to split the work up a bit, you know? I get to do all the really important people.' He beamed a smile at Renweard who looked as if one of Wat's smiles was a very dangerous thing to get close to. 'What can you tell me about

Lord Gudmund's departure?'

'Right.' Cwen turned back to the lad now that Wat was gone.

Hermitage looked left and right trying to work out what had just happened.

'It's all right to talk,' Cwen explained. 'Her Ladyship has asked us to look into the death of Lord Gudmund.'

'Look into it?' The lad clearly thought that was a very unpleasant thing to try and do.

'Not like that. We're going to try and find out what happened to him.'

'Oh, right.' The lad nodded as he understood this. After a pause he explained the whole thing. 'He died, you know.'

'Erm, yes,' Cwen started to look a bit concerned about how this conversation might go. 'We know that. We're going to try and find out how.'

'The normal way, I expect.'

'Normal way?'

'Yes, you know. Alive one moment, dead the next, that sort of thing.'

'That's it exactly,' Cwen smiled broadly, looking strangely impressed by this boy's thinking.

Hermitage considered that he hadn't yet seen evidence of any thinking at all.

'But what moved him from the one moment to the next, that's the question?'

'Is it?'

'Oh yes.' Cwen sounded very confident about this. 'What's your name?'

'Who, mine?'

'Erm, yes, yours.'

'Bart.'

'Bart, eh?'

'Yes.'

'Short for Bartholomew?' Hermitage suggested.

'Who is?' Bart looked around.

'I mean that your name, Bart, is a shortened version of Bartholomew.'

Bart looked at Hermitage as if he was simply humouring the sort of monk who spouted nonsense all the time.

'Bart.' Cwen ignored Hermitage completely. 'What do you know about Lord Gudmund? Apart from the fact that he's dead, obviously.'

'Know about him?'

'Did you ever have dealings with him?'

'Oh no.' Bart was very sure of that. 'It's not for the likes of me, is it?'

'What isn't?'

'Going and having dealings with his Lordship.'

Cwen sighed and breathed slowly. Hermitage recognised these signs and hoped that they weren't going to have an outburst.

'Do you know anyone who did have dealings with him? What did they say about him?'

Bart looked around him, clearly checking that no one was going to overhear his words. He was quite happy that Renweard was some way away. 'They say…,' he paused and looked around once more.

'Go on.'

'They say not to have dealings.' Bart got back to his walking as if happy that he had unburdened himself of this great confidence.

'Why?'

'Why?'

'Yes. Why not have dealings?'

'It's not good.'

'Not good, eh? I can imagine.' Cwen nodded as if this all made perfect sense to her. 'Otherwise why would they say not to have dealings?'

'You've got it exactly.'

'What sort of thing did he get up to then? Lord Gudmund. The sort of thing that made you not want to have dealings with him, I expect.'

'Exactly those sorts of things,' Bart nodded his agreement.

Hermitage was wondering if he'd get more sense by going to have a chat with one of the horses.

'And more,' Bart said significantly.

'Such as?'

'Schemes.'

'Schemes?'

'His Lordship had schemes, they say. And old Edling says to me don't get involved in any of his Lordship's schemes.'

'I bet he did.'

'Dangerous, he said.'

'Did he?'

'Risky.'

'Really. In what way? What sort of schemes were they?'

'Plots.'

'Plots?' Cwen was now sounding and looking absolutely fascinated by everything Bart had to say. Hermitage hadn't understood half of it, he just hoped she was getting something out of the conversation. If it even was a conversation.

'Always on the look out to advance his interests, they say.' Bart looked very sombre. 'Not that I had anything to do with that sort of thing.'

'Of course.'

Cwen dropped her voice 'Who was he plotting and scheming with, then? Or against?'

'Everyone.' Bart seemed to be growing into his role as distributor of his master's secrets.

'Everyone?'

'That's right. He couldn't cut a loaf of bread without having to have a scheme going on.'

Hermitage was becoming convinced that this was simple servants' chatter and complete rubbish.

'He comes to me one day to saddle the grey mare.'

'Did he?' Cwen asked as if this was the most significant thing she had ever heard.

'Me? What do I know about saddling mares?'

'Well, quite.'

'Of course, there's no telling him.'

'I can imagine not.'

'He's got a whole stable of grooms for that sort of thing, but I'm not to tell them.'

'Is that right?'

'How can I saddle the grey mare without the grooms knowing? What am I supposed to do, sneak the wretched animal out under my jerkin?'

Cwen shook her head at Bart's dilemma.

'It's a big thing, the grey mare.'

'I suppose it must be.'

'Them saddles aren't light, and the grooms don't let just anyone go and get one.'

'What did you do?'

'Looked stupid.'

'Well, perhaps Lord Gudmund thought you were a groom.'

'No, I mean I looked stupid. I put on my stupid look, as if I don't know where my feet have gone when I look up. It's a good thing to have, a stupid look. Someone asks you to do something you don't want to, so you look stupid as if you don't understand. They soon give up and ask someone else.'

'Erm, very clever, I'm sure.'

'That was one of old Edling's bits of advice.'

'Clever fellow, this Edling.'

'That he is. Or was.'

'Was? He was so old he died?'

'Oh no. He vanished.' Bart nodded his head in a slow and significant manner, the sort of manner that should accompany vanishings.

'Vanished?' Hermitage had to ask. This was something that he did understand. 'What do you mean, vanished?'

'You know, here one moment, gone the next. Had us all in a state of shock, I can tell you. Some reckons it was witches what done it.'

'Do they?' Hermitage hoped that this wasn't going to descend into superstitious nonsense. He knew people didn't actually vanish, but it was always amazing what the common folk would believe.

'But that's nonsense.'

'Of course it is.'

'Witches only take the head. The whole of Edling was gone.'

'Perhaps he just left,' Hermitage moved on quickly.

Bart scoffed at that, probably quite rightly. Servants couldn't just leave; they'd be caught and brought back.

'When was this?' Cwen asked.

'It'd be a while back now.'

'How big a while?'

Bart screwed up his face in thought. 'Be about the time Lord Gudmund went off with the king's man.'

'Perhaps he went with the king's man as well?' Hermitage suggested.

'Old Edling?' Bart obviously thought that was quite amusing. 'He'd be too old to fight in some battle.'

'But he was gone anyway.' Cwen pointed out.

'He was.' Bart now seemed to see that there might have been some connection.

'Why would Edling go with Lord Gudmund?' Cwen was sounding curious.

'He wouldn't.' Bart was sure of that.

'Not even for one of the schemes? The ones he seemed to know all about?'

Bart's eyes narrowed now, and he looked around him as if thinking that his proximity to Lord Gudmund's schemes might mean that he could be next. 'You mean he might have had a scheme down Hastings way?'

'Could be?'

'Oh,' Bart sounded even more concerned about this. 'That'd be a very dangerous thing to do, wouldn't it, what with the battle and all. Might get a man killed, a scheme like that.'

Caput VII

First, Plot your Scheme

'**W**ell, well,' Cwen said as they turned away from Bart to leave him to his new-found worry. 'Isn't that interesting?'

'I suppose it is,' Hermitage agreed. 'This poor Edling fellow must have got caught up in the whole business at Hastings and went the way of his master.'

'For goodness sake, Hermitage.' Cwen snapped at him. 'The schemes. Lord Gudmund's schemes and plots.'

'Oh, those, yes.'

'They could be very significant.'

'Or not,' Hermitage had to say. 'From what I've seen of noble folk, they are always scheming and plotting, usually against one another.'

'It's what they do best,' Cwen said. 'And the arrival of William would only make them worse. Those of them that were still alive, of course. Simply the news of his arrival and King Harold's journey from the north would get most of the nobles of the country into such a fit of plotting and scheming that they wouldn't know what to do with themselves. It would all present a marvellous opportunity for every one of them to think that they were going to come out on top. And they seem to like nothing more than coming out on top.

'Funnily enough, once they get there, they forget what it was they were going to do.'

Hermitage could only shake his head sadly at this state of affairs.

Cwen still hadn't finished with the nobility. 'They're all so stupid.'

'Stupid?'

'Yes. They all think that their own scheme is so devious and clever that it will never be defeated, simply failing to understand that every other noble in the country thinks exactly the same about their almost identical scheme.'

'Which could be good reason why Lord Gudmund might really have been murdered?' Hermitage suggested. 'Some other noble found that one of Gudmund's schemes didn't agree with him.'

Cwen clicked her fingers as she reached an exciting conclusion. 'And what better place to murder someone than the thick of battle?'

Hermitage frowned at that.

'It must happen,' Cwen insisted. 'All that sword swinging and arrow shooting. People must kill their own side by mistake sometimes.'

'I suppose it must be hard to know who is who,' Hermitage acknowledged.

'I've never been to a battle; but we've all heard about them.'

Hermitage nodded his agreement to that. Tales of battle were the most common sort. The country seemed to spend more time retelling the battle than they did fighting it in the first place. Even ancient writings frequently told of battles. As they must be such awful things in real life, Hermitage wondered why people were so fascinated by them.

'Complete chaos, from what I hear,' Cwen said. 'People and horses milling about in the mud. Pushing and shoving so close that you have to draw your sword before you get stuck in as there's no way you'll manage it once you've started.'

Again, Hermitage had no contradiction to offer.

'There you are, big sword in hand, about to swing it at the head of your mortal enemy when he ducks.'

'Ducks?'

'Yes, you know. Big sword coming towards your head, what are you going to do?'

Hermitage saw that getting out of the way would be for the best.

'The mortal enemy ducks and who happens to be standing behind him?'

'Who?' Hermitage was finding this tale quite exciting.

'Your mortal friend.'

'Mortal friend?'

'If you have a mortal enemy, you must be able to have mortal friend.'

Hermitage didn't think this was the moment for linguistic pedantry; which was unusual for him.

'Lo and behold you've taken your friend's head off by mistake.'

Hermitage could only widen his eyes at the awful thought.

'And arrows; don't get me started on arrows.'

He hadn't been going to get her started on arrows.

'You shoot an arrow up in the air, you don't really know where it's going to come down, do you?'

'I suppose not.'

'And if this friend of yours just happens to be in the wrong place, he's going to catch your arrow, isn't he?'

'He's having a very bad day, this friend.'

'That's two friends now,' Cwen pointed out. 'One by sword, one by arrow.'

It all sounded truly appalling, but Hermitage could see that there was no reason to deny the possibility.

'And if you actually wanted your mortal friend dead all

you'd have to do is get close enough.'

'Or shoot carefully.'

'Or shoot carefully. Exactly. Pat your friend on the back, wish him luck in the day's battle. Stride forth into the field with him. And then kill him. And no one any the wiser.'

Hermitage could only shake his head at this treacherous scenario.

'Of course, you'd have to make sure no one was watching. But then everyone else would be looking out for themselves, wouldn't they?'

'I imagine they would.'

'If Gudmund really did have some scheme going that was causing trouble, the field of Hastings would be the perfect spot to get rid of him.'

Hermitage considered this. 'Lady Gudmund said that he was old and would not get into the thick of battle. It would be a bit hard to walk up, chop his head off, and then claim that your sword slipped.'

'Have to be the arrow then. A lone arrow shot from the heat of the battle takes our Lord Gudmund off his horse, dead.'

'They shot the horse as well?'

'They could shoot who they like.'

'If this is the case, and I'm not for a moment saying that it is, how on earth do we find out who did it? The battle was huge, from what we hear. There were thousands of people there, it could have been anyone.'

'No, it couldn't.' Cwen looked quite sly. 'It would have to be someone who wanted him dead. Someone with a motive.'

'Like one of ten thousand Normans,' Hermitage suggested with some despair that they weren't making any progress.

'Yes,' Cwen admitted. 'That is still a possibility. But we

71

investigate using your melodic thing.'

'Melodic thing?'

'Yes, you know, motive, melody and opportunity.'

'Method, not melody.' Hermitage had a horrible image of a killer humming a tune as he went about his business.

'Oh, right. That makes sense now. I always wondered what music had to do with it. Anyway, the method is sword or arrow, doesn't really matter. The opportunity is the great big Battle of Hastings. All we have to do is find someone who had a very specific motive against Gudmund.'

'Through one of his schemes,' Hermitage said.

'Exactly.'

'How do we find out about them, now that he's dead?'

'Investigate, Hermitage, investigate.' Cwen even rubbed her hands at the prospect.

As Cwen, being a woman, wasn't allowed to be a full weaver, he imagined that she would also be prohibited from becoming the King's Investigator. Not that he would wish the role on his worst enemy, let alone his best friend, but she did seem more suited to it than him. She could investigate and he would assist, he'd be quite happy with that. In fact, he would be quite happy to let the assisting go as well, and just hear all about it later.

Before he could take any further instruction from Cwen, Wat re-joined them.

'Useful conversation?' he asked.

'Oh yes,' Cwen confirmed. 'Not only do we have it from his daughter that he was horrible, but we have it from his staff that he was a dirty little plotter.'

'I don't think Bart said dirty,' Hermitage corrected.

'Got to be dirty if it's a plot,' Cwen clarified.

'The picture grows murkier and murkier,' Wat said.

'Reading between the lines of Renweard's general contempt for everyone who is not Lady Gudmund, I'd say his Lordship was not highly thought of.'

'Not being highly thought of is hardly grounds for murder.' Hermitage knew that a lot of his fellow monks didn't think highly of him, but that wasn't really sufficient for them to kill him. Apart from the ones who said they wanted to kill him, of course. And those who actually tried.

'When I say, "not highly thought of", I mean in the Renweard sense.'

'And what's that?'

'It's the space occupied by people who, if you stuck your knife in them, you'd leave it there, rather than dirty your hands by taking it home.'

Hermitage tutted at the idea.

'Even I'm not as bad as "not highly thought of", apparently. I'm disgusting and a disgrace, but that's relatively acceptable. He even said that many people advised her against the marriage.'

'I don't see Lady Gudmund as the type to take advice,' Hermitage said. 'Even in her youth.'

'I quite agree. Even Harold said it was a bad idea.'

'King Harold?' Cwen sounded surprised. 'What did he have to do with anything?'

'He wasn't king then, but you know what nobles are like, always interfering in one another's business.'

'In which case, we have two problems,' Cwen said. 'One,' she held up a finger, 'it seems quite possible that Lord Gudmund could have been murdered after all. It sounds as if he might have quite a list of those who wished him harm. Hermitage and I have just been considering all the fine opportunities for murder that a really large battle presents.'

Wat nodded that this was very sound thinking.

'Two,' she went on, 'why does Lady Gudmund care?'

'Oh really, Cwen,' Hermitage said. 'The poor woman has lost her husband. She may simply have loved him dearly and is saddened at his departure. Had you thought of that?'

'Yes, obviously.' Cwen sounded disappointed that Hermitage was not giving her credit for thinking this through. 'But Lord Gudmund seems to be a nasty piece of work who most people would prefer dead, and Lady Gudmund does not strike me as the sensitive loving type. She's certainly not grieving very much.' Cwen puffed out her cheeks and did rather a good impression of Lady Gudmund. 'Husband's been murdered. Be a good monk and find out who did it.'

Hermitage's eyes widened at this heartless treatment of a poor widow.

'Why would she worry that this scheming, plotting, horrible husband who was not well thought of, is now dead? Could be good, having a dead husband. What was his is now hers and all that.'

'She's as bad as he is?' Wat suggested. 'And has her own scheme that requires locating and disposing of her husband's killer?'

'Quite possibly. Or she wants to find the killer for personal reasons.' Cwen suggested.

'Revenge?' Hermitage asked, knowing that revenge always made things so much worse, somehow.

'Could be. Or one of the others. Anger, greed, pride, that lot.'

'That lot.' Hermitage sighed at the nomenclature of the seven deadly sins.

'Can't be seen to be letting her husband go and get murdered. Shows weakness,' Cwen said. 'If people get the idea that they can murder the head of the Gudmund household with impunity, goodness knows what they'll try next. Or who they'll do next.'

Hermitage couldn't help but think that this was all getting a long way from a woman whose husband simply died in battle.

'This is the sort of thing nobles get up to all the time,' Cwen added. 'You know, "you shot my deer, so I kill your first born. You kill my first born, so I burn your manor down"'. She shrugged as if such nonsense was perfectly understandable. 'Only in Lady Gudmund's case she gets the King's Investigator to find out who did it, then deals with them.'

'Horribly,' Wat added.

'Of course.'

Hermitage worried that they were all getting too far ahead of themselves. 'We still don't know that he wasn't simply killed in battle. It is the most likely situation, after all. Consider a revision of Wat's very sound argument.'

Wat and Cwen looked a bit lost at this.

'Saxon nobles go to battle at Hastings,' Hermitage began. 'William and the Normans kill Saxon nobles at Hastings. One Saxon noble out of all of them is actually murdered by someone completely different.' He held his hands out to show that the ridiculousness of this argument was plain for all to see.

Unfortunately, Wat and Cwen seemed to have followed another track.

'Perfect opportunity for murder,' Wat concluded.

'No, no,' Hermitage protested.

'Could even have been other murders going on as well,' Cwen enthused rather disturbingly. 'Great opportunity to settle lots of arguments and feuds.'

Hermitage sighed as loudly as he could manage. 'William

and the Normans were just standing there watching while the Saxons all got on with murdering one another?'

'Don't be silly, Hermitage,' Cwen chided. 'You're getting carried away.'

'Yes, Hermitage,' Wat said. 'You know what you're like for being silly and getting carried away.' He winked for some reason.

'Did Renweard tell you anything specific?' Cwen asked. 'Give away what Gudmund was actually up to?'

Wat shook his head. 'He seemed to consider it his life's work to keep away from the man and his people. And to keep Lady Gudmund at a distance as well.'

'The marriage must have been a real disappointment to him.'

'That was pretty clear. Renweard obviously thinks that Lord Gudmund was so far below her Ladyship that he was lucky to lie on her floor.'

Hermitage couldn't understand that. 'But they did marry?'

'Absolutely. That was all as it should be, but she was the one with the money and the title. He was just some dashing knight who wandered into town.'

'Aha,' Cwen said with a knowing nod. 'Looking to make his fortune, eh? Luckily, Lady Gudmund already had one so he didn't need to bother.'

'Exactly. Renweard thinks that she could have done so much better.'

'But they do have a daughter,' Hermitage pointed out, not wanting to go into the details of that sort of thing.

'They do,' Wat agreed. 'And no son. Yet another failing on Lord Gudmund's part.'

Cwen sniggered at something or other.

'And I gather that he was not going to be allowed to try

again.'

'What a happy family.' Cwen was struggling to contain her mirth. 'Which makes it even more of a puzzle why Lady Gudmund is bothered about his murder. Unless she has a motive of her own.'

'Ulterior,' Hermitage said.

'Where?' Wat looked around as if expecting to see someone.

'It means further, or more distant. I considered it quite appropriate when we were looking into the business of King William's taxes.[7] If someone has a hidden motive, we could call it ulterior.'

'Could we?' Wat clearly didn't understand why it needed to be called anything.

'It's quite good, don't you think?'

'If you say so.'

'Meanwhile,' Cwen sighed, 'back at the murder in hand, if we may? This might explain why Lady Gudmund thinks her husband was murdered, being generally a bad sort. She may even have a few ideas about who it could have been. If she didn't do it herself.'

'Oh, come now.' Hermitage was not going to let that idea loiter. A thought did occur, though, and he didn't know where it had come from.

'A thought?' Wat asked.

'It is.' Hermitage almost felt as if he was looking at it from the outside, so unusual was it. Well, unusual for him, anyway. He seldom had thoughts of a material nature and spiritual murder was a rare occurrence; so rare he'd hadn't come across one yet. He even had to struggle to put it into words. 'What happens if you're killed in battle?'

---

[7] *The 1066 From Normandy* is your reference work.

'Erm, death?' Cwen suggested.

'Well, yes. I mean what happens to all your things? Your land, your money?'

'To the victor, the spoils,' Wat said, which Hermitage thought was a very interesting expression.

'Victori spolia?' he speculated on the Latin construction.

'Eh?' Cwen interrupted his thoughts.

'Sorry.' He tried to get back to his question. 'If, as a Saxon noble, you were killed in the battle at Hastings, your property would go to William?'

'I think William would be very disappointed if that wasn't the case.' Wat said. 'The whole conquest would be a waste of time.'

'But if you weren't killed in the battle, but were murdered?'

'Ah.' Wat and Cwen got the idea at the same time. 'Your property would stay with your family.'

'Possibly,' Wat said. 'Unless William came to steal it all anyway.'

'Yes, but it would be a good argument, wouldn't it,' Cwen followed the thought. 'Good King William, please don't take my estates. My husband didn't fight you at all, he was cruelly murdered by a wicked Saxon enemy.'

'Oh yes?' Wat replied as if he were the king. 'Which Saxon was this then?'

'Your own investigator found the wretch for me. I had him killed, just to be on the safe side. But Brother Hermitage will testify to the truth of it.'

'Oh dear,' Hermitage said, suddenly feeling that a simple death in battle had got a whole lot more complicated. It was bad enough that people went around killing one another, whatever the circumstances. If they were doing so with devious and dishonest intent, it somehow made things worse.

The biggest worry was that it made things worse for the investigator. If these people were prepared to benefit from the death of their closest relatives, what chance would a humble monk stand?

Caput VIII

A Peculiar Stori

Hermitage had no idea how to ask Lady Gudmund if her husband was a ne'er-do-well Saxon schemer who might have been murdered by a co-conspirator. The suggestion that her inheritance depended on his death being the right sort, was simply unthinkable. He found questioning people to be a terrible imposition and he generally tried to let Wat and Cwen do it. Cwen particularly, seemed to enjoy making people uneasy and forcing them to reveal themselves.

Perhaps a mild enquiry about who Lord Gudmund's associates were might be helpful.

Cwen was all for barging into the carriage and asking Lady Gudmund which of her husband's scheming little friends was most likely to kill him.

Wat suggested a touch of caution as they were in the midst of Lady Gudmund's host. If she really took against them, she could have Wat and Cwen dragged back to the workshop, leaving Hermitage on his own.

They all agreed that leaving Hermitage on his own to investigate a murder was not a good idea at all.

Given the circumstances of their departure from the carriage they thought it best to wait until evening before pursuing the matter any further. Perhaps Lady Gudmund would be better disposed towards them by then. And if Hermitage asked the questions, that would probably be helpful. Hermitage didn't think it was helpful for him but could see the reason. They already seemed to have established the situation where Wat and Cwen were the nasty investigators and Hermitage was the nice one.

His sense of direction was never terribly functional at the best of times, but he knew Bury St Edmunds was to the south. Apparently, it was quite a way east as well, and so they had left Derby on the old Roman road that pointed in the direction of far off Peterborough.

The Roman roads still provided the main thoroughfares for the country and Hermitage had had enough bad experiences on them to be very wary. They always seemed to be taking him straight to the scene of the crime, as if the murderers were committing their sins by the roadside just so that he could get there more quickly.

This particular road followed the pattern of most in the country, in that it was falling apart, having had most of its useful material taken away for building. Over and above this, it appeared that the Romans' own motivation for travelling east from Derby had not been great, and so they hadn't even bothered with a decent road in the first place.

As they moved along, the gaps in the path gradually became longer and longer until whole sections of it were missing altogether.

Saxon drove-ways tended to be simple, narrow tracks, along which livestock could be herded and simple, walking folk could make their way. Getting a large cart along was a trial, and Hermitage could see why the Ladies Gudmund needed such a large number of people with them.

As the last of the Roman roadway disappeared behind them, large wooden poles were extracted from somewhere under the carriage and were then fitted into slots on the sides of the vehicle.

A number of the men of the entourage then took up places

by these poles, which now stuck out in front and behind.

Bart passed them by as he took his place, giving them a very resigned shake of the head.

'What's going on?' Cwen asked.

Bart's voice was quiet. 'When we get onto the rutted old tracks, the carriage can't handle it, and so we have to help it along.'

'It must be heavy.'

'Really?' Bart sounded quite sarcastic. 'I hadn't noticed. You can have a go if you like.'

'No, it's all right.'

'Their Ladyships must not be disturbed by the discomforts of the road.' Bart sounded as if he didn't agree with this argument. 'They must be suspended above it; and we're the suspension.'

Just at that moment the cart's right wheels found a substantial hole in the path, and the men on that side took the strain with much groaning.

'It'll take forever to get anywhere at this pace,' Wat commented. 'Can't they get out and ride the horses?'

'What a suggestion!' Bart said, although he sounded as if it was quite a good one.

Wat just shook his head at the idiocy of the whole thing. 'I think I'd rather walk than be in the carriage.'

In the clear passages of the road, the cart made good pace and they had to walk quickly to keep up. Unfortunately, the clear passages were remarkable by their absence and most of the time they had to slow down to avoid getting too far ahead.

'Where are we heading?' Hermitage asked Renweard, who was walking up and down the line, berating the men for not responding quickly enough to the ruts in the road, or responding with too much enthusiasm.

Hermitage had noticed that some of the men seemed to be taking an unhealthy delight in letting the wheels drop into a rut, before using their poles to bounce it out on the other side with great vigour. It appeared to be some sort of competition to see how high they could get the wheels off the ground, before they crashed down again.

Apparently, a squeal from inside the carriage was a mark of success.

Renweard was too distracted by his task to be difficult. 'We have arrangements in place. We'll be able to shelter in a good house before nightfall.'

'And where would this good house be?' Wat asked, clearly thinking that there weren't many good houses in this part of the country.

Without giving the place any undue attention, Renweard simply spoke its name. 'Gotham.'

'Gotham?' Wat's voice carried a weight of disbelief. 'Are you serious?'

'Of course.'

Hermitage was extremely concerned that Wat was concerned. His own concerns were enough to cause him serious worry, if Wat was put out by the name of the place, Hermitage could see himself not lasting two moments. 'What's wrong with Gotham?' he asked.

'There's nothing wrong with Gotham itself,' Wat said. 'It's the Stori of Gotham that's the problem.'

'Why, what's the story?'

'Not that sort of story. Stori,' Wat spelled the word out. 'It's a him, and he's mad.'

'How dare you,' Renweard said. 'Lord Stori is a fine man.'

'Have you met him? Did you stay with him on the way from Bury?'

'Well, no. We came a different route, but he is well thought of.'

'Well thought of by the other mad men,' Wat suggested. 'If he's still there, of course, and hasn't gone the way of all Saxon landowners.'

Renweard simply tutted, turned his back on them and walked up to the front of the cart to berate the men there for getting off the track. He said that if their tracking didn't improve, he'd have them under the carriage changing the privy pot.

'In what way is this Stori of Gotham mad?' Hermitage asked gently. He asked gently in the hope that the answer would be gentle as well. A light eccentricity would be fine, perhaps a lively dance at inappropriate moments would be the limit.

'Not just one way,' Wat said, discouragingly. 'All sorts of ways all at once.'

'Oh dear.'

'Quite. And he's lord of a few manors around this part of the world, or he was. With any luck he'll have been dragged to Hastings with Harold and done the Saxon disappearing trick.'

'Is he dangerous? Have you met him?'

'He sent for me to do a tapestry once.'

'Ah.' Hermitage now had a much clearer idea of what sort of man this Stori was.

'And I refused.'

'Refused?' Hermitage was stunned for a moment. He couldn't imagine any image that Wat the Weaver would refuse to make. He had heard of many that should have been refused, most of them, in fact, but never one Wat had voluntarily turned down.

'What was it?' Cwen sounded intrigued by this.

84

'Black.'

'Black?'

'That's it.'

'He wanted a black tapestry? Tricky colour to get right,' Cwen said thoughtfully. 'Everything comes out dark brown,' she explained.

Hermitage understood this. His own Benedictines aimed for a black habit, but never really managed it. Even the Cluniacs, a relatively new order who thought that the Benedictines were a bunch of ineffectual slackers, hadn't achieved their desire for a habit as black as night; and being called the very, very dark brown monks tended to annoy them.

'You don't understand,' Wat said. 'He wanted a black tapestry.'

'Yes, you said.'

'All over black. Nothing but black. A great big tapestry of blackness.'

'What was the point of that?' Cwen asked.

'He was going to stare at it.'

'What would that achieve.'

'Make him even madder, as far as I could see. I think that was his hope.'

'Very odd.'

'Exactly. And I wasn't going to get involved in that sort of thing.'

'What sort of thing?' Hermitage asked, not seeing how black tapestries could be a "sort of thing".

'What next?' Wat asked. 'A tapestry without any wool?'

Hermitage couldn't see how that would work.

'Or hanging threads in a frame that symbolise the origin of tapestry. Perhaps just a sheep on a rope?'

'What are you talking about?' Hermitage was finding these descriptions rather disturbing.

'It's what happens when serious tapestry makers get together and muse about things.'

'Aren't you a serious tapestry maker?'

'Of course. I am a serious merchant of tapestry, supplying what the market needs in my own inimitable manner.

'But there are others who get so far into their own heads that they start producing work no one would recognise as tapestry at all. They ask themselves stupid questions.'

Wat changed his voice to be a rather airy but intense one. 'Why use a loom at all? It's so restricting. We should just throw the wool on the floor and let it land where the spirit takes it. I call it Loom Without a View.'

'Ah,' Cwen gave a broad smile. 'Stinley.'

'Yes, he's one of them.'

Hermitage recalled discussion of Stinley the weaver, colloquially known as Stinky.[8] As far as Hermitage could recall, the man was renowned for making tapestry out of things tapestry should not be made out of.

'And Stori just encourages them.' Wat complained. 'He's got too much money and he's as mad as a bucket of bats.'

'He seems known to the Gudmunds,' Hermitage pointed out.

'Yes, and that's a worry. If they think Stori of Gotham is the sort of person to offer a good house, they've got some very peculiar ideas about good houses. I think I'll sleep in the cart.'

. . .

---

[8] A Murder for Master Wat contains references to Stinley; they aren't nice references.

Arrival into Gotham was as normal as Hermitage could hope for. In the time taken to get there he had conjured a quite different place in his mind. The streets would be awash with people shrieking and pulling their hair out. The houses would be heaps of rotting wood from which bright eyes peered at him. And for some reason he had concluded that the safe house of Stori would, in fact, be a cave.

As in Derby, the people of the town emerged to see the disturbance that trooped along their street. And there seemed to be quite a lot of them. This Gotham was a large place and all the people in it looked completely normal. He began to wonder if Wat might not have been exaggerating.

At the end of the main street, as the last of the hovels and simple dwellings slipped behind them, the house of Stori appeared. It had to be the house of Stori, Hermitage couldn't imagine who else but the lord of the manor would live in such a place.

He cast a sideways glance to Wat as he considered the large Saxon hall that stood before them; a perfectly standard Saxon hall. It was a big one, but in all other ways no different from a hundred halls up and down the country. It did not look like the hall of a mad man.

'He's only fooling you,' Wat informed them.

The carriage was drawn around to the main entrance of the hall and the suspension breathed a collective sigh of relief. Renweard strode purposefully to the carriage door and beckoned one of the men to come and retrieve the steps.

The door to Gotham Manor was as imposing as it should be. A great slab of oak, studded with iron, told those who visited that this was not a place for the taking. Of course, a decent contingent of Norman soldiers would probably ignore the door and just knock the walls down, but still, it was a good door.

To one side of it a high stack of logs was piled under a simple shelter. To the other, a basic hand cart was parked, doubtless the vehicle for the collection of fresh logs when they were needed.

The overall impression was one of good order and organisation.

Renweard stood stiff and proud as the ladies Gudmund descended.

Hermitage noted that the overall impression was dishevelled and discomforted. For all the trouble of the cart and it's supporting entourage, the two ladies looked as if they'd rather walk. They even staggered slightly as the solid ground took their weight, instead of the swaying carriage.

Both of them adjusted their voluminous skirts, putting the folds back into some sort of order. This was followed by their hair, their shoes and finally they stretched their necks and arms to shake off recent discomfort.

Lady Gudmund gave Renweard a nod and the man strode up to the door of the hall and knocked on it with a heavy fist.

They waited for a response.

With a glance back at his lady, Renweard knocked again. Still no reply.

'Perhaps he's dead?' Wat suggested quietly to Cwen and Hermitage. 'Killed at Hastings, along with all the other Saxons?'

Cwen nudged Wat in the ribs. 'If he's rich we could get his widow to pay us to investigate.'

The Gudmunds were now looking rather puzzled. There was certainly no sign that this place had been abandoned. It looked well lived in and cared for. Hermitage glanced upwards and saw that there was a light drift of smoke coming from a central hole in the roof, so someone was in there; someone who didn't want to answer the door.

Renweard knocked for a third time.

He then screamed and jumped back, giving the impression that he wanted to hide behind Lady Gudmund.

Hermitage looked quickly around for any sign of what had startled the man. Perhaps there was a rat or a spider. He knew some people had trouble with rats and spiders; he was one of them.

There was no sign of anything unusual around the door at all. Apart from the logs that were moving, obviously. This sight was so peculiar that Hermitage didn't understand it enough to be alarmed. To begin with, he thought that the pile had simply been poorly stacked and was falling just at this moment. Then he wondered why the logs appeared to be walking towards them.

'Told you,' Wat said in his ear. 'Mad.'

'Aha,' said the walking logs.

Hermitage saw that this was a man with some logs attached to him. Lengths of twine secured them on top of his clothing at his legs, arms and chest, and his face had been smeared with mud. Now that was peculiar. Brother Bedling at De'Ath's Dingle frequently covered himself in mud, but then he was usually naked at the time.

This fellow had clearly been sitting at the log pile, but being covered in the things himself had been all but invisible. Actually, that could be quite clever. However, if Wat was right, and this was the Lord of the Manor, it could be quite mad.

'What do you think you are doing?' Lady Gudmund demanded of the man with the log collection.

'I am ready,' the logs replied in a very serious tone; serious for anyone, let alone someone wearing his fuel. The voice was deep and almost growling. It was a voice with no space for humour. The world was a serious place made up of serious events, things and people. It demanded a seriously serious attitude, and Stori had one. Even sitting in a log pile dressed as one of the logs was not a matter for levity.

'Ready for what?'

The log man looked to left and right and disclosed his confidence to them. 'Anything. I am ready for anything.'

'Except perhaps a fire,' Cwen muttered.

'We seek Stori of Gotham,' Renweard announced, recovering his composure and glaring at everyone to make it quite clear that his scream was never to be spoken of.

The logs crept closer. 'And you've found him, my friend.'

'Oh Lord,' Renweard sighed.

'Bucket of bats, I said,' Wat spoke up. 'But then I hadn't thought of logs.'

'You aren't Norman,' Stori accused him, ignoring the slur.

'Well, no.'

'I am ready for the Normans.'

'Got a thing about logs, have they?' Wat asked.

'It's a trap,' Stori explained, still taking himself far more seriously than anyone else was managing. 'They come into the hall past the logs and then I have them.'

'A hall full of Normans while you're dressed as logs.' Cwen clearly didn't think much of the idea.

'That's only half the trap.' Stori clearly thought they'd all be impressed by the other half. 'Once I have them in there I close and bar the door.'

'Well done.' Cwen looked around as if there might be an alternative good house close by.

'Then comes the clever part.' Stori was getting positively

intense.

They waited for the clever part.

'I burn the manor down.'

Silence greeted this cunning step.

'You burn your own manor down?' Wat was the first to ask.

'A manor full of Normans,' Stori explained as if no one could question such a master stroke.

'Which will only leave what, thousands in the rest of the country?'

'One step at a time,' Stori intoned.

Wat now looked to Renweard and the Gudmunds. 'Perhaps we'll be moving on? We'd be safer in Hastings standing just in front of King Harold at arrow time.'

'Ah, Hastings,' Stori nodded knowingly.

'You know about it?' Cwen asked, sounding surprised that this man knew where he kept his own ears.

'I was there,' Stori confirmed with grim now added to his seriousness.

'Didn't see Lord Gudmund by any chance?' Wat asked.

'I saw everything.' The fact that Stori was talking like a seer while still dressed as a decent sized fire was most disconcerting.

'You may be able to tell us what happened,' Hermitage said hopefully. If this Stori could confirm the death of Gudmund the whole investigation might come to a nicely premature conclusion.

'I can tell you everything. They are all in here.' Stori nodded his grubby head towards his manor.

'Who are?' Cwen asked.

'The Saxons.'

Hermitage felt his insides lurch at this. Was Stori hiding Saxons who had escaped from the battle? Could Lord

Gudmund be one of them? 'The Saxons are in your manor? Which ones?'

Stori considered them all with his sombre eye. 'All of them.'

'All of them?' Wat questioned this. 'All the Saxons from Hastings are in your manor?' He rolled his eyes towards the others. 'Of course they are.'

'Come. See.' Stori turned his back to them and made for the door.

As they followed, Hermitage noticed two small letters, carved into the top of the door frame.

'CV?' he asked, unable to resist some letters when they appeared before him. 'What does that mean?' He couldn't see how Stori and Gotham ended up as CV.

'Ah,' Stori intoned a bit. 'It is the motto of the house.'

'Motto?' To Hermitage's mind, two letters did not make much of a motto.

'Curriculum vitae,' Stori explained grandly. 'The course of life.'

Wat and Cwen looked to Hermitage to confirm that this was correct.

It was, but it still wasn't much of a motto. Perhaps the rest of it had been lost over the ages. 'Shouldn't it all be written out?' he asked the lord of the manor.

'All those letters?' Stori sounded shocked. 'I'm not made of money.'

He stood on his threshold and raised an arm, beckoning that they should follow. The raising of the arm caused the log that had been tied there to slip from its moorings and hit him on the toe.

With not a sound to indicate that anything had happened, Lord Stori limped into his manor.

Caput IX

The Secrets of Gotham

𝕿he inside of the manor of Stori of Gotham was surprisingly normal. Hermitage had prepared himself for something truly bizarre, judging from the behaviour of its lord. And he was never very good at anticipating the bizarre; it always turned out to be far more bizarre than anything he managed to come up with.

Unfortunately, it wasn't crammed with Saxon nobles tending their wounds and keeping their heads down in case a contingent of Normans dropped in. Which was not helpful in explaining why Stori had said all the Saxons were in here. That the lord of the manor was a complete loon would explain it.

This was a fine traditional hall. The floor was stone flags liberally covered with clean-looking straw, while small windows set low in the wall let some light sneak in.

At the far end, a simple wall of timber with wattle and daub infill separated off what was probably Stori's private space. The rest of the quite large interior was organised into an eating area with a large table and long benches, and a scattering of chairs and benches gathered around the fire.

A fire in the centre of the space warmed the place nicely while a high ceiling ensured that the smoke that didn't want to go out of the hole did not disturb the occupants unduly.

The area was hung with all the accoutrements of cooking. A large cauldron hung to one side on its iron stand, ready to be swung into position over the flames. A spit stood ready to take whatever animal was available, and tools hung from hooks above.

It was a very comfortable and well-maintained place and Hermitage thought that there was room for most of the population of Gotham to gather if they had to. They'd need to stand up and press together quite closely, but it could be done.

Which made it quite peculiar that the place was completely empty. A hall of this size should surely have servants and slaves attending to the place, as well as the lord's own family living within.

Lord Stori walked over to the fire, untied his wooden costume and threw each piece into the flames. He rubbed his hands once and then turned to face his guests.

Obviously, Lady Gudmund's humble servants were still outside as they weren't worthy, but Renweard was there, and his eyes were narrowed, as if he expected Stori to do something unexpected; and probably uncalled for.

'You want to know about Hastings,' Stori said, as if he was about to announce details of the forthcoming apocalypse.

'We want to know what you know about Hastings,' Cwen corrected. 'And in particular if there is anything you can tell us about Gudmund.'

Stori nodded seriously but did raise his eyebrows as if the name meant something to him. Hermitage had already concluded that the man did everything seriously, even dressing in logs.

'I shall fetch the book,' he said.

Ah, now that sounded much more hopeful. The thought that Stori might have anything useful to tell them at all was a serious doubt. After all, the man had disguised himself as a woodshed. Hermitage had serious doubts about the veracity of anything he had to say.

But if it was in a book, well that would be fine. Books were reliable sources of information. It briefly crossed his mind to wonder whether a book written by Stori would be any more reliable than the words that came out of his mouth, but he dismissed the worry. There was going to be a book.

Stori gave them all significant looks before leaving them and walking to the far end of the hall, where he disappeared behind the dividing wall.

'Where is everyone?' Hermitage asked quietly.

'Who?' Cwen looked about.

'All right, where is anyone? I suppose it's no surprise that the Saxons of Hastings aren't crowding the place, but Stori is Lord of the Manor, that isn't usually a lonesome role. Where are his servants, his family, anyone? Surely he can't live here alone?'

'Would you live with him?' Wat asked. 'I wouldn't stay in here if my lord's best secret plan was to burn the house down with all the people inside.'

'Is this man going to have anything useful to say?' Lady Gudmund was sounding quite impatient. 'He seems,' she searched for the word, 'distracted.'

'Distracted?' Wat obviously thought that was a very generous description. 'He's more than distracted. He's had his attention to the real world completely removed and buried in the woods. I told you he was mad.'

Even Renweard looked as if he was considering that the manor of Lord Stori might not be quite such the good house he had hoped for. He appeared to be looking around the walls for an escape route.

'Happy to bed down in the manor of Lord Stori?' Wat asked brightly.

Renweard glared as if this was all Wat's fault.

'Not that there's anywhere else to go now,' Wat added with some mischievous glee. 'Just have to stay awake all night, eh?' He patted Renweard on the arm.

The mood of the visitors was not helped by the noises that now came from the other side of the wall Stori had gone behind. They weren't unusual or worrying noises in their own right, in fact they would be perfectly insignificant in any other set of circumstances.

Hermitage couldn't help but swallow and move a little closer to Wat as he listened. He was positively certain that Stori was the only other person in the whole of the hall, so he found it very hard to understand why he was hearing quite an animated conversation.

It wasn't as if Stori was talking to himself, that would have been quite understandable. Everyone did that, particularly when they were looking for something. "Now where did I put it", "Oh, this is ridiculous", and "Aha there you are", were things perfectly normal people would say out loud.

The problem was that in Stori's case someone appeared to be answering back. It sounded just enough not like Stori to make the hairs on Hermitage's neck stand up. And he had already concluded that the lord of this manor was not perfectly normal at all.

'They want the book,' Stori said.

'I know they want the book,' nearly-Stori replied. 'I'm not deaf.'

'Well where is it?'

'Where you left it? Try there.'

'Here we are.' Stori had found what he was looking for.

'Do we trust them?'

'They are Saxons.'

'Are you sure? They could be Normans in disguise.'

'Normans in disguise?' Stori scoffed. 'Are you mad?'

Hermitage thought that was a very good question indeed. Unfortunately, there was no answer.

There was now some scuffling behind the wall, which made Hermitage even more concerned that Lord Stori might have moved on to fighting with himself.

He jumped as Stori appeared from behind the wall, lurching forward as if he'd been pushed.

'The book,' Stori announced with a glance back at the wall.

'Aha,' Hermitage said weakly. 'Very good.' He'd never been less keen to look at a book.

'Everything all right?' Wat asked with a nod back towards the wall.

'Yes,' Stori replied, looking puzzled. 'Why wouldn't it be?' He came forward with the book in his arms and despite the peculiarity of the situation, Hermitage couldn't help but feel the usual excitement he did whenever he met a new book.

This one was large and thick, and Stori took it over to the table where he laid it down before unwinding the thin cord that bound it shut.

'Now then,' he said as he pulled open the light-coloured leather of the cover. 'What did you want to know?' He looked at them all with his sombre and serious demeanour, as if he hadn't just been arguing with himself at all.

The others had moved over to the table to look at the book and they seemed to acknowledge that the monk in their midst would be in charge of book-related issues.

Hermitage considered the front page. Then he peered at it. Then he looked away before squinting closely.

'What's this?' he asked, holding out a hand towards the page.

'It's the book,' Stori said, as if it were the only one in the world. 'I thought you'd know about books, being a monk.'

'Well, yes. I know it's a book. I mean what's the writing?'

'Those are the words.' Stori imparted the information as if Hermitage might never have seen any before.

'All right. What language is it?' Hermitage didn't think he'd have to be this specific.

'My own.'

'Pardon?' Hermitage had heard the words, but they made no sense. Not that much of what was going on here made sense anyway. 'I thought you were Saxon.'

'I am.' Stori nodded to them all as if this was a most significant piece of information.

'But this language isn't Saxon.' Hermitage considered the words on the page once more. The letters were the normal ones, but the way they were put together was completely wrong. It wasn't old Saxon and it wasn't Latin. He knew some Greek and recognised a couple of the eastern languages and he could see that this was using the right alphabet, just in the wrong order.

'It's my own language. I made it up,' Stori informed them. He looked as if he was expecting congratulations for this achievement.

Hermitage's immediate reaction was to say, "you can't", but he resisted. He knew perfectly well that people weren't allowed to make up their own languages. Where would the world end if that sort of thing was permitted? He wasn't sure who was in control of the rules, or how they would be enforced, but making up a language that those in charge didn't approve of was ridiculous. Who would you speak it to?

The problem was that Stori had done just that. Well, he said he had. He had certainly done something with the letters but there was no telling whether it was any sort of language or not. 'Why?' was the next best question.

Stori held him with his steady gaze. 'So that no one can read it.'

This was getting completely out of hand. Hermitage was firm that people couldn't go round making up their own languages at all. Making one up that no one could read meant that it couldn't really be called a language in the first place.

'Except me,' Stori added.

Ah, now Hermitage saw something in it. He knew that some monks in the scriptorium would use Latin phrases or words that had secret meanings only shared between one or two of them. These meanings were almost always lewd if not positively revolting, so he never engaged in such goings on. For Stori to have made up a whole language was going a bit far though.

And if there was no one to share it with, what value was it?

Stori turned the first page over, and Hermitage recognised a list. A list was a list in any language, it seemed. Rows of letters marched down the page, each line stopping before it reached the right margin. If it looked like a list, it was probably a list.

'The Saxons,' Stori explained with a sombre nod.

Hermitage examined the page but still couldn't make any sense of the apparently random arrangement of letters.

The lord of the manor put his finger on the first line. 'Earl Leofwine,' he intoned.

Hermitage peered hard and tried to get his tongue around the nonsense. 'It says Lrae Eniwfoel.'

Stori nodded knowingly.

'Ah,' Hermitage called out the relief at understanding what was going on bursting out of him. 'It's backwards.'

Stori frowned hard.

'You've written the words backwards.'

Now Hermitage got a very had stare from Stori. 'How did you know that? Are you a Norman?'

'Of course not. I can see it.' Hermitage pointed at the line. 'The letters are backwards. He considered the next line. 'Erm, that one says Earl Gyrth.'

Stori took a step back now, clearly in shock that someone had untangled his devious secret.

'It's not very difficult.' Hermitage said, perhaps unwisely. 'Is this a list of all those who fell?' He glanced down the page and read several of the names. They weren't people he knew, but then he didn't mix in those circles. 'How did you get them?'

Stori appeared to be coming around a bit. At least Hermitage was showing genuine interest.

'I was there. I saw all.'

Hermitage was starting to find the unceasing gravity in Stori's tone a bit wearing. He suspected that if the man called for ale it would sound like a summons to his mother's funeral.

'But you survived,' Wat pointed out the obvious.

Stori nodded. 'I saw all. And I created the book.' He laid a serious hand on his book.

'Just so I understand,' Cwen spoke up. 'You went to the battle at Hastings, watched while all the Saxons were slaughtered and took a note of their names?'

Stori nodded once more. 'It had to be done.'

'Wouldn't they have preferred it if you'd helped a bit? You know, with avoiding the slaughter, that sort of thing?'

The lord of Gotham looked disappointed that Cwen didn't understand.

There seemed to be an unspoken agreement amongst the visitors that they wouldn't press this point. Better to move on and avoid any awkwardness.

'So.' Hermitage rubbed his hands. 'Lord Gudmund? Is he in the book?'

Unfortunately, Cwen hadn't silently agreed to anything. 'And if you didn't know their name, did you go up and ask just before they died?'

Everyone shushed her in the manner people do when someone is saying the most awkward thing that all of them are thinking anyway.

'Gudmund, Gudmund,' Hermitage scanned the page, looking for a Dnumdug somewhere in the list of the fallen.

'And I don't suppose you did any of the peasants,' Cwen called as she was helped from the room by Renweard and Wat, her feet not quite touching the ground.

'There is no Gudmund,' Stori growled his growl.

'No Gudmund?' Hermitage threw a look around the others. 'You mean he didn't fall?'

'Murder,' Lady Gudmund said with some satisfaction. 'Just as I said.'

'Or he's not dead at all.' Wat pointed out the alternative as he returned from depositing Cwen outside the door, where she seemed content to stay.

'I saw no Gudmund,' Stori said.

'He wasn't there?' Hermitage didn't understand that.

'You could have missed someone,' Wat said. 'After all, it was a big battle. Hard to take everyone's names, I'd have thought. Unless you checked them all in before they began? You know, "Harold? Here", "Leofwine? Here". And then at the end of the battle you just write down "not here anymore."' Wat lowered his head as it looked as if he might be the next to be escorted from the room.

'Lord Gudmund is known to me,' Stori said. He gave a

polite nod towards the ladies Gudmund. 'And I did not see him.'

'What about Edgulf?' Hermitage asked. Obviously Edgulf wouldn't be in the book, having survived the battle to bring word of Gudmund's death.

'Who?' Stori asked.

'Edgulf. One of Earl Waltheof's men.'

'Is he?'

'But then he survived,' Wat suggested. 'Looks like only the dead nobles get in the book.'

'Who is this Edgulf?' Stori asked.

Wat broke the silence that sounded quite worried and confused. 'He was the man who came and took Lord Gudmund to Hastings; and returned with word of his death.'

'He didn't get that word from me,' Stori rumbled. 'And I have the book.'

'Did Waltheof fall in the battle?' Lady Gudmund asked.

'No.' Stori didn't sound very happy about that. 'He submitted to William.'

'Did he now?' Wat sounded very interested in that piece of information and raised his eyebrows at Renweard. 'We now have good authority that the great Earl Waltheof surrendered at Hastings, his man Edgulf probably at his back, and that Gudmund was not even at Hastings.'

Hermitage wasn't sure that calling Stori "good authority" was at all justified.

'I am not sure Lord Stori here can be considered a good authority,' Renweard spoke Hermitage's thoughts, but it sounded more as if he was defending Waltheof and Edgulf.

'Quite,' Lady Gudmund agreed. 'And if any of this is true, Lord Gudmund could have been taken away to be murdered.'

'Nothing else has proved to be true in this tale,' Wat said. 'I wouldn't believe he's even dead if I were you.'

'There is one who may know,' Stori said, in a very conspiratorial manner.

'Really?' Wat sounded very doubtful about taking any advice from Stori of Gotham.

'I was preparing the book of the Saxons,' Stori said. 'There was also a book of the Normans.'

'I don't like the sound of that,' Wat even gave a little shiver.

'The Norman keeper of the book and I compared our records after the event. If there is any more to be told, he would know it.'

'Marvellous,' Wat moaned. 'Go and ask the Normans, eh? I don't think we'll bother.'

'He is no fighting man,' Stori explained. 'And I hear that he is travelling the country at the moment, gathering information about William's new realm.'

'Isn't that lucky?' Wat didn't sound as if it was lucky. 'And who is this record keeper?'

Stori breathed the name with even more seriousness than Hermitage thought possible. 'Ranulph de Sauveloy.'

The others exchanged looks and shrugged that the name meant nothing to anyone.

'We can keep an eye out for him.' It was clear that Wat was intending to do no such thing.

With nothing further to be gained from discussion with Stori, there was further silent agreement that no one wanted to spend the night in this place. The ladies would sleep in the cart and the men would camp around it. Even if there was an attack in the night there was no point summoning the Lord of Gotham for help. Perhaps he would throw some logs if it came to it.

As they moved to leave the hall, Hermitage glanced back

for one last look. He started and clutched Wat's arm.

'What is it?' Wat asked.

'Oh, nothing, nothing.' Hermitage let go again. He saw little to be gained from reporting that just by the side of the wall at the back of the hall he thought he saw a pair of eyes looking at him. He didn't know whether to be relieved that Stori had not been talking to himself after all, or even more worried about what was back there. He concluded that saying nothing and pretending everything was all right would be for the best.

Stori had final words for them at the door. 'You must beware of Ranulph de Sauveloy.'

'Oh yes?' Wat asked quite sincerely. 'You said he wasn't a fighting man. Is he dangerous?'

'Dangerous? No.' Stori shook his head as he picked up some fresh logs and started to strap them on himself. 'But he is a bit peculiar.'

Caput X

The Book of The Battle

'That's that then,' Wat said brightly when they were out of Stori's earshot. 'All sorted out nicely.'

'What's sorted out?' Cwen asked, joining them and looking as if nothing had happened.

'Turns out that Edgulf was with Waltheof the surrenderer and Lord Gudmund wasn't even at Hastings in the first place.'

'Oh dear,' Cwen commiserated with Lady Gudmund. 'So he might not be dead after all. I am sorry.'

'Apparently, the only thing we can do is go looking for some Norman called Randolph and ask him.' Wat said with a smirk.

'Ranulph,' Hermitage corrected.

'Yes, one of them.'

Cwen gave a light laugh. 'As if we're going to do that. Go looking for a Norman. Ha ha.'

'Quite. Time to go our separate ways, I think. At least we didn't get too far from home before solving your problem for you.' Wat smiled at the Gudmunds. He was looking very expectant and had even started rubbing his hands together. It seemed this was the moment that payment for their services would be welcome.

'Solving our problem?' Lady Gudmund asked.

'Yes, you know. Dead husband? Gone south with the king? Actually, not gone south with the king and maybe not dead. Glad we could sort it all out so quickly.'

Hermitage knew that they had answered a number of

questions, but they still didn't know what had happened to Lord Gudmund. He wasn't confident that Lady Gudmund would be satisfied with this outcome.

'I am not satisfied with this outcome,' Lady Gudmund said.

Hermitage took little pleasure from being right.

Wat simply shrugged. 'What else can we do? You asked us to find out who killed your husband. Turns out that it could be no one. Edgulf reported his death, but then he was with Waltheof doing some surrendering. Is he to be trusted?'

'We don't know that Lord Gudmund was not murdered,' Renweard said. 'And Edgulf is a good man, I would swear to it. He was probably only following his master's order.'

'Then we have to find out,' Lady Gudmund instructed.

'Ah, well.' Wat sucked air in through his teeth as if he'd just been asked to reduce the price on one of his tapestries. 'It's the King's Investigator, you see.'

Hermitage didn't know why this was going to be his fault. He would just have to listen to Wat and find out.

'What about him?' Renweard and Lady Gudmund both considered Hermitage.

'Murders.' Wat nodded as if that was all that needed to be said.

'Yes?'

'He does murders. Investigates them.'

'We are aware of that.' Lady Gudmund was impatient. 'If you recall, it's why we came to you in the first place.'

'There you are then. If there hasn't been a murder, we've got nothing to investigate. Hermitage only does murders.'

Hermitage definitely didn't like the sound of that.

'Then he can investigate whether there has been one,' Renweard stated.

'It doesn't really work like that.' Wat was now shaking his

head sadly as if he'd love to help but there was really nothing he could do.

'And it wouldn't have anything to do with the fact that the next piece of information to be found is in the hands of a Norman?' Renweard was clearly questioning Wat's courage.

'Of course not.' Wat managed to sound mortally offended. Whether he was or not was a completely different question. 'We deal with Normans all the time. The king, even.'

'And Le Pedvin,' Cwen added helpfully.

'And Le Pedvin,' Wat confirmed. 'This Branulf is no worry to us.'

'Ranulph,' Hermitage corrected once more.

'So there's nothing you can do?' Lady Gudmund asked this in a rather peculiar tone, as if she had given up on securing Wat's aid very quickly indeed. That really wasn't like her. 'No help you can offer in finding out what happened to Lord Gudmund?'

'Sorry,' Wat gave his helpless shrug once more.

Lady Gudmund now held out a hand towards Renweard.

When her servant looked puzzled, she gave him a significant-looking nod, and beckoned with her fingers that he should hand something over.

With a reluctant cough, he did so, not seeming at all keen.

Lady Gudmund now stepped to Wat, took his arm and lifted it so that his palm was upwards. Into this she deposited a heavy looking purse that chinked pleasingly as it landed,

Wat looked at his hand. He considered the ladies Gudmund and Renweard. Finally he considered Hermitage and Cwen.

Hermitage was simply surprised. Perhaps Lady Gudmund was being true to her word and was paying Wat for the work they had done this far.

Cwen had her arms folded and was glaring at Wat with her "don't you dare" look. It was one that Hermitage had come to recognise.

'Find out what happened to Lord Gudmund?' Wat said, sounding as if he'd been talking about a completely different Lord Gudmund. 'Well, I suppose there might be something we can do.'

'I thought there might be,' Lady Gudmund said with some contempt as she turned to prepare for her night in the cart. Wat got a clip round the ear as he nodded and smiled to young Lady Gudmund.

'What was that for?'

'Everything,' Cwen said. 'Just about everything.'

'What just happened?' Hermitage asked Cwen.

'I hit Wat's ear.'

'I mean about the purse?'

'Wat sold our services for a mess of pottage.'

'Pretty solid sounding pottage' Wat chinked the purse in their faces. 'Oy!' he said as Cwen snatched it from his hand.

'This belongs to the King's Investigator.' Cwen bowed her head and handed the purse over to Hermitage.

He simply looked at it, never having even had a purse, let alone one full of coin. He didn't know what to do with it, but he had a very strong urge not to even touch it. The root of all evil was the only thing that sprang to mind.

'I'll look after it for him,' Cwen said, securing the purse at her waist.

'Lady Gudmund gave that to me,' Wat protested rather feebly, but didn't try to retrieve the money.

'And now I've got it.' Cwen smiled sweetly.

With the camp of the Gudmunds settling for the night, the investigative triumvirate found their own spot, close by the walls of Gotham manor. The weather was fine, but it would still be cold sleeping out in the open.

'There is a nice fire indoors, you know,' Wat said with a nod towards the building.

'And Stori of Gotham between us and it,' Cwen pointed out.

'I'm sure he wouldn't mind. Not sure he'd even notice.'

Hermitage had to speak up. 'There was someone else in there,' he whispered in a low voice.

'In where?'

'In the manor, behind the wall.'

'You mean Stori really was talking to someone else?' Wat checked. 'I had him down for the sort who issues written instructions to the animals.'

'I only saw a pair of eyes.'

'Perhaps that's where he keeps his pairs of eyes?'

'They were watching us.'

'Generally the sort of thing eyes do, I imagine.'

'Well,' Cwen said with bright enthusiasm. 'Let's go and see.'

'Go and see?' Hermitage had thought that his report would be enough to make sure that was exactly what they didn't do.

'Only one pair of eyes,' Cwen pointed out. 'We've got three. And if there is someone else, they might know more than Stori is telling.'

'Do you think he was deceiving us?' The thought hadn't even occurred to Hermitage, after all, Stori had a book.

'Who knows? He is a man who travels all the way to the battle at Hastings, the one where the Saxons are defending their country from conquest, and he takes notes. At best it doesn't sound like the action of a sensible person, and at worst he's up to something that makes sure he stays alive.'

'Or he's simply one turnip short of a stew,' Wat suggested.

'I think he's that as well. Come on.' Cwen moved back towards the door. 'I'm quite prepared to risk a pair of eyes for a nice warm fire all night.'

Hermitage gave her a weak smile.

'I'll go first,' she assured him.

'Good plan,' Wat said.

They passed Stori of Gotham without difficulty. Hermitage thought there was a slight nod of acknowledgement from the log pile, but it was hard to tell. He'd never had logs nod at him before.

Back inside, the building was warm and very comfortable. If Lord Stori had this place at his side but still chose to sit on the log pile all night, there really was something wrong with him.

'Behind the wall, you say?' Cwen asked loudly.

Hermitage just nodded.

Cwen strode across the empty space and walked around behind the wall. She then came out of the other side, holding the ear of an old man between her fingers.

Fortunately, the old man was still attached and was accompanying his ear with small squeaks of complaint.

'Cwen, what are you doing?' Hermitage asked.

'I found the pair of eyes.'

'And a pair of ears, by the look of it. Leave the poor fellow alone.'

Cwen released the ear and the man rubbed it with a glare for Cwen.

'Who are you?' she asked.

'Who are you?' the man replied, quite reasonably, Hermitage thought. 'Come in here grabbing peoples' ears. It's not right.'

'Just answer the question.'

'Where's Lord Stori?'

'Outside with his logs. Or vice versa.'

'We are here with the Gudmunds,' Hermitage explained. He and Wat walked over to join Cwen, hopefully to deter any more earache. 'We were the ones in here looking at the book to see if we could find any trace of Lord Gudmund, who has gone missing. Lord Stori was helping us. You probably saw.'

The old man looked as if he was prepared to accept this, as long as Cwen kept her distance.

'Gudmund, you say?'

'That's right. Lord Stori could not find any record of him in the book.'

'Well, of course he couldn't.' The old man now seemed to think Hermitage was some sort of idiot for asking.

'Because the name is not there,' Hermitage nodded.

'Partly. But mainly because Lord Stori can't read.'

'Erm.' Hermitage really didn't know what to say to that. The lord of the manor had gone over the book with him, he had explained about his secret language, which wasn't very secret at all. How could he do all that if he couldn't even read? Then he recalled that Stori was outside dressed as a log, he supposed anything was possible. But he had recited the house motto, such as it was. The man obviously knew c and v at the very least.

'But,' Cwen began. 'The book?' she tailed off.

'Oh, he likes to have the book and hold it and tell people what's in it, but he can't understand a word of it.'

'It is all written backwards,' Hermitage said. Perhaps Lord Stori could read one way but not the other.

'Har har,' the old man coughed his laughter. 'My little joke. Every time he goes on about his precious book, I know that anyone looking at it will see that it's backwards, but it's too much for the idiot of the manor.'

'I, er, think I may have told him.'

'You did. And others have as well, but as he doesn't understand how words work in the first place; he's not interested in which way round they are.'

Hermitage tried to think all this through. His first conclusion was that if Lord Stori couldn't read the book, it was very unlikely that he had written it. 'You wrote the book.'

'I did.' The old man nodded with some pride.

'So you were at Hastings?'

'I was. I was the one urging the Lord of the Manor of Gotham to get stuck in and defend his country. He was the one who would rather hide behind an old man and a book.'

'Ah,' Cwen said knowingly.

'Ah, indeed. If King Harold had survived, he'd have had a few words to say to Lord Stori; "Goodbye and where would you like to be buried", probably.'

'You were the record keeper, not him.'

'That's it. Harold's forces came by here on their way south. They expected Stori to go with them, demanded it even.'

'He was reluctant,' Cwen snorted.

'That's why he now spends his time hidden in the log pile; in case another king comes by wanting him to go to war. Not keen on war, is Lord Stori; or battle, skirmishing, combat or loud arguments.' The old man spat his contempt. 'I was only too willing to go and do my bit.'

They all looked at him and concluded that in a big battle none of his bits would last very long.

'But I'm not as young as I used to be.'

'I'm not sure he's as young as anyone used to be,' Wat muttered quietly.

'But I asked what I could do to serve my king.'

'Very loyal,' Hermitage observed.

'One of us had to be. The king said I could accompany them and make a note of the victory. He promised to get it all written in a great book; the tale of the defeat of the Norman invaders.'

'A pretty thin book now,' Wat observed.

'But I still kept the record. Then, when we left Hastings, or as I prefer to call it, "ran away", I put everything in the book, only backwards to show Stori for the cowardly fool he is.'

Hermitage couldn't do anything but accept this tale. It all made sense, in a very nonsensical sort of way. And Lord Stori was a very peculiar fellow. 'There was mention of Ranulph de Sauveloy, who wrote the book for the Normans? You compared your records?'

'Awful man,' the old fellow summarised. 'The only comparison he wanted to make was how much better his book was than mine.'

'He may not be able to help us then?'

'That man wouldn't help the helpless; apart from criticise them for not getting any help.' There was yet another spit on the ground. Hermitage was having to dodge them.

'I read the book though,' he said. 'And I saw no mention of Gudmund. Perhaps it's in the later pages.'

'No,' the man said blankly.

'So it's not there.'

'No, it isn't.' The old fellow seemed to have become quite annoyed at this question.

'Because he wasn't there?' Cwen asked.

The man held them all with his gaze which was now serious and sombre. 'The name of Gudmund is not in the book for a very good reason.'

'Really?' Wat sounded intrigued. 'And what is the reason?'

They waited for the aged record keeper to draw breath and give his explanation; but were disturbed by a strange noise that grew in volume before coming to a rapid conclusion.

Hermitage could only describe it as "whoosh, thud".

The *whoosh* part had come from the direction of one of the low windows in the wall. The *thud* had been when the arrow finished its journey in the old man's chest.

None of them could do anything but gape at the scene as the poor victim simply collapsed onto the floor, probably dead by the time he got there.

'What the hell?' Wat eventually spat out.

'He's been shot,' a horrified Hermitage confirmed the event.

'He's been killed.' Cwen knelt at the side of the body. She quickly looked from the dead man to the window the arrow had come from. Jumping up, she ran for the door and burst out of it.

'I, I, can't believe it,' Hermitage said. He considered the body before him and he really couldn't. He'd investigated more murders than he cared to consider, but he'd never seen one done right before his eyes. Yes, Brother Ambrosius had died what seemed like years ago, but the main issue with that hideous business was that it had happened right before his eyes and he hadn't noticed.[9]

There was no getting away from noticing this.

It was horrible.

Murders were horrible, of course. What was done to people was beyond simple sin, it was evil. Dealing with the dead bodies and finding out who did what was truly revolting.

Standing right in front of someone when they were shot to death was more than anyone could cope with.

He was sure this sort of thing was normal in a battle, but

---

[9] *The Heretics of De'Ath*, where the whole debacle began.

then it would be expected. No one would go along to a battle and then be surprised by all the fighting.

A discussion with someone in the middle of a quiet manor was not the place for shootings.

He was so stunned he didn't really know what to do.

Wat seemed in no better condition as he just stood at Hermitage's side. 'We didn't even know the old boy's name,' he said sadly.

'No one there,' Cwen panted as she entered the hall again. 'A few scuffle marks around the window but no sign of anyone. Whoever shot him made a quick escape.'

'Good Lord,' Hermitage said. He had been so shocked that he hadn't even started a prayer for the poor man. He now did so.

'Well, well,' Cwen said as she considered the body, apparently far more nonchalant about the whole business than Wat or Hermitage. 'This is ridiculous, isn't it?'

'Ridiculous?' Hermitage hardly thought that was the right word.

'Yes. Someone is about to reveal the secret that makes everything clear, and they get shot as the words are coming out of their mouth? You wouldn't even make that up to put in a story. No one would believe it.'

'Someone really doesn't want us to know about Gudmund, do they,' Wat said.

'They don't?' Hermitage finished his short blessing. There would be time for more considered supplication on behalf of the dead later.

'He's just about to tell us why Gudmund was not in the book, and he didn't seem happy about it when, whoosh, thud.'

'Oh, Wat, really,' Hermitage chided.

'And that's another thing,' Cwen said.

'What is?'

'People don't really die from whoosh, thud, surely?'

Caput XI

Whoosh, Thud

'I hardly think that's a key issue,' Hermitage said, giving Cwen a disappointed shake of the head.

'It's what children do in the fields, isn't it?' she said. 'When they're playing battles, they run around with their arms held out pretending to be archers, going "whoosh, thud, you're dead."'

'Do they?' Hermitage couldn't recall that from his childhood, but then that was hardly surprising. He didn't play battles, although he knew the other children did. Now he thought about it, perhaps some of them had shouted "whoosh, thud, you're dead" at him as he was passing by, and then complained when he didn't die properly.

'If I recall,' Wat said quietly. 'When someone got you with "whoosh, thud" you clutched your chest, said "argh" and rolled over on the ground. Then you got up after you'd served your time dead and re-joined the battle.'

Cwen nodded that this was the case.

'You didn't drop to the floor never to rise again.'

'Poor old man,' Cwen seemed genuinely saddened. 'He went all the way to Hastings with Harold, was willing to put his life on the line and then he gets shot through a window in his own home.'

'We had best tell Lord Stori,' Hermitage said.

'Had we?' Wat said thoughtfully as he squatted at the side of the body and considered the arrow that had removed one life from the room. 'And what if Lord Stori was our bowman?'

117

Wat flicked the feathers at the end of the weapon. 'Can't see anything unusual about this. Standard longbow, I'd have thought. The fletching isn't brilliant, but then I suppose it didn't have far to travel.'

'Lord Stori was the killer?' Hermitage couldn't believe that.

'It was someone outside,' Cwen said. 'There's only three people we know didn't do it; us. Well, four if you count the victim.'

'The man could hardly shoot himself through a window, could he.' Hermitage thought Cwen was being rather flippant about this.

'It would be tricky,' Cwen acknowledged. 'So, it had to be someone outside, and Lord Stori is outside. He must be a what-do-you-call-it.'

'I don't know, what do you call it?'

'Suspect, that's it. A person about whom there is suspicion.'

'Well, yes,' Hermitage had to admit the possibility. 'But if Lord Stori wanted the man dead he could have done it at any time.'

'The old man wasn't about to reveal the secret of Lord Gudmund at any time, was he?'

'I wonder if we could find the bow,' Wat mused. 'If we discover a longbow out there, it would be a big help in finding who shot it.'

'How could we tell that the longbow shot this arrow?' Hermitage asked. 'The things are all the same as far as I know. Any bow could shoot any arrow.'

'Hm. It would still be suspicious though.'

'I think our first step has to be to lay this poor fellow to rest.' Hermitage bowed his head. 'And we'll probably need some help with that. Gotham must have a priest we can summon.'

Wat said nothing but was looking thoughtful.

'Or do you think we should take him to the church?' Hermitage asked. 'Perhaps the Gudmunds would let us use their carriage.'

'I'm thinking,' Wat said.

Hermitage couldn't see what there was to think about. There was a dead man at their feet who needed the ministrations of the church. 'About what?' he asked.

'Hear me out,' Wat said, which told Hermitage that the weaver's thinking was going to be of the shocking variety. 'What if we put him behind the wall?'

Hermitage couldn't immediately see what that even meant. Put a body behind the wall?

'The only people who know that he's dead are the three of us and the killer, yes?'

'Well, yes,' Hermitage could see that was the case.

'Ah,' Cwen nodded her agreement to whatever was being proposed. 'If we go out there and say nothing, we may be able to see who's behaving suspiciously.'

'Particularly as it only seemed to be us and Lord Stori who knew the old man was in here in the first place,' Wat went on. 'Of course, someone could have been loitering out there to find out what we were doing. Then they saw the old man and heard what he was going to say.'

'And they were loitering out there with a longbow, were they?' Cwen clearly thought that was going a bit far.

'Someone was,' Wat insisted. 'I don't think you can make an arrow go "whoosh" by just throwing it. First thing we can do is go and see what Stori is up to. If he's behaving strangely, we'll know he might have had something to do with this.' Wat nodded towards the body.

'If he's behaving strangely? How much more strangely does

he have to behave?' Cwen asked. 'At least the old man wasn't shot with a sharpened log; that would have been a complete give-away.'

'Will you two stop it,' Hermitage pleaded. 'We have an old man who has just been murdered right in front of us. You're now suggesting we do nothing about it and pretend it hasn't happened?'

'Only so that we can catch the killer,' Wat insisted. 'That's what you'd want to do anyway, isn't it?'

'Of course. But this hardly seems a decent way to go about it. We cannot simply prop a dead body behind a wall while we go round seeing who looks suspicious.'

'I don't think we could prop him anywhere,' Cwen pointed out. 'Not stiff enough yet.'

'Cwen, really!'

'All right,' Wat made placating gestures with his hands. 'There's no need to get excited about this.'

'Excited?' Hermitage raised his voice before lowering it again in case someone heard. 'I'm not getting excited; I am simply asking that the dead be treated with respect and not used like bait in some trap.'

'Look,' Wat said, 'you can go off and find the priest, how's that?'

'That's better,' Hermitage was glad that they were seeing it his way.

'Only before you go, help us get the body behind the wall, and when you do go, take your time about it.'

'What?'

'While you're getting the priest, Cwen and I will do a quick visit outside and see who looks like they might have just shot someone.'

'And what do people who might have shot someone look

like?'

'Worried, probably. I haven't seen any of the Gudmund party who look like hardened killers, in which case shooting an old man in the chest would be quite a shock.'

'How awful for them,' Hermitage said despondently.

And they may have tell-tale signs.'

'Such as?'

'A longbow in their luggage? Not many places you can hide one of those things.'

'Perhaps in a log pile?' Cwen suggested with a heavy dose of accusation.

'Could be,' Wat agreed. 'But we didn't know we'd be looking for an archer until now, so we can try and spot the signs.'

'What signs?' Hermitage had watched archers, naturally, but he didn't know they had signs.

'Strong arms and back,' Wat said. 'Hitting someone in the chest, even from short range, is not the sort of thing anyone could do. And from that low window?' Wat nodded towards the source of the arrow. 'It would take quite a bit of skill. We're looking for someone who knows how to handle a bow and has had a lot of practise. Hence strong arms and back.

'They've probably got marks on the arm as well, either where the bracer is strapped, or some cuts from where they shot without one.'

'Would they do that?' Even Hermitage knew that the string of a bow could inflict a nasty cut on the forearm if there was no protection.

'If the need to shoot was urgent, and they didn't have time to prepare.'

'Such as them discovering an old man was about to reveal a great secret,' Cwen nodded.

'And if it was a rushed job, there might be scratches to the pulling fingers as well, if they didn't have a chance to put their tabs on.'

'You seem to know a lot about archers,' Hermitage observed.

'I did a tapestry for one once.'

'Oh yes?' Hermitage was cautious about hearing any more about this. He dreaded to think what sort of thing Wat had made; although naked archery sounded like a bit of a dangerous pursuit.

'Well, I did two, actually.'

'Two?'

'Only because the first one wasn't right. Apparently.' Wat didn't sound very happy about this. 'It was a perfectly good tapestry with all the bits he'd asked for in all the right places, but then he said I'd put the bracer on the wrong arm.'

'Ah,' Cwen said. 'One of those.'

'One of those?' Hermitage asked.

'The customer who complains that the tiniest details aren't quite right when they don't really matter. This is a spring scene and the deer would have shed their antlers, why have you got antlers on that deer in the background? That sort of thing.'

'Ah,' Hermitage nodded. 'Accuracy.'

'Call it what you like, this archer had a whole list of things I'd got wrong and had to be put right before he'd pay.'

'Why did you bother?' Cwen asked.

'He was a very well-paid archer and I wanted his money.'

'Oh really,' Hermitage sighed.

'And I'm afraid there's one other thing I learned that we really need to find out about.'

'Oh yes, what's that.'

Wat nodded down at the body. 'Arrowheads.'

'Arrowheads?' Hermitage didn't understand the problem.

'There are lots of different arrowheads. Cheap ones, expensive one. Ones for hunting, ones for battle. Ones only a decent archer would use and ones for any old jack-a-trade. The arrowhead could tell us something about who the archer might be.'

'You mean the arrowhead that is currently on the inside of a dead old man?' Cwen asked.

'That's the one.'

'We have to pull it out?' Hermitage asked with some horror.

'It's got to come out sometime. Can't bury him like this.'

'Don't we just break it off?'

'Not if we want to see what the arrowhead looks like.'

'Oh Lord.'

'And there's another problem,' Wat said.

'Another one? Oh good.'

'It might be barbed.'

'Barbed?'

'Yes, it means there are little edges to it that…,'

'I know what barbed means.'

'Good. So you know that pulling it out the way it went in will make a bit of a mess.' Wat shrugged that there was nothing he could do about this.

Hermitage swallowed, hoping that his food wasn't going to come out the way it went in.

'We have to push it through?' Cwen asked. Even she sounded a bit put out by this. 'I don't like the sound of that.'

'I'm not too keen myself, funnily enough,' Wat said. 'Pushing arrows through old men was not how I planned to spend the evening. Mind you he is quite thin.'

Hermitage felt his cheeks bulge as his stomach told him that it had heard quite enough.

There was already quite a bit of blood about the place, the arrow having released the sanguine humours to leak all over the old man's front and onto the floor. There was no telling if some vital area had been pierced, or the poor fellow had simply passed from the shock of being shot. A young man might be able to take an arrow and survive, but the elderly never managed surprises quite so well.

'Perhaps I will go and find the priest,' Hermitage suggested. He thought that there was no way Wat would ask him to push the arrow out, but he didn't even want to be there to see how it was done.

'Good idea,' Wat said. 'Right, Cwen, let's roll him onto his side so we can get at the arrow.'

'I know he looks dead, but do you think we'd better check first?'

'I suppose so. If he isn't, pushing the arrow all the way through would probably finish the job.'

Cwen knelt down and put her ear to the old man's chest. 'Can't hear anything. No breathing, no nothing.'

'Right. Dead it is then.' Wat joined Cwen at the man's side. 'Let's just hope we don't hit bone on the way through.'

Hermitage decided that he would quite like to go and fetch the priest right now.

Leaving the two of them to their awful task, he quickly made his way to the door and out into the evening air. A glance at the log pile showed that Lord Stori was not there. He quickly concluded that this was another suspicious thing and he made a note to tell Wat and Cwen when he got back.

Before he moved on, he went up to the logs and reached out to touch one or two, just to make sure that Stori hadn't become so absorbed that he was no longer visible.

No, there was no man there at all. Just real logs. And he peered over the back of the pile, which was only three layers deep, to make sure there was no longbow sticking out.

Satisfied that he hadn't discovered anything useful, he turned to head into the village. He bumped straight into Renweard.

'Ah, Brother monk, I was coming to look for you. Lady Gudmund would like a word.'

Hermitage didn't like the sound of that. There were ways of asking for a word and this wasn't the nice kind. In De'Ath's Dingle he was frequently asked if some Brother or other could have a word, and he learned which ones to very wary of.

There was no choice here so he followed Renweard back to the carriage where the servant beckoned that he should enter.

'Brother Hermitage,' Lady Gudmund smiled as he climbed in. She indicated that he should sit opposite her, next to her daughter. He gave the young Lady Gudmund a nod and a smile, which was returned. This wasn't seeming like such a bad encounter after all.

'I have a rather delicate matter to raise with you, Brother.'

'Ah,' Hermitage said. He didn't like delicate matters, they always tended to be quite awkward and embarrassing and he never knew where to look.

'It's about your friends.'

Hermitage wondered who she could be talking about for a moment. If she meant friends in general, Hermitage didn't really have any.

'Your fellows in investigation.'

Ah, Wat and Cwen. Yes, they were definitely friends, but over the time they'd been together, Hermitage had come to think of them not as friends but as family.

'How can I put this?' Lady Gudmund mused. She pursed her lips and cast her eyes to the roof of the carriage.

Hermitage thought this must be very delicate if Lady Gudmund couldn't bring the words to mind, given her natural domineering manner.

The lady eventually chose her words. 'Can they go away?'

'Go away?' Hermitage didn't understand.

'Yes, just so. Go away. Go home. Leave us. Depart.'

'Erm..,'

'They are a trying pair.' Lady Gudmund seemed to be warming to her task. 'The weaver is flippant, plainly greedy and disrespectful, and the girl is rude and disrespectful. You are the King's Investigator so I would like you to continue the work. They can go back to their weaving. There. It is said.'

It certainly was. Hermitage knew the others could be a bit difficult now and then, but no one had ever asked them to leave before. And if they did go, he didn't know how the investigation would proceed. He needed them to point out the things he missed. All of them. Quite frequently.

Perhaps he could just ask them to behave themselves. Not that he'd had much success with that in the past. He was just formulating his response when there was a loud knock on the carriage door.

'Yes?' Lady Gudmund asked.

The door opened and Renweard appeared. 'One of our number is missing, my lady.'

'Missing?'

'Bart.'

'Who?'

'One of the cart-men.'

Lady Gudmund looked bemused. 'If you say so. And what do you mean, missing? He's probably just gone off into the woods.'

'No, my lady, we've searched and called, and he is nowhere to be found.'

'Run away?' young Lady Gudmund suggested.

'Very unlikely,' Renweard reported. 'He was not a troublesome fellow. Never run off before.'

Hermitage's heart was thumping in his chest. Could it be that Bart was the one with the bow? Had he killed the old man and then run off. In which case, why? Was there more to Bart than met the eye?

'And what do you want to do about this?' Lady Gudmund asked, making it quite clear that missing cart men were not really her problem.

'Look for him, my lady.'

'Really?' Lady Gudmund clearly thought that if you lost a cart man, you simply got another one; wherever it was cart men came from.

'We suspect he may have been taken.'

'Taken?' Lady Gudmund sounded sceptical.

Hermitage was positively fretful. Had Bart witnessed the murder and been dealt with?

'There are signs of disturbance,' Renweard reported. 'And we found this.' He stepped back and held up a fine-looking longbow.

'And who does that belong to?' Lady Gudmund asked.

'We don't know,' Renweard said. 'Never seen it before.'

Hermitage couldn't help but cough. All eyes turned to him.

'Do you know anything of this, Brother?' Lady Gudmund asked, much more her old self.

'Not exactly,' Hermitage said. 'But I may know where there's an arrow to go with it.'

Caput XII

All Fall Out

The arrow was held up for examination. It was not a pretty sight, but then neither was the dead man lying on the floor who had been its previous recipient.

For a few moments, no one had anything to say. Hermitage was quite pleased about that as he imagined many of the things would be questions. Questions for him, and he didn't have any answers.-

They were all gathered in the hall now. The Ladies Gudmund had left their carriage to see the significance of this arrow for themselves. They had discovered that things didn't get much more significant when it came to arrows than being killed by one. Young Lady Gudmund was clearly distressed by the scene; the elder Lady Gudmund, not so much.

Renweard stood closer, as if he'd seen this sort of thing before.

Lord Stori was kneeling at the side of his erstwhile critic.

They had found him under the Gudmund carriage, claiming that he was waiting out of sight so that he could spring out and attack any Normans who dared to show their faces. The ladies and Renweard seemed ready to accept this, while Hermitage tried to hide his scepticism.

'Ah, Osbern,' Stori wailed. 'What have they done to you?'

'They've shot him,' Wat explained quite heartlessly. 'Through the window, with a bow. This one.' He took the bow from Renweard and held it out for Stori to look at.

'Woe is me,' Stori sighed.

128

'Woe is me?' Cwen treated the expression with some contempt and a roll of the eyes.

'I don't suppose you've ever seen this bow before?' Wat asked bluntly.

'How dare you,' Renweard spoke up. 'Lady Gudmund is right; you truly are a disrespectful fellow. Lord Stori is mourning the death of his, erm, old man here, and you accuse him.'

'With good reason,' Wat replied. 'And being disrespectful to potential killers is what I do best.'

'As if a man of Lord Stori's standing would stoop to the use of the bow.'

'He doesn't hunt then?' Cwen checked.

'Hunting is one thing. Shooting old men through windows is completely different. You'll be accusing me next.'

'I can if you like,' Wat said. 'What reason did you have to kill Osbern here?'

'None at all.' Renweard's outrage was getting the better of him. 'Just as Lord Stori had no reason.'

'Ah,' Wat said very knowingly. 'That's where you'd be wrong.'

'Wrong?' Renweard looked to the ladies for some support.

'Wrong as wrong can be. We found out a few things from Osbern here before he died.'

Hermitage noticed that Lord Stori gave them a sideways glance at this, forgetting his grieving for a moment.

'The great book of the dead at Hastings, for example. Not written by Stori at all, it seems.'

'Not written by Stori?' Renweard dismissed this suggestion as if it were the mumbling of an idiot.

'There's very little written by Lord Stori as it happens. Mainly because he can't write.'

Lord Stori stood from Osbern's side now and considered Wat with a sad look and a solemn shake of the head. 'You have been taken in by the old man's ramblings?' he asked. 'I suppose you would know no better.'

Wat ignored the comment. 'It was Osbern who wrote the book. Just as it was Osbern at Hastings.'

'Of course, Lord Stori would take his man with him.' Renweard snorted at the idiocy around him.

'And Osbern had something to tell us about Lord Gudmund. But that was before he was shot.'

'Tell you?' Lady Gudmund asked.

'Just so. He said there was a very good reason why Gudmund was not in the book and he was on the verge of telling us what it was when the arrow arrived.'

Lord Stori was simply shaking his head, the way people do when they want to make it clear that the person they are dealing with is so comprehensively wrong that arguing with them would be a waste of words.

'So,' Wat summed up the situation. 'Lord Stori here could have wanted his man dead before he revealed any more secrets about his master than were comfortable, perhaps some connection to the disappearance of Lord Gudmund?'

Another sad shake of the head from Stori.

'Or someone wanted him silenced before he could tell the truth about Lord Gudmund.' At this suggestion he gave hard looks at every member of the Gudmund household currently present.

'What truth?' Lady Gudmund demanded.

Now it was Wat's turn to look disappointed at those around him. 'You'll recall the man was silenced *before* he could tell? The man with the arrow hole?' He nodded at dead Osbern. 'That means we don't know.'

Hermitage noticed that Lady Gudmund was looking quite dangerous now. She didn't like Wat before, and he wasn't making things any better.

Stori found his voice now, and it was full of sympathy for Wat's stupidity. 'Poor Osbern. He always wanted to give more than he was capable of. I humoured him, naturally. He had been with my father, you know. He gave himself airs but they were mostly harmless. He told you that he wrote the book, eh?' Stori looked as if that was just the sort of thing old Osbern would do.

'We could get you to read us some more names from it then?' Wat offered.

'You have seen the book. There's no more to be gained from that.'

'I see.' Wat made it clear that he didn't believe that for a moment.

'Enough!' Lady Gudmund barked. This was so authoritative, that Hermitage was surprised Osbern himself didn't sit up and pay attention.

'I had already asked the King's Investigator here to send you two home.' The lady gave them a look so stern you could have put a boat in front of it.

'Good luck with that,' Cwen muttered, giving Hermitage wink.

'You are impudent beyond measure. I overlooked the disgusting nature of your trade on the generous assumption that you would assist this investigation. I see that you are no help at all and so you are dismissed. Be gone.'

'Dismissed?' Wat asked, sounding interested in the idea, rather than actually taking any notice.

'Exactly. You have my money, take it and go.'

Wat took on a very thoughtful look, as if he was weighing

up an interesting proposal, instead of responding to an instruction from a member of the nobility.

He faced Cwen and gave her a resigned look. 'I suppose there's nothing for it.' He held out his hand.

Cwen smiled and gave Wat a nod that said she was very pleased with his behaviour. She took the purse of money from her belt and handed it over.

He weighed it once and then nonchalantly threw it to Renweard. 'I don't really need any more money,' he said.

Hermitage was aghast. He would have to remember that.

'An old man has been murdered here,' Wat was very serious. 'An old man who did not deserve it. An old man who was poorly served by his master; and may even have been killed by him. I choose to believe Osbern. He went to Hastings. He wanted to serve his king, and this was his reward. Well, we're going to find out what's going on here whether you like it or not.'

This was all very awkward, but Hermitage felt quite proud of Wat. He'd never seen him so passionate.

'And Hermitage was right,' Wat went on. 'The idea that Lord Gudmund was murdered at Hastings is ridiculous. If he was there, he was killed in battle with his king as is right and proper. More likely he was avoiding the battle, like Stori here.'

Lord Stori was still looking at them with the natural sympathy due to the deranged.

Lady Gudmund looked ready to snatch the bow and shoot them all. 'You are no longer in my service and so you will leave.' The words were ground out as if trapped between two very heavy stones in a mill. 'I thought that the king's own investigator might be able to help with this, but I can see that even he has been tainted by your company.'

Hermitage was fairly sure that he hadn't been tainted by

132

anyone.

'You are quite right,' Wat agreed. 'We are not in your service.' He gave them each a little bow. 'We are in the service of King William. Brother Hermitage is the King's Investigator, not yours. And knowing his majesty as well as we do, I am sure that he would want us to find out what is going on here.'

From their experience thus far, Hermitage was confident that the king wouldn't want anything of the sort.

'When we see him again, we can report on all that we find. He's bound to be sending for us soon. Murders all over the place, you know. And he always likes to hear what his new subjects are getting up to. Particularly the ones with a bit of land.'

Lady Gudmund now looked prepared to give up on the bow; and push an arrow through Wat with her bare hands.

Instead, she drew herself up, considered the room briefly and then turned to leave. As she did so she gave them all the very familiar look; they were now beneath her notice.

'Bye,' Cwen called as the party exited the hall, Lord Stori in tow.

Hermitage gazed on, getting deeper into confusion with every step. If the Gudmunds were not going to talk to them, as now seemed clear, how were they going to be able to find out anything useful?

'Well,' he said, not having anything more constructive to hand.

'Nobles,' Wat breathed the word and simply shook his head. 'Do any of them do anything useful at all, do you think?'

Hermitage couldn't even begin to understand that question. It was like asking if the trees did anything useful. Nobles were nobles and other people weren't. What more was there to discuss?

'Not that lot,' Cwen said. 'But do we really think Stori shot Osbern?'

'Probably not,' Wat accepted.

'What?' Hermitage was a bit shocked by that conclusion. They had just had a very uncomfortable few moments with the Saxon nobility on the basis that one of them might have been a killer. Now they were saying that he wasn't?

'Don't think he's got it in him,' Wat shrugged.

'But we just got dismissed from Lady Gudmund's service, partly on the basis of accusing Stori of being the murderer.'

'They're hiding something,' Wat said.

'And they've got their purse back,' Hermitage pointed out.

'Yes,' Wat nodded solemnly. 'Maybe I did go a bit too far?'

'You went just right,' Cwen comforted him at his loss.

'Perhaps it's not so unreasonable,' Wat suggested. 'Shooting an old man through a window is just the level of bravery I'd expect from Stori.'

'It must take bravery simply to go anywhere near somewhere like Hastings,' Hermitage said, not wanting to hear Stori completely dismissed.

Wat shook his head. 'I suspect Stori always knew he wasn't going to get involved. And anyway, those who genuinely want to go to battle aren't brave. If there's no fear, where's the courage?

'The brave are the ones who don't want to go to battle, but go anyway, in the middle of their fear. And they fight for their life because they are terrified of losing it. The loons like King William and Le Pedvin aren't brave, they like fighting and killing. You wouldn't call me brave for making a tapestry. But what if I was terrified of wool? Then I'd be very brave.

'And what's a coward? Not someone who is shaking in their

boots or crying in their beer at the prospect of battle. They're the bravest of the brave. The cowards are the ones like Stori who avoid it and blame others. Who leave the Osberns of the world to stand for them. And then try to take the credit.'

'Ah,' Cwen said. 'The way of the world, you mean.'

'That's it,' Wat cheered quite quickly. 'And we've got the chance to find out what one collection of them is up to.'

'We know so little,' Hermitage said. 'Apart from Osbern's account of Stori, we don't know any more about the death of Gudmund than we did when we started.' He recalled why they'd all gathered in the hall in the first place. 'And now Lady Gudmund doesn't have us to find out for her.'

'Her annoyance got the better of her,' Cwen observed. 'She may regret it later, but as soon as Wat starts annoying her again, she'll see the sense of it. She'll have to find some other way of discovering her husband's fate. She's got too much pride to come back to us again.'

Hermitage didn't know whether to be pleased or disappointed by that. 'Did the arrow tell you anything?'

'Not really.' Wat held it up. 'Certainly nothing special about it. There are thousands like this in the world.'

'Renweard reported that Bart had gone missing,' Hermitage said. 'That's when he produced the bow.'

'That cart boy?' Cwen asked. 'I don't see him having anything to do with this.'

'Me neither,' Hermitage agreed. 'But he's missing. And there were signs of some sort of struggle, apparently.'

'Interesting,' Wat mused. 'We certainly didn't see this bow before now.'

'It could have been hidden somewhere,' Cwen said. 'Somewhere on the cart would be the best place.'

'Which brings us back to the Gudmunds.' Wat nodded.

'Who are the ones who wanted us to investigate the death of Gudmund in the first place. Oh, I'm confused.'

'That's good,' Wat said.

'Good? How is it good?'

'It means there's plenty to investigate. The only time you're not confused is when you say "aha" and point out who did it.'

'I'm a long way from that. Apart from Osbern here, we don't know that anything's been done at all.'

'One dead body is enough to go on, I'd have thought. And we know how this one was done. There's your method and opportunity. And we know the motive.'

'He was about to tell us about Gudmund,' Cwen said.

'Yes, but what?' Hermitage could not feel his confusion abating in the slightest.

'If we knew that, I suspect we could all go home.'

'What can we do about any of it?' Hermitage asked. 'Lady Gudmund certainly won't accommodate us anymore. Not even me.'

'We follow them,' Wat said.

'Follow them?' Hermitage thought that sounded a bit rude.

'They could be going to look for the missing Bart?' Cwen suggested. 'And we could do with finding him as well. Was he the bowman, or has he been taken?'

'Lady Gudmund didn't seem particularly concerned about him at all.'

'Now that does ring true,' Wat said.

'And if this is all connected with Gudmund, we need to follow them anyway.' Cwen sounded quite keen on some following.

'Will they allow us?' Hermitage asked.

'Do they get a choice?' Cwen replied. 'What are they going to do, shoot the King's Investigator?'

That hadn't even occurred to Hermitage, but it did now.

'Oh dear,' he fretted.

'Cheer up,' Cwen encouraged. 'At least they stormed out and left us with the nice warm fire while they get a horrible cold cart.'

'And a dead body,' Hermitage pointed out.

'Think of it as keeping vigil. Stori will have to deal with him in the morning.'

Hermitage just shook his head gently as he thought that the ridiculous situation of Gudmund's supposed murder had become a horrible one in very short order with Osbern's real one. And now it had got awkward as well with the falling out. He didn't know which was worse. He hated awkwardness. Still, Cwen was right, at least they had comfortable lodgings for the night.

'All right, you lot,' a voice barked from the door.

It was Lord Stori accompanied by four of the Gudmunds' largest cart bearers.

'You needn't think you're staying in my hall for the night. Out, out, the lot of you.'

With an exchange of glances, they knew that they really had no claim on the hall. It did belong to Stori, after all.

As they trooped to the door, Wat patted the lord of the manor on the shoulder. 'Look after Osbern. We thought we heard his spirit moaning a while ago. It was either that or the devils come to take his soul. Just keep out of the way, you'll be fine. Probably.'

As they walked out of the door, Hermitage heard the Lord of Gotham whimper in his dark abode.

Caput XIII

On the Trail of Bart

The following morning, Hermitage, Wat and Cwen watched as the camp of the Gudmunds prepared to move on. Work was done that they took no part in. Orders were issued that they ignored. Preparations were made that they remained unprepared for.

It was as if an order had gone out that the three of them were to be simply ignored; and the order was being obeyed.

'Nothing to stop us simply walking along behind them,' Cwen said. 'The speed that cart moves we'll have no trouble keeping up.'

'Do you think they'll allow us?'

'Oh, Hermitage. You're the King's Investigator. You can go where you like and do what you like.'

Hermitage had never seen it like that.

'They really can't shoot you,' Wat tried encouragement. 'Shooting the king's man would cause all sorts of trouble.'

'I'll bear that in mind.' Hermitage sank slightly in his habit.

'Come on, looks like we're off.'

The order of the Gudmund parade had been restored and the men stood ready at their poles to help the cart along. The fact that Bart was missing meant that someone had to be put in his place.

This was a rather elderly fellow who did not look or sound pleased at his new role in life. He protested that the first time he tried to lift the cart his arms would fall off, but this was to no avail. Renweard simply offered to strap the pole to man's back if that awful event came to pass.

With a creak and a crunch, the cart of the Gudmunds set off along the trail.

Lord Stori stood by his entrance watching the departure and Hermitage determined that the look on the man's face was worry. He wore it so often himself that it was easy to recognise in others. And he could see why the Lord of the Manor had cause for concern. He was now alone, without even Osbern for company, and the protection of the force of the Gudmunds was leaving.

Wat's hearty, 'Give our regards to the Normans,' as they moved away, did not do anything to cheer the Lord of Gotham's mood.

There was no sign of hurry in the passage of the Gudmunds, even though one of their number was missing. Mind you, Hermitage thought that if the cart tried to hurry on these roads it would probably fall apart.

After a few moments of desultory walking, Cwen spoke up. 'I think we'd better go ahead and let them follow. At this rate Bart could have got to Spain and back before we arrive in Bury.'

Wat nodded his agreement. 'If the lad's been taken, or is running away, he's hardly likely to do it this slowly.'

'If they're even looking for him at all,' Hermitage added. 'I know the sight of the body was disturbing, but I didn't get the impression Lady Gudmund, Renweard or even Lord Stori were genuinely concerned.'

'I'm absolutely sure they weren't,' Cwen said. 'After all, he was only a servant. Come on then.' She strode off, passing by the carriage and giving a cheery wave to the men who were already taking the strain of the cart as it rumbled through the ruts.

The others followed and soon left the Gudmunds behind.

'Do we even know where Bart is going?' Hermitage asked after the train had been left far behind. 'He could have gone in entirely the other direction. If he did shoot Osbern he's hardly likely to go home, I'd have thought?'

'We can hardly cover the whole country,' Wat said. 'We'll just have to go ahead and see what we can pick up.'

'Track,' Cwen suggested. 'You know, like tracking. From the Latin *vestigare*, investigate?'

'Don't remind me.' Hermitage shivered.

'We'll just have to carry on to the next settlement and see if there's any word. You know, ask if anyone's seen a young man who looked like he was running for his life.'

'Or was tied up, being dragged along screaming,' Wat suggested.

'That's the sort of thing.' Cwen smiled. 'Either way, he won't have gone unnoticed. Even a stranger trying his best not to be spotted will be. You know what people are like.'

'Particularly in this day and age,' Wat said. 'Everyone has to be on the lookout for a passing Norman. Look at Lord Stori of Gotham.'

'Do we know what the next place will be?' Hermitage asked.

Wat thought for a moment. 'Rempstone, I'd think. That's where we'd join the road heading towards Bury.'

'It's a good job you are well travelled,' Hermitage commented.

'Anyone in Rempstone likely to chase you out of town with rocks in their hands?' Cwen asked.

Wat shrugged as if this was a perfectly reasonable question. 'No. Only ever passed through before. Small place, nothing to it, really.'

They found no sign of Bart on the way to Rempstone, but

Hermitage didn't really know what he was looking for. The young man sitting by the side of the road would have been good.

Wat was right, it was a small place, smaller than Gotham, certainly. A place of little interest to anyone, Hermitage thought, which made him wonder why the Normans were here.

The sight of the simple and crude castle that had been constructed by the side of a modest Saxon hall made them pause before venturing into the place.

'Oh dear,' Cwen voiced their thoughts.

'Oh dear, indeed,' Wat agreed. 'What are they doing here? Can't be anything of interest in this place.'

'Apart from the road, itself?' Hermitage suggested.

Wat nodded reluctantly. 'I suppose it is a crossroads and they could keep an eye on people coming and going. Build a nice castle here so that they can come out and threaten people.'

'In which case they'll have seen Bart if he did come this way,' Hermitage said.

'Not if Bart saw them first.'

They loitered in the shelter of the trees by the side of the road, each of them unwilling to step out into the gaze of a Norman fortification.

As Hermitage considered it, he thought that it was a very modest one, there was no troop of heavily armed Normans stamping about the place.

The usual great mound of soil had been piled up, doubtless using the forced labour of the locals, and on top of this a simple wooden stockade had been built. This too was a rather haphazard looking thing, as if it had been put up in a great hurry.

'I don't think much of that,' Cwen said. 'They must have thrown it up while they were on their way somewhere more interesting. Doesn't even look very well manned.'

'Could be just to stamp their mark on the road,' Wat suggested. 'Show the Normans are here, so behave.'

'I can't actually see anyone at all,' Hermitage said. 'Not even any horses.'

Everyone was familiar with the Norman use of horses; the main use being to trample all over Saxons.

'There's some life at the hall.' Wat nodded towards the gentle plumes of smoke that were coming from the roof of the Saxon building. 'I think that if we stick to the trees, we can get to it without being spotted.'

Agreeing that this looked perfectly possible, the three of them worked their way around the side of Rempstone until they could approach from the rear of the hall. Creeping along the side of the building, they were pleased to reach the main door without any alarm being raised.

Wat banged his fist against the wood, clearly hoping to make as little noise as possible.

'What is it?' A voice called from the inside.

They all gave resigned sighs. They'd gone to all this trouble to avoid being spotted by the Normans and here was a plainly Norman accent, asking them what they wanted.

'I suppose it might be more comfortable in here than in their castle,' Cwen said. 'And if they own the place anyway?'

There was nothing they could do now. Saying, "oh nothing really", or, "sorry, wrong hall," was hardly going to get them away from the attention of the Normans.

'Just travellers passing by,' Wat called though the door, trying to sound as uninterested as possible. 'But if you're busy, we can carry on passing. No problem.'

Unfortunately, this reply seemed to be enough to encourage the Norman to come to his door. The sound of bolts being drawn on the inside indicated someone was about to appear.

Hermitage momentarily wondered what sort of Norman would bolt himself inside a Saxon hall. He knew they bolted other people in their homes, but never bothered with locks themselves.

The door creaked open and a large shape blocked the entrance.

'Yes?' it asked, the Norman lilt of the voice being even more pronounced now.

'We're, erm, just in the area,' Wat said rather hesitantly. 'And we're seeing if a friend of ours came through. Young lad by the name of Bart?'

The door swung open now and the large shape was revealed as one large man. He was clearly someone of wealth and good standing as he must have been eating for most of his life. He was of that simple shape that began below the chin and ended somewhere above the ankles; a simple shape that required a lot of maintenance. It was no surprise that this fellow had chosen to live in a low Saxon hall and not at the top of a steep Norman hill.

His dress was clearly in the Norman fashion and he even had a Norman helmet under his arm, the sort with the long metal piece protruding from the front to protect from any attack on the nose. There was something a bit odd about it though, even to Hermitage's eyes, which were not well versed in helmet design.

Wat was giving the man very intense scrutiny.

'I have seen no one,' the man said in a rather final manner, as if inviting them to leave at the same time.

'Who are you then?' Wat asked.

Hermitage was shocked at the blunt manner of the question. It was hardly the most sensible way to ask a Norman anything.

'Who am I?' the man sounded mightily offended at the question. 'I am Roger de Bully.'

The name didn't mean anything to Hermitage, but it sounded nicely Norman.

'Really?' Wat's reaction was quite peculiar. 'You don't look like a Norman conqueror.'

'And what do Norman conquerors look like?'

'Like fighting men who have just got off their horse.'

'You wretched Saxon,' Roger de Bully snarled a bit. 'You can see my castle.' He gestured towards the pile of soil and the palisade on its top.

'I can see *a* castle,' Wat agreed. 'Well, I can see some soil with a bit of wood on top.'

'Not many Normans though,' Cwen pointed out. 'Apart from you, obviously. That's one.' She folded her arms.

Hermitage wasn't sure what was going on now. Insulting a large Norman and his castle seemed to be a very rash thing to do.

'You wouldn't be a Saxon at all?' Wat asked politely.

The man went very red and looked angry to go with it. 'How dare you? I'll have your head.'

'A Saxon who's piled up some soil and put a few bits of tree on top to make everyone think the Normans have arrived?'

'Ridiculous.'

Hermitage thought it was ridiculous as well.

'Hardly going to be attacked by the Normans if they think you're one of them,' Wat explained helpfully.

'There's a bit of a pattern in this part of the world,' Cwen said. 'We've got the lord of Gotham hiding in his wood pile while down the road in Rempstone, people are pretending to be Norman.'

'I am not pretending anything,' Roger said, although Hermitage noticed that his accent seemed to have changed a bit. 'The great Norman people are in charge of the country now, and they have taken this manor.'

'Of course they have,' Wat sounded as if he was talking to a child. 'Although I doubt they even asked for it. Get your surrender in first, eh? It's an interesting tactic. The chances of survival must be quite high.'

'I don't know what you are talking about.' Roger de Bully seemed to recover his accent. 'You are all disgusting Saxons by the look of it. Be on your way.'

Wat tried to peer around the man into the hall, not an easy task as Roger was only slightly smaller than the door. 'If I recall correctly a fellow called Godric was lord of the manor hereabouts. Didn't used to be called Godric before the Normans arrived, did you?'

'I shall set my men on you,' Roger threatened.

'I think I'd like to see that,' Cwen smiled, looking round and making it quite clear that she couldn't actually see any men.

Wat considered the hall, and the castle and the man before him. 'Are you seriously telling me that you are a Norman invader and not the local Saxon lord dressed up as one?'

'I have no idea what you mean.'

'That helmet is not an old pot polished up with a nose-piece stuck on it then?'

Roger de Bully shifted his helmet until it was behind his back.

'I imagine you are just waiting for the arrival of your Norman friends who, seeing you as one of them, will not burn your hall down with you inside it.' Wat shook his head more in amusement than disappointment. 'Didn't get the idea from Stori of Gotham, did you?'

'I don't think you made it as far as Hastings,' Cwen said. 'Coming from either direction.'

'What do you people want?' Roger de Bully asked, if this was even him.

'We're looking for a killer,' Cwen said with some glee. 'Someone who shot an old man through a window.' She appraised the figure before her. 'And that was a small old man. Not much of a target at all.'

'Shot an old man?' Roger sounded quite worried now.

'Exactly. And he might have come this way.'

'I've seen no killer.'

'Well, you won't, not if he shoots you through the window.'

Roger looked quite concerned at this idea. 'And why are you looking for him?'

'Ah, well.' Wat drew himself up to full height. 'This,' he beckoned towards Hermitage, 'is King William's investigator.'

They all heard Roger de Bully swallow. He considered them as he tried to assimilate this information.

Hermitage suspected that his assimilation had stopped after the words "King" and "William".

'You must come in then.' Roger tried to sound enthusiastic and welcoming but could only manage nervous and more nervous. 'Why didn't you tell me who you were? Letting me keep King William's, erm, man, waiting at the door. What will you think of me?'

'We already know what we think of you,' Cwen said as they stepped into the hall.

The interior of the place was very similar to the hall at Gotham, but then there wasn't much you could do with a Saxon hall to make it stand out. A large fire burned in the centre of the space and a stone floor stretched from wall to wall. A large old table for eating, with chairs scattered about was off to the left, while the back of the hall was divided for the lord's private quarters.

'I wonder if he's got an old man back there as well?' Cwen asked, as if all Saxon halls came with old men at the back.

'Our royal majesty has sent his man to look for this killer, eh?' Roger was now managing to sound as if he had been in on this plan all along. He beckoned them to take seats at the table.

'Something like that,' Wat said.

'If I had seen such a fellow I would naturally have dealt with him myself. On behalf of the king, you know.'

'Oh, of course.' Wat's head bowed slightly, probably under the weight of sarcasm.

'But I have seen no one. These are very quiet times.'

'They are,' Cwen agreed. 'Quiet because all the Saxons went off to fight for their king and didn't come back. Well, not quite all, obviously.'

'You say an old man was killed.' Roger managed to avoid any of the accusations against him. 'Anyone in particular.'

'Fellow called Osbern,' Wat said.

'Osbern.' Roger nodded and considered the name carefully. 'Osbern, eh. Poor fellow.'

'You knew him?' Hermitage was hopeful that there might be some more information here.

'No, never heard of him.'

Before Hermitage could express his irritation at being led on like that, the door to the hall crashed open.

'Sanctuary, sanctuary!' A desperate voice cried out.

They all started and looked over. Roger de Bully even seemed ready to run.

Hermitage couldn't quite make out the shape as the light was behind, although there was something familiar about It. Whoever this was, they weren't very well informed. This wasn't holy ground so how could they claim sanctuary?

The man staggered into the room now and threw himself at Wat's feet, the weaver being the closest.

It was Bart.

'Sanctuary, sanctuary,' he cried once more.

Hermitage stepped over, taking care not to get too close in case Bart had another longbow about him. The look on the young man's face convinced him that there was no danger. The poor boy looked absolutely terrified. 'I don't think we can actually offer sanctuary,' he said, wanting to be scrupulously correct, as usual. 'This not being a holy site. But why do you want sanctuary anyway?'

Bart looked up at him with eyes so full of fear they were brimming over. 'I have done something awful,' he wailed.

Caput XIV

The Interrogation of Bart

It took a while before Bart could be calmed enough to say anything sensible at all. He jittered and fidgeted about, constantly looking over his shoulder to the door, as if expecting pursuit to fall upon him at any moment. All he would say was that it was awful; whatever *it* was.

He certainly wasn't behaving like a hardened killer with expertise in shooting people through windows.

Cwen instructed Roger de Bully to fetch some wine, which the man went to do, before he paused to wonder why he was taking orders in his own hall. He gave a glance towards Hermitage and did as he was instructed.

Bart gulped the wine down and it seemed to have some effect.

'Tell us what has happened.' Hermitage said. 'What is this awful thing you have done?'

Bart's eyes skittered from one of them to the other, the most nervous glance was for Roger, as there seemed to be no telling what he might do.

'I cannot say,' Bart didn't say as he wrung his hands.

'But you must. How can we help you if we don't know what it is you did?' Hermitage felt quite bad about this line of questioning. He knew that the most recent bad thing in the area was the shooting of Osbern, and that Bart was a suspect. He had to admit that was a very bad thing indeed, but he wanted to hear it from Bart himself. It could be that this was a completely different very bad thing and he didn't want to leap

149

to any conclusions.

He didn't imagine that the young man had run screaming for sanctuary because he'd broken a pot. Mind you, he didn't know how strict the Gudmund household was.

'You can tell us,' Cwen encouraged gently. 'We're not your masters, and Hermitage is a monk.'

Hermitage wasn't clear how being a monk helped in a situation like this.

Bart considered them all.

'You can ignore him.' Cwen nodded towards Roger, who looked mightily offended at the remark. 'He's just some Saxon hiding from the Normans.'

'I am Roger de Bully,' Roger announced haughtily. 'I'm Norman.'

'No, you're not,' Cwen dismissed the idea and gave her attention back to Bart.

'And this,' Cwen tipped her head towards Wat, 'is Wat the Weaver.'

Bart's eyes now widened. '*The* Wat the Weaver?' he asked with some awe.

'The only one,' Wat smiled.

'So,' Cwen said, 'you can imagine how many really awful things he's done in his lifetime. What can you have done that's worse?'

'Do you mind?' Wat complained half-heartedly.

Bart did relax slightly at this exchange. He lowered his head and spoke to his own lap. 'I have done worse than anything else,' he mumbled. 'I have done the worst thing that there is to do.'

'Which is?' Cwen encouraged.

Bart took a deep breath. 'I have killed a man.' The final words shuddered from him, but he seemed to take some relief that they were out now.

'Really?' Wat sounded as if Bart claimed that he'd had flown here on the back of a pigeon.

'I have,' Bart insisted.

'I see. And how did you do this?'

Bart swallowed and lowered his face into his hands. 'I shot him.'

Hermitage couldn't contain a small gasp. Despite his behaviour, Bart obviously knew that someone had been shot and was claiming to have done it.

'You shot him. And with what did you shoot him?' Wat enquired politely.

Bart looked up, seemingly puzzled by the line of questioning. 'With a bow, of course.'

'Of course. Bit of an expert with a bow, are you?'

'Well,' Bart hesitated. 'Not really.'

'Ever shot one at all before?'

'Erm, no.'

'But you shot this man who's now dead.' Wat paused for a moment. 'Can I ask a very odd question?'

No one objected.

'How do you know you shot a man?'

Hermitage thought that this was a very odd question indeed. People who shot other people usually knew they'd done it, surely. All that business with the bow and the arrows and such forth. Whoosh, thud, as Cwen had so eloquently put it.

'Were you playing with the bow when it went off?'

'I was told.' Bart was starting to sound a little annoyed that people weren't believing his confession.

'You were told you that you'd killed someone?' Hermitage wasn't following this at all now.

'That's right.'

'Did you not remember it yourself?' Hermitage had come across some casual killers in his time, the Norman, Le Pedvin being top of the list, but forgetting that you'd just killed someone really was going too far.

Bart looked rather shamefaced. 'I do things when I'm asleep.'

'I beg your pardon?' Cwen was now the one sounding incredulous.

'I do things when I'm asleep, I always have done. I can't help it.'

'What sort of things?' Hermitage asked.

'Talk, wave my arms, kick. I even get up and walk about sometimes.'

Hermitage was reaching a conclusion about this. He hardly felt that using "aha" was justified when he concluded who was not the killer, but something had to be said. 'I hardly think that getting up and walking about is the same as taking a bow and shooting someone.'

'I was told,' Bart repeated.

'Who told you?'

'I don't know.'

Now Wat buried his face in his hands for a moment. 'Let's get this straight. Someone you don't know came and told you that you'd got up in your sleep, picked up a longbow, just the sort you've never used before, and shot someone to death.'

Bart nodded that this was a succinct summary.

'Before you went back to bed,' Cwen checked.

Hermitage had a key question in his head. 'What were you doing in bed? The man was shot in the early evening.'

'I was only having a doze. It's hard work lugging that cart around all day. When we stopped and finished unpacking, I sat down and nodded off.'

'During which doze you shot someone.' Wat shook his head.

'And how come you didn't know the person who told you?' Hermitage asked.

'He was wearing a hood.'

'It all becomes clear,' Wat said.

Bart looked at him hopefully.

'A hooded figure comes and tells you that while you were having a little sleep you found a longbow from somewhere, along with the arrows. You then crept along to the window in Gotham hall and shot an old man in the chest. After that you dropped the bow, went back to your resting place before being woken with the news.'

Bart hung his head dolefully.

'Except you didn't.'

'I didn't?'

'Of course you didn't. The whole thing is completely ridiculous. For a start you've never used a bow before in your life. They are not easy things to master. Shooting someone in the chest through a window is the work of an expert. When most people pick up a bow, the first thing they shoot is the ground about two feet in front of their own feet. Show me your hands.'

Bart held his hands out, palms down.

'Other way up.'

Bart turned his hands.

'There you are.' Wat took Bart's hands in his own and peered at them. 'Neither of these hands has ever shot a bow, never mind in the last day.'

They all considered the hands, even Roger de Bully who seemed to be taking an interest in developments.

'No callouses on the fingers from regular use. Do you use your right hand for most things?'

Bart nodded.

Wat dropped the left hand and held the right up as if giving a lecture. 'And if this was the first time he'd used a bow, his fingers would be bruised and battered from just one shot. And you can't tell me that in his sleep he also managed to put tabs on. Show me your left arm.'

Bart frowned but did as he was told. Wat rolled his light sleeve up and pointed to the young man's forearm. 'There you are.'

Hermitage agreed that this was indeed a forearm.

'No mark of the bowstring. If you fire a bow you have to wear protection on your left arm as that's where the string will hit after the arrow has gone. And it hits hard. There would be a mark. And there isn't.'

Everyone was nodding appreciatively at this erudite explanation.

'Now stand up and hold your arms out.'

Bart did so.

Wat tapped the underside of each arm. 'This is no bowman. Strong lad, probably from lifting her Ladyship's cart, but both arms seem the same and the right would need to be stronger. He might be able to pull the string, but not loose an arrow with any accuracy.'

'That's a very well-constructed argument,' Hermitage was impressed.

'It's the same one that the archer used on me,' Wat explained. 'Showing me how completely useless I'd be with a bow, seeing as I was utterly weak and pathetic. I think that's what he said.' Wat shrugged that he didn't really want to be an archer anyway, so he wasn't worried about it.

'Are you saying I haven't killed anyone?' Bart asked very cautiously.

'I can't say that,' Wat shook his head. Bart's worried expression deepened.

'You could have killed someone for all I know, after all, we've only just met. How do I know what sort of thing you've got up to in the past? Could have been killing people left, right and centre. What I am saying is that you have not shot anyone. Not yesterday. Not ever, I suspect.'

Bart's look was now confused but grateful.

'Knife, poison, pushed off a cliff,' Wat went on with some enthusiasm. 'You could do all those, but not a bow.'

'And the man was killed with a bow,' Bart said. 'That's what the man told me.'

'He was right about that,' Wat agreed. 'We were there.'

Bart's eyes widened. 'Then you saw who did it?'

'Afraid not. Like we said, old Osbern was shot through the window.'

'We were talking to him,' Cwen explained, 'when whoosh, thud.'

Hermitage gave her a disapproving look.

'Not even whoosh, thud, argh. Poor fellow was dead straight away.'

'But you didn't do it,' Wat assured Bart.

'Then,' Bart thought carefully. 'Why..?'

'Why did some hooded figure tell you that you had?'

Bart nodded.

'That is a very good question. In fact, it's the key question, isn't it, Hermitage?'

Hermitage agreed. 'The chances are that the fellow who said you had done it is the one who actually did it. He was trying to throw the blame on to someone else.'

'And someone who is known for doing things in their sleep might believe it themselves.' Cwen sounded as if this step in events was largely Bart's fault.

'Why did you run away?' Hermitage asked. 'If you thought you'd shot someone wouldn't you stay to find out if he was all right?'

'I was going to, but the one with the hood said I had to get away.'

'I bet he did,' Wat snorted.

'He said I'd killed the Lord of Gotham's servant and that Stori would want my head.'

'He even helped you leave,' Wat said.

'He did. He got me out of the camp and sent me off.'

'I think we need to find our fellow with the hood,' Wat said. 'I'd wager he carries the marks of a bowman.'

'Where did he and the bow come from though?' Hermitage asked. 'We know that we didn't see one in the Gudmund's party. Bart, had you ever seen one about.'

'No.' Bart shook his head. 'Lady Gudmund always made it clear that none of us were to carry any weapons. Apparently, the Normans don't like it.'

'She's right there,' Cwen complained.

'And there was nothing about the hooded man that you recognised?' Hermitage checked.

Bart shook his head. 'Lots of people have hoods,' he explained unhelpfully, nodding towards Hermitage.

Wat now paced up and down the side of the table. 'We have to assume the man with the hood is one of the Gudmund party. We've not seen any strangers about. And a bow's a big thing,' he mused. 'There can't be many places you could hide one.'

'On the carriage,' Cwen said. 'Or under it. Maybe even

disguised as part of the thing itself.'

'It's certain no one could carry the thing without being spotted,' Wat agreed.

'And why would anyone leave it behind?' Hermitage asked. 'They sound like precious things.'

'If you want to make it look like Bart did the shooting and then ran off you might leave it,' Wat said. 'And if it was someone in the Gudmund group, they've got it back now.'

'I think we need more words with the Gudmunds,' Wat said.

Hermitage wasn't too keen on that. 'We've already upset them so that they don't want us anywhere near. We can't make them answer us.'

'True, but we can look for where a bow might have been hidden. And examine their hands to see if anyone's shot a bow before.'

'That's not going to be much easier.' Hermitage couldn't see how this was to be done with people who didn't want to cooperate. He could never do anything with people who didn't want to cooperate; surely that was their essence.

'We don't ask, obviously,' Cwen said. 'We just do it.'

'How? They're heading for Bury; they may pass by here, but they won't stop.'

'We'll just have to make them.' Cwen looked as if she already had a few ideas about how to stop a carriage. 'Carriages are hitting stones and breaking wheels all the time,' she explained. 'This time the stone will hit the carriage and break the wheel. Well, it will if we throw it hard enough.'

'Oh Lord,' Hermitage fretted. 'And how are we supposed to get a look at peoples' hands?'

'Could you get them to pray?'

'Could I what?' Hermitage didn't understand what was

being suggested but knew that it was appalling.

'Get them to pray. You know, put their hands together.'

'How are we going to see the inside of their fingers if they've got their hands together,' Wat criticised the idea.

'Prayer is for God,' Hermitage pointed out as plainly as he could. 'I can't get people to pray just to have a look at their hands.' Surely, they both saw the explicitly sinful nature of the request.

'Maybe you could give out money,' Cwen suggested to Wat. 'They'd hold their hands out for that.'

'Don't be disgusting,' Wat was clearly horrified at that suggestion. 'We'll have to think of something else.'

'Won't they get me for killing the old man?' Bart asked.

Wat sighed. 'You didn't kill the old man, remember?'

'Oh, yes.'

'For heaven's sake try and get that bit right or we'll all be in trouble.'

'Didn't kill him,' Bart repeated the lesson. 'Right.' He had relaxed now that he wasn't a killer anymore and put his wine down on the table.

Wat watched him with a worried expression, as if not knowing whether he could trust the boy not to confess to something he hadn't done. 'I say.' He looked at the table.

'What?' Hermitage asked, hoping that he might have come up with a better idea for hand examination than fake prayer.

'Look at this.' He stepped up to the table and pointed at the surface. It was scarred and damaged from years of service, and several people had carved in it, as was quite normal. If anyone had really enjoyed their host's hospitality, the least they could do was gouge holes in the furniture.

There were images of crude animals and some just plain crude images. There were a couple of swords and some faces, very badly done. There were also letters. Someone of learning had carved this table.

'See that,' Wat pointed to one specific area.

Hermitage looked. 'Oh,' he said. 'CV.'

'Just so. CV, eh, master Roger.'

'If you say so,' Roger responded. 'I wouldn't know, it's not my table after all.'

'You being a recently arrived Norman,' Cwen said disparagingly.

'Quite.'

She looked at the table as well. 'I suppose Stori could have been here to eat and carved his letters in the table.'

'The same Stori who can't read?' Wat asked.

'I'm sure he could learn C and V,' Hermitage said. 'Even if he didn't understand them. Particularly as it's his family motto.'

'Hm,' Wat didn't sound convinced. 'It shows that Stori the Hider knows our mysterious Norman here.'

'I've never heard of the fellow,' Roger complained.

Cwen sighed. 'Can you stop talking as if we believe you.'

Bart had wandered over to look at the table as well.

Hermitage pointed out the letters they were discussing, naturally assuming that Bart couldn't read.

'I know,' the young man said.

Hermitage immediately felt bad about his assumption.

'I've seen them before.'

'On Stori's house, that's right.'

'No, on Lord Gudmund's.'

Hermitage, Wat and Cwen exchanged meaningful glances. Hermitage just hoped it was the same meaning.

'Now that is interesting.' Wat rubbed his hands as he looked forward to a new experience. 'I think we just got a whole host of new questions to ask the Gudmunds.'

Caput XV

To Trap a Gudmund

Hermitage found the preparations for the arrival of the Gudmunds positively alarming. He could appreciate that they needed further discussion, but Cwen in particular seemed to be preparing for war.

At one point she'd suggested digging a large hole in the ground and covering it with branches. The plan was that the cart would drive over this and fall in. The occupants would then be held in the hole until they answered the questions, after which a ladder would be lowered to let them out.

The problems with this plan were numerous and insurmountable, but it was only when Hermitage pointed out that the horses would be the first to fall into the trap, and that they probably wouldn't have any pertinent information to offer, no matter how hard they were questioned, that Cwen started to relent. He further pointed out that horses couldn't climb ladders, but Cwen said he was only being difficult.

The fact that they hadn't got a ladder, anything to dig a hole with or enough branches to disguise a cart-sized hole, were mere details and Hermitage suspected that Cwen was now saving this plan up for another time.

Wat also reminded them that the Gudmund party was quite a large one. All the retainers and servants would be hard to manage between the three of them, let alone if half of them were in a hole. He suspected that the others would not take this calmly.

Bart said that he was willing to help, even if it meant

jumping into a hole. He obviously found being wrongfully told that he was a murderer quite annoying and was keen to see whoever had tricked him brought to justice.

Roger de Bully simply looked on in bemused interest, shaking his head every now and again, and muttering about the strange things that these Saxons got up to when they were left alone.

Simply stepping out in front of the train and holding their arms up was not seen as a viable strategy. Wat suspected that Lady Gudmund would be quite happy to let her cart simply drive right over him, after which her troop could trample on his body.

The others could only nod that he was probably right.

'And Renweard is not going to let Lady Gudmund be bothered by any of us,' Hermitage said. 'She's even lost confidence in me. If we make any attempt to talk to them again, I suspect they will simply ignore us.'

'We have to break the cart somehow,' Cwen said thoughtfully. 'If it's damaged in some way, they'll have to stop.'

'It is a pretty solid thing,' Wat said.

They had already dismissed Cwen's original idea of simply throwing rocks at the wheels until they broke. As someone in the entourage now possessed a bow and some arrows, and one of them was obviously a capable archer, they concluded that he who cast the first stone would soon after receive the first arrow.

'What about those stupid lengths of wood they use to carry the thing. We could probably break one of those.'

'Yes,' Wat agreed. 'If we had an axe and asked them if they minded waiting for a few moments while we chop bits off their cart.'

'Why don't we just ask them?' Hermitage suggested.

Cwen snorted at this pathetic idea. 'You've already said they won't talk to us. Why would they stop at all?'

'I could call out that I have new information concerning Lord Gudmund.'

Wat nodded slowly. 'If Cwen and I were nowhere to be seen, they might stop for Hermitage. He could tell them that he'd sent us home in disgrace as we'd behaved so badly.'

'I don't think there's any call for falsehood,' Hermitage said.

'I think it might help. If you tell Lady Gudmund that you are truly sorry about your awful friends, that you have dismissed us and will be dealing with us later, she might soften a bit. You could even say that we will be reported to the king. She'd like that.'

Cwen's face now took on a very calculating look and she even stuck her tongue out of the corner of her mouth as she considered some new scheme.

Hermitage did not hold out much hope that this one would be any better than the last. It was almost certain that it would involve more violence.

'The king,' she said slowly.

'What about him?'

She now focussed her eyes on Hermitage, which made him very nervous indeed.

'You are the King's Investigator.'

'Lady Gudmund already knows that,' Wat said. 'And she's become less and less impressed with the fact.'

'But if the king were here, she'd stop,' Cwen smiled.

'Are you suggesting we go and find William and ask if he'd mind helping us hold up a carriage?'

'No.' Cwen was full of confidence. 'We use another Norman.'

'Another Norman?'

'Our own Roger de Bully.' Cwen turned her fearful gaze upon the man.

'What?' Roger asked, not paying much attention.

'You're a Norman,' Cwen said.

'At last. I'm glad that you see the truth of it.'

'So you can stop the Gudmunds when they come by.'

'I can what?' Roger didn't sound quite so keen on being a Norman anymore.

Cwen warmed to her thoughts. 'What are these wretched Saxons doing tramping across your land without permission, eh? You are completely within your rights to demand they stop and explain themselves.'

'If not pay a toll of some sort,' Wat suggested with a little gleam in his eye.

'I can't do that.'

'You are Roger de Bully the great Norman conqueror, yes?' Cwen now managed to look surprised that there could be any doubt about his identity.

'Well, yes.' The doubt that had been floating around now seemed to have landed on Roger.

'There you are then.'

'Erm.' Roger cast his eyes around, looking for something. 'My men.'

'What about them?'

'They're, erm, all off hunting at the moment. We'd have to wait until they get back, by which time it could be too late.'

'Lady Gudmund is nervous enough about the Normans to be brought to a halt by just one, no problem.'

'And,' Wat snapped his fingers. 'You can say that you are now hosting the King's Investigator and are very disappointed at the way he's been treated.'

'Ah, now,' Hermitage could see this getting completely out of hand in no time at all.

'And his friends,' Cwen added. 'Who does this Lady Gudmund think she is? You'll have her land and titles off her if she gives you any trouble.'

Roger had now started wringing his hands.

'What's the point of conquering a country if you can't order the locals about?' Cwen encouraged.

'Can we just ask her to stop,' Hermitage said, seeing that this had already got out of hand and nothing had actually happened yet. 'Master Roger can simply stand by his manor and hold a hand up to enquire of their business. In a perfectly normal manner. There's no need to start inviting trouble.'

Roger seemed a bit happier about that approach, although Cwen had her invitations ready.

'And,' Hermitage went on, thinking that he might placate her a bit, 'we can still combine the two plans.'

'Push the cart in the hole once they've stopped?' Cwen asked brightly.

'No, not the hole. We are not doing the hole.'

Cwen muttered something about some people having a lack of ambition.

'I can be to hand and can report that you and Wat have been sent back to Derby.' Hermitage wondered if they'd mind actually heading back to Derby, even if it was only for a while, just so that he could be telling the truth. He knew the chances of getting their cooperation were slim.

'What are you doing here then?' Cwen asked. 'You've been dismissed by the Gudmunds as well; why have you come to Roger's?'

'I am the King's Investigator; I am visiting Roger de Bully as I am close by.' Hermitage was starting to feel a bit wobbly about this whole situation. He knew that it was better than throwing rocks or digging holes, but not by much. Once again, an investigation was requiring that he lie. He reminded himself that Osbern was dead, and that someone in the Gudmund party had done it. Surely such an act justified a little deception.

Now he worried that not only was he lying, but he was justifying it at the same time.

'We can lie in wait,' Cwen said.

'Waiting for what?' Hermitage was even more worried about the idea of Cwen lying in wait for anything.

'Just in case.'

'It won't be necessary,' Hermitage assured her. 'You must not be seen, otherwise the Gudmunds will know that it is all a ruse.'

Wat seemed more content with this plan than Cwen. 'It could be useful,' he said. 'Hermitage and Roger can occupy the Gudmunds while we sneak around and have a look for the hiding place of the bow and ask a few more pointed questions.'

Cwen smiled at this suggestion, while Hermitage's stomach started churning.

'The Gudmund girls and Renweard are bound to attend upon a noble Norman in person. They'll leave the rest of the place free.'

Hermitage wasn't happy referring to the ladies Gudmund as girls, but he took the point.

'And Bart can help us go over the cart in quick time.'

Bart nodded that this would not be a problem.

'We just need Hermitage and Roger to keep the Gudmunds occupied.'

'How?' Hermitage asked, already fretting over his task.

'Ask about CV?' Cwen reminded him of why they were doing this at all.

'Ah yes.'

'And they won't dare leave a Norman without permission.' Cwen nodded at Roger. 'If he invites them to stay the night they'd have to say yes.'

Roger did not look at all keen on having a hall full of visitors. Particularly ones with a history of shooting people.

'Although I expect his men will be out hunting all night,' Cwen said with a shake of the head. 'He'd better send the Gudmunds on their way at some point.'

'Excellent,' Wat rubbed his hands. 'All agreed then. What we need now are some Gudmunds to play with.'

He, Cwen and Bart retreated to the back of the hall, away from the road, where they could see what was going on but could not be seen.

Hermitage and Roger stood outside the hall door, each looking nervously at the other. Hermitage gave a rather weak smile, which was returned with even less strength.

'Have you been here long?' Hermitage asked, unable to bear a silence for more than a few moments.

'Since ten sixty six,' Roger replied with little enthusiasm.

'Of course.' His next question would have been about Roger de Bully's home and whereabouts in Normandy that was. As he was now coming round to the idea that Roger wasn't Norman at all, he felt this would be a bit awkward.

'We've not had much rain recently,' he said instead.

'No, indeed.'

Another pause arrived which needed to be sent on its way.

'Your castle is very impressive.' Hermitage considered the very unimpressive castle.

'Thank you.' Roger took a breath. 'King's Investigator, eh?'

He tried to sound nonchalant but there was a slight squeak to the voice.

'That's right.'

'Have many, erm, dealings with the king then?'

'Oh yes.' Hermitage's disappointment at this aspect of his role was clear. 'He frequently calls upon us.'

'Really?' Roger's voice was now losing control.

'Him and Le Pedvin.'

'Le Pedvin.' This came out almost as a sob.

'A difficult fellow.'

'Difficult, yes, I'd heard.'

'You don't know him then?' Hermitage kept forgetting that this was not a real Norman.

'I am a very minor fellow,' Roger sounded rather pleading now. 'I have very little to do with the likes of Lord Le Pedvin.'

Hermitage's reply of "I don't blame you" was on his lips before he managed to bite it back.

It was just a few more moments before a noise could be heard off in the distance.

The two men moved onto the track and looked hopefully along to see if the Gudmunds were arriving. Hermitage had not really been looking forward to this, but it was better than standing in awkward silence with Roger.

There was definitely something coming. The shouts of men as they issued and followed instructions became gradually clearer. The Gudmunds' cart was obviously having a hard time with the track.

'Aha,' Roger said rather pointlessly.

Hermitage nodded his agreement to this.

More moments dragged before the first people could be seen coming along. Hermitage and Roger moved out into the middle of the road, unable to disguise their nervousness at standing in front of rapidly approaching horses; a nervousness that was not assuaged by the fact that the horses weren't actually approaching rapidly.

'I think you'd better go first,' Hermitage said to Roger, who seemed to be hiding at the back.

'Ah, yes. Quite so.' The Norman conqueror stepped forward.

The lead men of the party now spotted that there were two people in the road and paused as they considered what to do.

Reporting back seemed to be best and so they turned and headed for the cart and its horses, which were now grinding their way along at slightly less than walking pace.

Unsurprisingly, it was Renweard who appeared first of all. He briefly peered ahead and then seemed to recognise Hermitage. He dropped all caution and strode purposefully up the road.

'What are you doing here?' he demanded of Hermitage, casting a disinterested look at Roger.

Hermitage found the courage to nudge Roger in the back and encourage a response.

'Ahum. What are you doing on my land, then?' Roger asked.

Renweard gave him a rather offended glance now.

'Your land?' Renweard asked.

'Of course. I am Roger de Bully, liege man of King William, and you are on my land.'

Renweard squinted a bit now, as if trying to discern whether this was serious or not.

'Who are you, and where are you going?' Roger now demanded, growing into his role.

'I am servant to Lady Gudmund and we are travelling to her estates in Bury Saint Edmunds.' Renweard sounded as if he wasn't prepared for any sort of debate about this.

'*Her* estates?' Roger asked. 'I think it's for King William to decide what estate belongs to whom. And the King's Investigator here tells me that there has been a murder.'

Renweard seemed to lose a touch of confidence now.

'We can't have murders,' Roger said, as if they were spoiling the view. 'And you can't go dismissing the king's own man. Who do you think you are?'

'Erm,' Renweard was flustered now.

'I think we had better consider this further,' Roger said, getting quite impressively high and mighty. 'You and this lady of yours will join me before you go any further. There's some explaining to do.' And with this, Roger turned on his heels and gave Hermitage a peremptory wave that he should follow him into the manor.

'We will await you within,' Roger called back. 'Be quick about it.'

Hermitage could do nothing but follow in Roger's footsteps, leaving a bemused Renweard to stand and stare at them both.

As they entered the hall once more, Hermitage was about to congratulate Roger on his handling of the situation when he was brought to a halt by bumping into the man as he stopped by the door.

Roger de Bully, the great Norman conqueror was holding himself up with one hand, just before he was sick on the floor.

Caput XVI

Saxon vs Norman

'What is the meaning of this?' Lady Gudmund demanded as she stood in the hall of Roger de Bully.

Roger faced her and said nothing, while Hermitage stood out of the line of fire.

Renweard was at his lady's side as usual, while young Lady Gudmund loitered behind.

'Well?'

Still Roger kept silent, and Hermitage suspected this was because the poor man was terrified. He pursed his lips, and Hermitage hoped that he wasn't going to be sick again, that wouldn't make a very good impression at all. And they'd only just managed to clear up the last event before the Gudmunds arrived.

Roger said that it must have been a bad deer he'd eaten, but Hermitage often felt sick after a confrontation with some abbot or other and so sympathised with Roger's position. The poor fellow probably thought that pretending to be Norman would mean that people would leave him alone. Facing down anyone did not seem to be in his nature, let alone organised Saxons and their demanding mistresses.

The ever-lengthening silence seemed to be annoying Lady Gudmund intently. She looked to Renweard for some explanation, but all he could do was shrug, indicating that he didn't have a clue either.

Next, the lady cast her critical eye at Hermitage. He only offered a weak smile, hopefully giving the impression that he was waiting upon Roger like the rest of them.

'Speak, man,' Lady Gudmund ordered.

Roger glanced around, saw a chair close by and sat.

Hermitage imagined that his legs wouldn't hold him up anymore.

He then folded his arms, crossed his legs and to Hermitage's eye, looked as if he desperately needed the privy. He couldn't take his eyes off Lady Gudmund, as he probably thought that was the direction the attack would come from.

Renweard gave a slight cough.

Lady Gudmund looked at him, and he replied with a strange series of expressions that passed Hermitage by completely.

The lady seemed to understand the communication and didn't look very happy about it. Mind you, in the short time Hermitage had known her, she'd spent very little time looking happy.

Still Roger stared and kept his peace.

Next, Lady Gudmund gave Renweard a very annoyed look indeed. All this got was another shrug that there was nothing else to be done - whatever it was that was being suggested.

Lady Gudmund turned her attention back to Roger in his seat. She took a deep breath and appeared to be forcing herself to do something that she would really rather not.

Very stiffly, and with a face frozen in discomfort, she gave a very cursory nod. 'My Lord,' she somehow squeezed the words out between her teeth.

'That's better,' Roger said. 'Wasn't hard, was it?'

Hermitage heard the squeak in the voice, but Lady Gudmund seemed not to notice.

'And I believe I get to say, what is the meaning of this?'

Lady Gudmund looked quite put out by this. She was

clearly not used to being challenged, that much was obvious from her response to Wat. What she really found disturbing was being challenged by someone who had every right to do so.

The lady seemed to be fighting some internal battle and was barely in control. 'We are travelling to Bury Saint Edmunds,' she managed to say.

'So this fellow told me,' Roger waved a disinterested arm at Renweard. 'What are you doing travelling anywhere, that's the question?'

'I...,' Lady Gudmund began.

'And what's this about a murder?' Roger interrupted.

Lady Gudmund was *really* not used to being interrupted and didn't take it at all well.

She now drew in a very deep breath, clenched her fists and let it out slowly. This seemed to help a bit. 'It is a long story.'

'We have plenty of time.' Roger now beckoned that she and her party were allowed to sit.

They did so, and Hermitage sat as well, but back by the table, so that he could listen but not really be noticed.

The lady took a moment to consider her words. 'My husband was murdered, I believe.'

'Your husband?' Roger was puzzled. 'And he was shot through a window?'

'Shot through a window?' Lady Gudmund looked at him as if he was spouting gibberish. 'No, of course he wasn't shot through a window. We don't know how he was killed. That's why I got this monk here to try and find out.'

'The King's Investigator,' Roger reminded her.

'Just so.'

'But he says the man was shot through a window.' Roger glanced at Hermitage and seemed to be getting lost.

Lady Gudmund frowned as she tried to make sense of this.

'That was another man,' Renweard spoke up.

'Another one?' Roger managed to sound shocked. 'How many murders are following you people about?'

Lady Gudmund had never in her life been referred to as "you people" and she didn't know how to respond. Or rather she did but knew that she couldn't slap a Norman round the face.

'He was only a servant of some sort,' Lady Gudmund explained. 'And he wasn't even mine.'

'He's still dead though?' Roger checked.

'I suppose so.' Lady Gudmund obviously didn't think servants died in the same way as nobles.

'And he was shot through a window?'

'Yes.'

'After which you dismissed King William's investigator.'

'It was nothing to do with that,' Lady Gudmund protested. 'He has an awful weaver and his girl with him. Where are they?' Lady Gudmund looked rather nervously around them all, as if expecting Wat and Cwen to jump out on her; that being just the sort of thing they did.

'I, er, sent them home,' Hermitage had no option but to speak. It could be true that he had sent them home, that didn't mean that they'd actually gone.

'That's one good thing then,' Lady Gudmund said. 'They were completely hopeless in discovering what happened to Lord Gudmund, the monk included.' She gave Hermitage a withering glance; probably the one she longed to throw at Roger. 'So I dismissed them.'

Roger considered this for a moment. 'Is it for you to dismiss the king's servants?'

'Well, er, that is..,'

'Exactly.'

'I took them on in the first place,' the lady protested, a bit too much.

'Yes,' Roger drawled. 'And I'm not sure you were entitled to do that either. Diverting the King's Investigator to look into some minor family matter.'

'Minor family matter? My husband is dead.'

'A lot of husbands are. Particularly the Saxon ones. I'm more concerned about people being shot through windows. We can't have that sort of thing going on you know, not without permission. What would the king say?'

That seemed to stump Lady Gudmund.

'This is a Norman country now,' Roger explained. 'We don't have people being murdered all over the place.'

Hermitage thought he would have to disagree with that.

'Who did it?' Roger asked.

'We don't know,' Renweard spoke, Lady Gudmund didn't look capable of engaging any further.

'Well, you'd better find out then, hadn't you? Can't have murderers wandering the country shooting through windows. Where would it end, eh?'

Neither Renweard nor Lady Gudmund looked as if they had the first clue where it would end.

'And you can have the King's Investigator back. There you are.' Roger sounded as if he was giving a magnificent gift.

Hermitage was pretty sure he didn't want to be given to anyone, let alone the Gudmunds, who he knew were not keen on him anyway.

'Now,' Roger continued with a confident rub of the hands. 'Do you have servants with you?'

'Erm, yes?' Renweard made a question out of the answer.

'Excellent. They can come and prepare food for us. My men

are all out hunting and won't be back for hours.'

Hermitage thought that Roger was pushing his luck a bit now. Better to lie a bit low perhaps. It seemed that the role of Norman conqueror was going to his head; probably helped by the response of the Gudmunds.

'While we wait, you can tell me all about yourselves,' Roger said.

Renweard and Lady Gudmund didn't look enthralled by that prospect.

'For example,' Roger encouraged, 'who is this Edmund and why have they buried him in your home?'

. . .

Once the Gudmunds had gone into the hall, Wat, Cwen and Bart headed for the carriage and the people milling about. They had briefly discussed trying to be discreet about it, but thought that the three of them sneaking about searching would be hard to miss. They hadn't even gone three paces before someone saw them.

'Hello Bart,' one young fellow said. 'Why aren't you dead.'

'Dead?'

'It's all over the place. Apparently, you got caught in a bow string and it cut your head off. Everyone knows.' The fellow now peered rather closely at Bart's head, obviously wondering how it had got attached again.

'No, it wasn't him,' another of the Gudmund servants came over. 'Bart here killed a man.'

'I didn't,' Bart protested.

The second man wasn't having any of that. 'Oh yes, you did. I know. I heard it from Peter.'

The first man nodded, looking very impressed. It was clear

that this Peter was a source of information to be trusted.

'You flew in through a window and took his heart out with your own bare hands.'

Bart looked at his hands. 'That's ridiculous.'

'That's not what Peter said.' The second fellow sounded mightily offended that Peter's version of events was being challenged.

'If I was supposed to be there, I should know,' Bart complained.

The second man gave this a very dismissive shrug, as if Bart was the last person to be trusted in a situation like this.

'Can I just make things very clear,' Wat said forcefully.

They gave him their attention.

'The man was shot through a window by someone with a bow. It was not Bart.'

'And you'd know, would you?' The second man was clearly still in Peter's camp.

'Yes, we were standing next to the victim when it happened. Now show us your hands.'

'Show you our hands?' The first man clearly thought this was a very strange request, and probably the precursor to something really unwarranted.

'Yes, I want to see if either of you was the killer.'

'And you can tell that from our hands, can you?' The second man's contempt for them was having a wonderful time.

'I certainly can.' Wat reached out and grabbed the hands and considered the palms of both. 'No,' he shook his head. 'Dirty and revolting but no sign of firing a bow.'

'Firing a bow, pah.' This was treated with equal contempt. 'It's Bart's hands you want to look at. And ask him what he did with the heart.'

'I have looked at his hands and he didn't do it either.'

'Right master know-all, aren't you?'

'Yes,' Cwen stepped forward. 'He is. Which makes you,' she paused to give the next words their full force. 'An old gossip.'

The man staggered back under the power of the insult. The others even cast surprised eyes at Cwen. That really was going a bit far. Calling a man a gossip?

'How dare you?' was all the fellow could come up with.

The first man drew breath at the egregious slur.

'Perhaps we can get on?' Cwen suggested. She ignored the second fellow, who looked as if he was gathering his strength for a response to the most outrageous abuse that he had been subject to. 'We want to look at the cart.'

The first man gave Cwen a very cautious look and decided that he had better things to do somewhere else. 'Do what you like,' he said as he walked away. 'The Gudmunds are in the hall, so be quick about it.'

Cwen nodded towards the cart and they made their way over, leaving the one accused of gossip to recover.

'Oh yes?' Another man asked. 'And what would you want?'

This fellow was standing at the side of the cart and was dressed in a long leather apron of some sort. He had a nonchalant, confident air about him as he leaned against one of the wheels.

'We want to look at the cart,' Cwen said.

'Well you can,' the man agreed. 'No touching though.'

Cwen shook her head at this nonsense. 'No, we need to examine it. We're looking for something.'

'I'm sure you are, but you're not doing it on my cart.'

'Your cart?' Wat asked with interest. 'Lady Gudmund's cart, surely?'

'And I am her cart man.' The cart man puffed his chest out

at this, as if being a cart man was one step away from nobility. 'As Bart there well knows.'

Bart had said nothing and seemed to be in awe of the cart man.

'Not dead then?' the cart man asked nonchalantly.

'No,' Bart confirmed.

'I thought as much.' This sounded as if the cart man considered Bart not being dead as just one more of the young man's failings.

'Cart man, eh? Excellent.' Wat smiled. 'You can show us the cart then.'

'You can see it from where you are.'

'I know, but it's so impressive.'

The cart man swelled even further at this.

'And the King's Investigator really wants us to have a look. He sent us with specific instructions. And we're supposed to report anyone who gets in our way.'

These words seemed to sow a level of confusion into the cart man that he didn't know how to deal with. He was clearly trapped between further patronising bluster and fawning servility. The result was that he didn't say anything at all.

'The king,' Cwen repeated to help resolve the conflict. 'William, that is. The Norman.'

'And Harold before that,' Wat added.

The cart man seemed to reach a conclusion. 'Then of course the great king's man shall be obeyed.' He spoke brightly, as if there had never been the slightest doubt about this. He held an arm out that they were more than welcome to examine the cart in as much detail as they pleased.

With a snort of derision, Cwen went first and stepped into the cart to look around.

Wat nodded Bart to climb up to the driver's position, on a

platform high at the front, which left him to do the underside.

He knelt on the ground and tipped down so that he could get his head underneath.

'What exactly are we looking for?' Bart called.

'Any sign,' Wat shouted back. 'You know. Where something could have been hidden.' He clearly didn't want to say too much and alert the cart man. 'If it was on the cart, we'll know that it was someone with access.'

This cart man was now looking simply confused. It was all well and good people wanting to admire his magnificent equipment, but crawling all over it like this was hardly decent, king's man or not.

'If you was to tell me what you'd like to see I could probably show you,' he offered.

Wat found nothing under the cart, no secret box or hidden straps to tie a bow in place. He stood now and moved around the outside. On the back, between where the two rear wheels stuck out, there was a storage platform for luggage and supplies. There was no way of telling if a bow had been kept here or not. At the back of the platform there was a long, low case of wood, probably for securing valuables away from the weather. It had a lock on it, a sophisticated and expensive thing to have on a cart.

'What's in here?' he called to the cart man.

The fellow wandered around to the back of the cart, and was joined by Bart and Cwen who had had no luck with their search.

'That?' the cart man asked with little interest. 'It's just the strong box.'

'And what's in it?'

'Not my place to know,' the cart man was sure of this.

'Do you have the key?'

The man was shocked. 'Certainly not. That is Lady Gudmund's strong box. It's not for the likes of me to go knowing what's in it.'

'It's about the right size,' Cwen commented.

'And if it's kept locked, no one would know what's it in,' Wat said. 'Who does have the key?'

'Lady Gudmund,' the cart man said, as if that was the end of the questioning.

'Just her?'

'And Master Renweard, as is right and proper.'

'Better open it then.'

'I said,' the cart man repeated slowly, 'that only Lady Gudmund and Master Renweard have keys.'

'Who are only needed if you use a key,' Wat said with a knowing smile. He reached to the purse at his belt and extracted a thin stick of metal.

'What's that for then?' the cart man asked suspiciously.

'Oh, this and that.' Wat leaned over the box and fiddled around with the lock using his little stick. There was a loud click.

'Oh dear, perhaps I've broken it.'

Cwen was standing with her hands on her hips giving Wat a most disappointed look. 'How many times have you done that before?'

'Never,' Wat protested his innocence. 'On my heart.'

'Never on the strong box of Lady Gudmund, you mean.'

'That's right,' Wat nodded his agreement as he lifted the lid of the strong box.

They all peered in and eight eyebrows were raised at the sight.

'Oh, bloody hell,' Bart swore.

Caput XVII

Weapons of Individual Destruction

Nobody moved for several moments. There was certainly no urge to lean forward and set hands on the instrument revealed.

'Is that…?' Bart breathed. 'Is that the bow that killed this Osbern?' He seemed to be considering it as if worried that it might jump up and shoot him if he was rude to it.

It was certainly a fine-looking bow. Well-made and strung ready for firing. It had been covered with a cloth, but this was thrown to one side, as if someone had carelessly tossed the weapon into the box when they'd finished with it. And putting a bow away still strung was odd. Any bowman would know to unhook the string for storage; unless they were planning to use it again quite soon.

Wat also took breath and slowly shook his head.

'Awful,' Bart said. 'To think a piece of wood and some string could kill a man.'

'You need an arrow as well,' Cwen pointed out. 'Although I expect you could use just the bow if you knew what you were doing. Stab someone, strangle them, trip them up near the edge of a cliff.' She considered her options for a moment. 'Overall, I think the use of the arrow is best.'

Bart and the cart man gave her very odd looks.

She shrugged that she was only being helpful. 'Anyway,' she added, 'this isn't the bow that shot Osbern.'

Bart couldn't follow that. 'It isn't?'

'Well, it isn't the one Renweard showed us.'

'There are two?'

'Could be more than two. Could be dozens of the things.'

'Lady Gudmund doesn't allow weapons,' the cart man stated the fact, as if the bow would now helpfully disappear.

'You'd better tell that to Osbern, I'm sure he'll feel much better about being shot to death with one.'

Wat faced the cart-man. 'You say only Renweard and Lady Gudmund have keys to this box?'

'And you,' the cart man said bluntly. 'Or so it seems.'

'Yes, but I didn't shoot Osbern.'

'So you say.'

'As I was standing next to him when he took delivery of his arrow, I can't have done.'

The cart man didn't look convinced by this argument. After all, Wat was a stranger and everyone knew the sorts of things strangers could do.

'And if Lady Gudmund doesn't allow weapons?' Cwen left the question in the air.

Bart and the cart man looked at her expectantly.

She sighed. 'It would have to be Renweard?'

'Ah,' Bart got it. The cart man was still frowning.

'Of course, Lady Gudmund only says there must be no weapons,' Wat said. 'Doesn't mean she follows her own instructions.'

The cart man looked mightily offended at this suggestion.

'It's a dangerous country,' Wat went on. 'You'd have to be a little bit mad to travel the roads without some sort of protection. Locked away in a box might be best. Any Normans would not see a band carrying weapons and so wouldn't slaughter the lot of you on the spot. Any robbers on the other hand? They could be dealt with.'

'What?' Cwen was contemptuous. 'Ask the robbers if they'd

mind waiting while you find the key for your strong box, get your one bow out and start shooting?'

'You'd see them coming,' Wat retorted.

'Ah, of course. You're right. A bow in a strong box is excellent protection against all those very stupid robbers who let you know that they're on the way.' She shook her head at Wat's poor thinking.

'The point is,' Wat ignored her, 'that we have found a bow in the strong box. It's not the bow that shot Osbern, but Renweard has a key.'

'So Renweard shot Osbern?' Cwen asked.

'He's favourite at the moment.'

Wat puzzled over this while Bart and the cart man simply looked increasingly incredulous.

'Why?'

'Why?' Wat asked.

'Yes, why? Why would Renweard shoot Osbern?'

'He was about to reveal something about Lord Gudmund.'

'That would be good, surely. The Gudmunds want us to find out why he was murdered, Osbern's information could have been useful.'

Wat considered this for a moment. 'Or embarrassing?'

'Embarrassing?' Now it was Cwen's turn to be incredulous. 'You don't shoot people because they're embarrassing. If that was the way of things half the country would be dead.'

'Perhaps he was going to reveal something that Renweard did not want known.'

'Such as?'

'I don't know, do I?'

'Renweard didn't like Lord Gudmund, remember?' Cwen said.

'That's right,' Bart spoke up. 'Never did.'

The cart man seemed to be urging him to keep his peace, but he wasn't urging very hard.

'We heard he thought his Lordship was less than Lady Gudmund deserved,' Cwen encouraged some more details.

'He certainly never had a good word for him.' Bart said. 'Even I knew that and I'm about as low in the household as you can get. We'd often hear him muttering about his Lordship and what a waste he was.'

'There you are,' Cwen said to Wat. 'Renweard is more likely to murder Gudmund himself, than do Osbern because he might be embarrassing.'

'I'm trying to be helpful by thinking about what might have happened,' Wat protested, his clear implication being that Cwen wasn't helpful at all.

'In any case,' Cwen said, 'this isn't the bow that killed Osbern. And it's locked in a strong box.'

Wat did now lean over and picked the bow out of the box. He weighed it in his hands and seem impressed. Holding it at the end of his outstretched left arm, he gave the string a gentle pull with his right hand. Again he nodded appreciatively. 'Good piece of work,' he said.

'Lady Gudmund wouldn't have any rubbish,' the cart man said.

'No rubbish weapons when she's said no weapons at all, eh?' Cwen asked.

'Shame there's no way we can find out if it's been fired recently,' Wat mused.

'What?' Cwen snorted. 'Like a notch on the bow for every dead Osbern?'

'It is odd that it's kept strung and ready,' Wat said.

'So the robbers not only have to announce their arrival, but they have to wait while you string the bow, do they?' Cwen asked. 'Perhaps you can ask them to line up nicely and stand still while you shoot them?'

Wat simply looked at the bow and had nothing else to offer. 'I could ask someone to line up while I shoot them,' he muttered.

'I think we need to have a word with Renweard,' Cwen ignored him. 'I can't see Lady Gudmund as the type to kneel down outside a window and shoot Osbern.'

'We don't even know that it was him.' Wat put the bow down again, admitting that there really wasn't much to show Renweard as the killer.

'But he needs to explain why there's a nice bow locked up in a box when there aren't supposed to be any weapons at all.'

Wat nodded at this. 'He will be surprised to see us again.' He gave a mischievous smile.

. . .

For a warm afternoon, the inside of the Manor of Roger de Bully was positively frosty. The conversation was painful and awkward and Hermitage thought that Roger was doing very well to keep as silent as he did.

Using silence as a weapon was not something Hermitage had ever considered. He tried to avoid silence as much as he could, which was difficult with those monks whose vows required as much of it as possible. He always found it embarrassing and difficult.

Some of the Gudmund servants had been summoned to tend the fire and prepare food for the noon meal, and Roger seemed quite content to simply sit and watch them.

Lady Gudmund was clearly in no mood for small talk and Renweard was not going to take a lead. Young Lady

Gudmund sat demurely in her mother's shadow and once the pleasantries, which weren't actually very pleasant, were out of the way, there was nothing left to say.

Hermitage still had to raise the question of the C and the V seen at Lord Gudmund's house, but as there was no conversation of any sort, it was hard to break the topic in.

Once the origin of Bury Saint Edmunds had been dealt with, and the death of Lord Gudmund briefly considered, Roger seemed content to let the Saxons stew in a silence of their own making.

Hermitage suspected that the man was the most nervous in the room, and that any detailed conversation might give away the fact that he wasn't Norman at all. Best to let the Gudmunds draw their own conclusions.

And the silence was having its impact on the lady and her two attendants. They shifted on their seats, exchanged glances and worried looks and generally looked as uncomfortable as a Saxon should in the presence of the Norman who holds their life in his hands.

That they didn't know about Roger only made things even more awkward for Hermitage. Having the urge to speak during silence was simply part of his nature, knowing that anything he said would be wrong, was making him positively twitchy. Eventually, he could stand it no more. He stood from his chair at the table.

'I'm, er, just needing to, erm, go outside,' he said.

No one showed the slightest interest in what he needed, so he quickly made it to the door and the relief of any space that didn't have people in it. He breathed a great sigh and felt his body sag. He was really not keen on going back in again.

'Ah, Hermitage, there you are,' Cwen called as she approached with Wat and Bart.

Hermitage cast a nervous glance at the hall door, hoping that no one inside could hear.

'Keep your voice down,' he instructed. 'I told Lady Gudmund that I'd sent you home.'

'Doesn't mean we'd go though, does it?' Cwen said brightly.

'That's what I thought.'

'How's it going?' Wat asked.

'Awful.'

'Really?' Wat sounded as if awful was quite good.

'No one's talking to anyone. Roger is doing a good job of pretending to be a Norman and the Gudmunds just sit there.'

'Silence, eh?' Cwen sympathised. 'You must be suffering.'

'And Roger has told the Gudmunds that they can't dismiss me because I'm the king's servant.'

'That's good,' Cwen nodded.

'Really?' Hermitage didn't think it was good. 'And now he's said that I can investigate the death of Osbern.'

'Even better.'

'Have you found out about C and V?' Wat asked.

'I haven't had a chance to find out about anything. How can I, when no one will say a word?'

'You're the King's Investigator,' Cwen encouraged. 'Demand that they tell you what you want to know.'

Hermitage simply looked at her as if she should know that was not going to happen.

'What are you doing out here, anyway?'

'I said I needed to be excused and no one stopped me. I had to get out.'

'There you are then. When you go back you can say that you've just remembered something.'

Hermitage supposed that might work. At least his entrance should disturb the appalling peace a bit.

'And there's something else you need to find out about,' Wat said.

'Oh yes?'

'A bow.'

'The one that shot Osbern?'

'No. We found another one.'

'Another one?'

'Locked in Lady Gudmund's strong box, and only she and Renweard have the key.'

Hermitage's thoughts were sent into a spin by this. A bow? In Lady Gudmund's strong box. When the apparent instruction was that there should be no weapons. This really was very suspicious. Even Hermitage could spot that. There was one key question that had to be asked about this.

'How did you get in Lady Gudmund's strong box when only she and Renweard have the key?'

'It fell open.' Wat grinned.

'Doesn't sound very strong.'

'He helped it a bit,' Cwen explained.

Hermitage now understood what had happened. 'You broke into Lady Gudmund's strong box and found a bow.'

'There are some as might put it like that,' Wat agreed.

'Then how on earth am I going to ask the Gudmunds about it? Oh, excuse me, but I believe there's a bow locked in your strong box that no one knows about?'

'Be mysterious,' Cwen suggested.

'Mysterious?' Hermitage was starting to think that the horrible silence of the hall was better than this.

'Yes. Say that you are the King's Investigator and that this is the sort of thing King's Investigators know about.'

'And that how you know is none of their business anyway,' Wat added.

'From my judgement of Lady Gudmund's current mood, she would very much like to kill someone now. If I go in and say anything like that, it will be me.'

'You've got to ask something,' Cwen said. 'Work round to it.'

'Work round to knowing what's in a locked strong box?'

'Ask if there are any other bows about.' Cwen was getting impatient. 'You know. A bow shot Osbern and we have that. Where did it come from? Does anyone else have a bow? You know there's one, see if they lie.'

'See if they lie.'

'That's it.'

'And then what?'

'Then you'll know that they're lying and it can all go towards "aha".'

'Aha.'

'When you say "aha", you know who did it.'

Hermitage could only shake his head sadly. He felt that "aha" was still a long way off. And it wouldn't even be the "aha" for the murder that caused this whole mess in the first place. Now that was a thought.

'Do you think the person who killed Osbern could have killed Gudmund?' he asked.

'Certainly could,' Cwen agreed. 'If you've killed one person it probably makes it easier to do another one. But would they? What's the connection?'

'Murder near the Gudmunds,' Hermitage said wearily. 'It's getting worryingly common.'

'Come on Hermitage,' Wat encouraged. 'Get back in there and put the fear of God and King William up them.'

Hermitage was already well stocked with the fear of God and King William.

'C and V and bows,' Wat reminded him. 'Two very helpful topics of conversation.'

Cwen now pushed him back towards the door, which he thought was unnecessary. He gave them his resigned and reluctant shrug.

'They don't even know we've found Bart,' he said, looking at the young man.

'That's all right,' Cwen replied. 'The camp think he's dead anyway. Or that he killed Osbern. Or both.'

'Means I don't have to go back to work,' Bart said, seeming quite happy with the current situation.

'That's another thing you can ask them,' Wat said. 'What are they doing about Bart? He's either killed someone or been done himself, you'd think they'd be curious.'

'You know,' Cwen nodded. 'Investigate things.'

Hermitage supposed that there was nothing for it. He would have to go back in there and ask pertinent questions. But it wasn't easy. He felt as if he were Daniel walking into the lion's den, when the lions were all sitting around sticking thorns in one another's paws.

Caput XVIII

Do You Mind if I Ask?

No one even looked up as he re-entered the room. They all seemed lost in their silent reveries; either that or they were all so nervous of one another that they didn't know what to say.

The servants busied about the place and a large pot now hung over the main fire. Every now and again someone would throw something into it and give it a stir. Even the servants kept their peace though - although they probably did that most of the time anyway.

He did notice that wine had been distributed. The Ladies Gudmund and Renweard held goblets which they largely ignored. Roger had his own, much larger goblet, and a flagon at his feet from which he was already topping up.

Hermitage sat back at the table, deliberately kicking his chair as he did so. This did get reactions from the room, even if they were scowls of annoyance.

'Well,' he said, hoping it would be a precursor to something like a useful conversation.

Roger now looked at him hopefully, as if there were about to be some relief from this awful situation. Lady Gudmund glared at him as if he had interrupted Mass.

'C and V, eh?' he bleated rather hopelessly.

'C, V?' at least Roger was playing the game.

'Yes, here on the table.' Hermitage indicated where on the table, but the Gudmunds were showing no interest. 'The letters C and V are carved.' He paused. Nothing. 'The same letters that appear at Gotham hall, Lord Stori's family motto. Curriculum vitae, "the course of life", apparently.'

Lady Gudmund now simply sighed at this apparent idiocy.

This was enough to move Hermitage on from subjugated inferior, to mildly irritated King's Investigator. After all, this woman had approached him in the first place to find out about her husband. Now here she was treating him like dirt on her carriage wheels. He rarely felt ire at the actions of others, and he hadn't really gone to that extreme here, but it was slightly annoying.

'And I am told that these letters appear on the hall of Lord Gudmund.'

Lady Gudmund now looked as if someone was blowing her up like a pig's bladder. She seemed to be inflating as she sat there, growing bigger and more imposing with each moment.

That wasn't really the reaction Hermitage had been after; a simple "oh really", would have sufficed. Perhaps C and V had struck home.

'What do you mean?' Lady Gudmund enunciated each word as if it had its own barbed point.

'The letters, C and V,' Hermitage repeated, retreating back towards subjugation.

'What do you mean, Lord Gudmund's hall?' the lady specified her question.

'Oh, er, well...,'

'The hall is the hall of my father and his father before him,' Lady Gudmund clearly thought this was the most important issue of the moment. 'Lord Gudmund may have been my husband, but the hall is my family's.'

Hermitage supposed that made sense, after all, they had heard about Lord Gudmund marrying above himself, but it did seem to be a very touchy point for her Ladyship.

'There we are then,' Hermitage was happy to agree with whatever she wanted. 'The letters C and V are yours?,' he said.

Now Lady Gudmund looked thoroughly confused. 'What are you rambling about, monk?'

'What are you rambling about, King's Investigator,' Roger corrected.

This did nothing for Lady Gudmund's mood, but Renweard laid a cautioning hand on her arm, before she did something stupid to a Norman noble.

She forced her next words out, with obvious discomfort. 'What do the letters have to do with anything?'

'Exactly,' Hermitage was glad she was getting it now.

'Exactly, what?' Renweard spoke, perhaps before Lady Gudmund said something very regrettable.

'The letters C and V appear in three different places,' Hermitage explained. 'Gotham and here may be explicable, after all, the halls are not far apart and Stori probably visited, erm, some time ago.' He was very proud of stopping himself saying "Roger".

'But if the letters are at Gudmund, erm, Lady Gudmund's hall, it seems more than a coincidence.'

Renweard shook his head as if he agreed with Lady Gudmund's assessment of Hermitage, but wasn't going to be quite so rude about it. 'The letters C and V have nothing to do with our hall. Or the family. I've never seen them anywhere.'

'Really?'

'Yes, really. Why on earth did you think they had anything to do with us?'

'I was told,' Hermitage said, before he'd thought about what the next question was going to be.

'By whom?'

There it was.

'By whom?' He thought repeating the question might make it go away.

'That's it.'

Hermitage managed to think through his options here. He could simply say who had told him, that would be the honest approach. But it would also be an unhelpful one. It would get Bart in trouble, it would reveal that they had found the young man, and it would give the family the opportunity to repudiate the information as servants' gossip.

'I cannot say,' he managed to come up with.

'You cannot say?' Renweard found this hard to believe. 'Someone told you nonsense about some letters and you don't know who it was?'

'I know who it was,' Hermitage said. 'But I cannot say.'

Renweard only frowned more deeply at this.

'I cannot tell you,' Hermitage was explicit. 'It is confidential.'

'Confidential?' Renweard sounded as if he had never heard the word before.

'It's from the Latin confidentia.' Hermitage thought that everyone should know that.

'I know what it means,' Renweard was sounding a bit annoyed now. 'What I don't know is why you're using it.'

'He's using it,' Roger spoke quietly from his seat, 'because he doesn't want you to know who told him about the letters. It's all due to your suspicious behaviour.'

'Our what?' Lady Gudmund nearly exploded.

'Creeping about the country, using the king's servants for your own devices, getting people murdered. You're lucky my men are away or I'd have you all locked up.'

Hermitage worried that Roger really was going too far with his part. Doubtless the wine, which was still being drained and topped up with increasing regularity, was loosening his restraint.

Once again, Renweard had to hold Lady Gudmund back from doing something very rash.

'So you have never seen the letters before?' Hermitage asked, hoping to divert the hall away from a potential battle between the Gudmunds and de Bully. Roger was a lone man, even if he was a big one. He suspected that Lady Gudmund could deal with him all on her own.

'No,' Renweard confirmed. 'We have never come across the letters before. They have no significance to the Gudmund family.'

Such was the irritated disinterest in this topic that Hermitage had to conclude that Renweard was telling the truth. He considered what alternatives there were.

'Lord Gudmund himself, perhaps?'

'What about him?'

'Did he use the letters?'

'What do the letters have to do with murder?' Renweard asked in some despair. 'They're only letters, they could mean anything. Yes, for Lord Stori they say curriculum vitae, but that's not the only use for two letters, surely?'

'Of course not,' Hermitage admitted. 'But it's the coincidence. Lord Stori's hall has them. Osbern was murdered there when he was about to say something of Lord Gudmund. We then have a report that Lord Gudmund used the letters himself.'

'Excellent,' Renweard rolled his eyes.

Hermitage couldn't see what was excellent about it.

'The letters did it then.'

Now the man was spouting nonsense.

'Look, King's Investigator.' Renweard leaned forward and looked at Hermitage, but used his title in a rather disrespectful manner. 'There is a problem with Lord Gudmund using these letters for whatever mysterious purpose you are imagining.'

'And what's that?'

'He couldn't read or write.'

Hermitage saw that might be a problem. 'Neither could Lord Stori.'

'So his dead old man said. If you believe him.'

Hermitage didn't know who to believe. He did wish that people would simply tell the truth when he was investigating a murder; it would make the whole thing much less complicated.

'Let us assume,' Hermitage began. Even as he did so he thought that this was an interesting approach. He could assume all sorts of things and then follow them until he found out whether they were right or not. All his upbringing and training had told him never to assume anything, only rely on teaching and the interpretation of experts. Could it be that he was an expert? No, absolutely not. Still it had to be worth a try as he wasn't getting anywhere by any other means.

'Let us assume that Lord Gudmund used these letters, even though he could not read or write. And that you did not know anything about it. Let us further assume that Lord Stori did likewise.' Heavens above! Piling assumption upon assumption, where would this giddy dance lead?

'All right,' Renweard accepted the assumptions. 'Now what?'

Hermitage didn't know now what.

'It's suspicious,' he said.

'Oh good,' Renweard sighed. 'We can put it with the shooting of an old man then.'

'We don't know what it means yet,' Hermitage said. 'But it will all come together at the end.' He sincerely hoped that this was the case. He momentarily thought that there must come an investigation when he couldn't actually work out who did it. Either his "aha" would be wrong, or he wouldn't be able to come up with an "aha" at all. Perhaps this was it.

'If we're all still here at the end,' Renweard muttered. The implication of his tone was that they would have all got bored and gone off to do something else; or died of old age.

'We'll put the question to one side now, to see where it will fit.'

'What about the dead man?' Roger said from somewhere towards the bottom of his latest flagon of wine.

'Which one?' Renweard asked.

'Fellow with the arrow.'

'Osbern,' Hermitage said. 'We know that Osbern was shot with an arrow.'

'At least that's not an assumption.' Renweard was sounding quite weary about the whole business now.

'And we have the bow. You'd never seen it before?' Hermitage asked Renweard.

'Never. And it's quite a nice one.'

'Or the arrow?'

'Arrow's not much use without a bow.'

'But you had never seen the arrow before, either?'

'Who can tell,' Renweard sounded disinterested. 'All arrows look alike as far as I'm concerned.'

Hermitage paused for a moment to think about how to move this line of questioning on. "what about the bow in your carriage then?" seemed a bit blunt.

'There are no weapons kept about your party, in case of urgent need?'

'Absolutely not,' Lady Gudmund spoke up. 'We know better than to carry weapons in these times.' She glanced at Roger who was smiling at his wine now. Hermitage suspected it wouldn't be long before he started talking to it as well.

'We know that the Normans frown upon such things,' Renweard explained.

Hermitage acknowledged that, knowing that a Norman frown could be quite fatal.

'But there are still robbers abroad,' he said.

'Which is why we travel in numbers. Robbers would have to be pretty foolish to attack all of us at once.'

Hermitage tried to steal a glance at Renweard's hands and arms, looking for the signs Wat had suggested. As the man had long sleeves and was fiddling with his wine goblet, it was impossible to tell.

He thought he would take a chance with his next question. Assumptions and now chances, he didn't know what was coming over him. 'You use a bow yourself,' he stated the fact.

'Of course,' Renweard admitted. 'The Gudmund land is good for boar.'

That was an interesting answer; interesting and unhelpful. Hermitage had forgotten that people used bows in the normal course of life, instead of just for killing people. The signs on Renweard's hands and arms would be there, but not at all connected to the death of Osbern. Well, not necessarily connected.

Oh dear, this was not getting any easier.

'Where could the bow have come from?' he now tried.

'Where do bows usually come from?' Renweard asked dryly. 'Some sort of tree, I imagine.'

'I don't mean where do bows come from in principle, I mean where did this one come from? They are big things, hard to hide.'

'I suspect the killer brought it with them,' Renweard suggested rather contemptuously. 'It could have been someone from Gotham who had a long-standing grudge against Osbern. And if you're planning to shoot someone you probably think about taking a bow with you before you set off. You know, "now, have I got everything? Flask, staff, hat, yes. Bow, arrows? All good to go.'

'But no one knew Osbern was about to say something about Lord Gudmund,' Hermitage pointed out. 'It really would have to be a coincidence for a long-planned murder to happen at just that moment.' He was quite excited by this thought. 'Someone must have been listening to the conversation and quickly decided that Osbern had to be dealt with.'

'And they happened to have a bow with them?'

'Exactly. A bow that came from somewhere. We saw no strangers about. Cwen ran out of the hall as soon as Osbern was shot and saw no one. And you found the bow.' Hermitage was quite surprised by this thought and wondered why it hadn't occurred to him before. 'Cwen didn't find it, and she was first to the window. Where did you find it?'

'In the woods by the servants' camp. They were making a fuss because they couldn't find Bart. I went to see what was going on and this was in the trees.'

'In the trees?' Hermitage wondered what the bow was doing up in a tree.

'Amongst the trees,' Renweard corrected. 'On the ground.'

'Just lying there?'

'It wasn't doing anything else. Why, do you think it's a

magic bow that can shoot people of its own free will?'

'No.'

Renweard's annoying manner was helping Hermitage take courage and make suggestions that were really quite offensive. 'What I'm thinking is that Osbern was shot with a bow by someone with experience. Wat told me that shooting accurately at all takes some skill, never mind through a window.

'I am further thinking that while you say there are no weapons in the Gudmund entourage, one turns up out of nowhere. There are no people from Gotham about and Cwen finds no one outside the hall.

'Then you, an experienced bowman, happens to find a bow just lying in the woods.'

Renweard didn't look interested in any of this.

'And Osbern was shot just before he revealed something about Lord Gudmund, a man we know that you despise.'

'Aha,' Roger slurred the expression and dribbled some wine at the same time. 'He did it.' He pointed a wobbly finger at Renweard.

'Don't be ridiculous,' Renweard dismissed the accusation with little concern. 'If Osbern had something bad to say about Lord Gudmund, I'd have been happy to hear it.'

'Now then, Renweard,' Lady Gudmund spoke up. 'We cannot have ill spoken of Lord Gudmund. It would reflect badly on the family.'

Renweard hung his head but to Hermitage's eye looked as if he had something that he really wanted to say.

'Anyway,' Lady Gudmund continued. 'Lord Gudmund has been murdered, that's where all this began, and that's where the King's investigator,' she managed to get the words out, 'must focus his attention, not on some servant.'

'A dead servant with an arrow in him,' Hermitage pointed out, his earlier irritation now rising to out and out pique. 'An arrow that came from a bow.'

Lady Gudmund waved this away as obvious.

'Just like the bow hidden in your carriage.'

Renweard coughed and spluttered wine all down his front.

Caput XIX

Take a Bow

'There is no bow in my carriage,' Lady Gudmund was at her most imperious.

'Oh yes there is,' Hermitage said.

'There is not. I think I would have noticed a bow. And I have told you that I permit no weapons.'

Roger slurred a helpful addition. 'What you permit and what actually goes on are frequently two different things.'

'Where is this so-called bow then?' the lady demanded.

'Hidden about your carriage.'

'Hidden about my carriage? Ridiculous. And you have seen this thing?'

'Well, no, but I am assured that it is there.'

'Oh really?' Lady Gudmund clearly considered Hermitage capable of making things like this up.

'It has been discovered.'

'Discovered?' The lady now sounded more horrified that people were going through her things than that a bow was amongst them. 'Who is discovering things in my carriage.'

'Wat and Cwen,' Hermitage said with some satisfaction. He longed to add that he had told Lady Gudmund they helped with his investigations, but saying, "I told you so" was never something he did.

'You said you'd sent them home,' Lady Gudmund complained.

Yes, Hermitage had said that, hadn't he? How awkward. 'All part of the investigation,' he said, thinking that it sounded quite reasonable.

'I will not have the likes of those two going through my possessions.'

'Even if those possessions include bows, the likes of which just killed a man.' Hermitage couldn't believe how difficult he was being.

Roger now stood and wobbled about a bit on his feet. 'I say we have a look at this bow,' he burbled through a mouthful of wine.

'Quite so,' Lady Gudmund agreed. 'And we shall see that it is either a figment of this monk's imagination or...,' she paused, and her face took on a very thoughtful look; thoughtful and rather nasty.

'Or what?' Roger asked.

'Or that weaver and his girl put it there themselves.'

Hermitage didn't understand that. Why on earth would they do that? 'Why on earth would they do that?' he asked.

'Because you have not the first idea who killed the servant and you need to show that someone did it. You have picked on me.'

'Why would we pick on you?' Hermitage was completely lost now. He had realised that Lady Gudmund was a difficult woman, but this really was going too far.

'You are supposed to be the King's Investigator, and here you are in the hall of a Norman noble.' She nodded her head towards Roger, apparently acknowledging for the first time that he was entitled to some recognition. 'You need to show Lord Roger that you are worthy of the king's service so that he will report favourably upon you.'

Hermitage didn't want to be in the king's service at all. He certainly didn't want any good reports going back to the king and Roger wasn't even a proper Norman. There was very little of this he felt he could impart to Lady Gudmund.

The Lady stood and drew herself up to her full height. 'As far as I have been able to discern, you are a perfectly useless investigator.'

Well, that was a bit rude.

'I asked you find out about my husband's murder and you've achieved nothing at all.'

'But...,'

'And that was days ago. What sort of investigator can't work out a murder, for goodness sake?'

Hermitage was reasonably confident that Lady Gudmund wouldn't have experience of any other investigators by which to judge him, and in any case, finding out about a murder in a battle that happened ages ago wouldn't be straightforward for anyone.

He thought that her reaction to the mere idea that there might be a bow on her carriage somewhere was a bit extreme. Uncharitably, he thought that it was easy for her to go on the offensive when she was quite offensive to begin with.

'You come along with a couple of disgusting weavers and call yourself the King's Investigator. And you took my money.' Lady Gudmund seemed to be suggesting that she had been tricked. 'How do I know you are who you say you are at all?'

'You came to me,' Hermitage protested. 'And we didn't ask for your money, you offered it. And now you've got it back.'

He was used to standing in silence while some abbot berated him for his life's failings, but he didn't see why he had to put up it with from this woman. She was unveiling a whole new side to Hermitage that he didn't know he had. He felt a strong compulsion to prove that she had something to do with the death of Osbern, and then hand her over to William.

Better still, Le Pedvin. That'd show her.

He took a breath and calmed himself.

'What we need to do is look at the bow,' he said simply, and gestured towards the door, indicating that she could go first.

'There may well be a bow,' she grunted. 'Doesn't mean it has anything to do with me.'

'I think,' Roger slurred and got their attention. 'I think that this one here knows all about it.' He pointed a wobbly finger at Renweard.

'Knows all about what?' Lady Gudmund demanded.

'This bow thing. Soon as it was mentioned he threw up his wine.'

'The shock at the monk's impertinent suggestion. Come,' Lady Gudmund commanded. 'We shall see this bow and then be about our business. The sooner we resume our journey the better. I see no reason to loiter here with a fraudulent monk and a drunk.' And with that she swept from the hall.

The rest of them followed on, the young Lady Gudmund once again giving Hermitage an apologetic look, as if her mother was all her fault.

'Oh, hello,' Cwen said brightly as the party emerged from the hall. 'Look what we've got.' She held up the bow for all to see. 'Did you ask them about C and V, Hermitage?'

Hermitage could only give a little shrug to indicate that he had made no progress on anything. Perhaps Lady Gudmund was right and he wasn't a very good investigator. Now, if only the king could be made to appreciate the fact, he might be able to get back to being a proper monk.

'Bart?' Renweard asked as he saw the young man.

Bart dropped his head and tried to shrink from view.

Renweard frowned and considered him in uncomfortable detail.

'What's that thing?' Lady Gudmund asked with a nod of little interest.

'Called a bow,' Wat explained. 'Put it together with an arrow and you can shoot people.'

'Really.'

'It's true.' Wat assured her. 'And we found this one in your strong box.

For once, Lady Gudmund seemed lost for words. That Wat the Weaver had been through her strong box was simply too much to bear.

'But it's not the one that killed Osbern,' Cwen said.

Wat held up a finger. 'Or is it?'

'Is it?' Cwen asked.

'We've only got Renweard's word that the bow he had was found in the woods. It could well be that there were two in the box all along. Either of them could have been the murder weapon.'

Cwen nodded and smiled that this was a good thought. 'So they both belong to the Gudmunds.'

'Could be.'

'Enough!' Lady Gudmund bawled at them all and stunned them to silence.

'There was no bow in my strong box,' she stated the bald fact. 'Tell them, Renweard.'

They all looked to Renweard who didn't exactly look away but appeared to want to.

'Tell them that there were no bows in the strong box.'

'Erm,' Renweard said.

'Renweard,' Lady Gudmund used the name to get right inside his head and frighten his soul.

There were a few moments of awkward silence before Renweard broke down. 'It was only there for urgent need,' he wailed. 'I know you said no weapons, but we couldn't go traipsing all over the country without some sort of protection. We wouldn't have got it out if it wasn't desperate. We'd never have let any Normans know it was there. We wouldn't even need to have fired it. It would be enough for robbers to know that we had one. Deterrent, that was it, it was a deterrent.'

Lady Gudmund had folded her arms now, and from the look on Renweard's face this was a very bad sign indeed.

'So, you did have bows in the strong box,' Wat said. 'I thought so.' He nodded as if content to have what was only a vague theory confirmed. 'Bows just like the one that shot Osbern.'

'Why did you say you had never seen the bow before?' Hermitage asked Renweard. 'In fact, why produce it at all, when you knew they were hidden in the strong box.'

'Because that one really isn't ours.' Renweard said this with a glance to his mistress that knew he was not being believed. And probably never would be again.

'I only put one in the strong box, that one.' He nodded to the bow in Cwen's hand. 'I'm not completely stupid.' This seemed to be as much a plea to Lady Gudmund as anything. 'If the Normans caught us with a host of bows, we'd be in trouble, but one could be reasonable for anyone to carry.'

'Who else knew the bow was in the box?' Hermitage asked.

'No one. I swear it. I put it there just before we left and only I have the key to the box, apart from her Ladyship.'

'Who never opens it herself,' Cwen observed. 'Having you to do that sort of thing for her.'

'We'd never had to use it,' Renweard went on. 'And now we were on the way home. We'd get back, I'd put it away, and no one need ever know.'

'Apart from Osbern,' Wat observed.

'Who was shot with the other bow,' Renweard insisted. 'At the same time Bart disappeared.' He looked at the young man, clearly anxious that someone else should become the focus of attention as soon as possible.

'Bart who was told that he'd shot Osbern in his sleep,' Cwen said.

'That's ridiculous,' Renweard almost laughed; only almost, as if he was going to have to seek permission to ever laugh again.

'Quite. Some hooded figure told him that he'd done it and advised him to run away.'

'And you believe him, do you?' Lady Gudmund asked with some contempt.

'Good job we didn't believe you when you said you had no weapons,' Cwen replied. 'Yes, we believe him,' she went on. 'He's got no signs of ever having fired a bow in his life.'

'Well, that's excellent,' Lady Gudmund considered them all disparagingly. 'We still have a mysterious bowman who shoots people through windows and we still have a King's Investigator who has not the first clue who did it.' She gave Hermitage a personal look intended to cause distress. 'When he was standing in the room at the time. Very impressive.'

'Shot through a window while you were outside it at the time,' Cwen replied in similar vein. 'And you had a bow in your carriage. Even more impressive.'

Lady Gudmund looked as if she were ready to step forward and bite Cwen's head off.

Hermitage had an overwhelming urge to step into the middle of this fray, if only to calm it down a bit. It was true, he had no answers to offer anyone, but it was not helpful for them all to just stand there accusing one another.

He also had an urge to do no such thing and retreat quietly, leaving them to get on with it.

Without really knowing what had happened, he found himself between the Gudmunds on one side, and Wat, Cwen and Bart on the other.

Roger simply stood swaying slightly.

'People, people,' Hermitage held his hands up. He quickly dropped them again. 'There is no point simply accusing one another without evidence.'

'Evidence like a bow?' Cwen asked.

Hermitage gave her a disappointed frown and was pleased to see that she looked slightly apologetic.

'Let us assume, for the sake of argument, that the bow Renweard found is not from the strongbox of Lady Gudmund.'

There was a bit of grumbling about this from one side of the crowd, but no one actually objected. Hermitage thought that assuming things for the sake of argument sounded quite exciting.

'Let us further assume,' he said, getting a bit carried away, 'that Bart really was told by some hooded figure that he had killed Osbern.'

The grumbling was from the other side now.

'This means that we really are looking for another person. It was no one in the Gudmund party.' He nodded towards Wat and Cwen to stifle their complaints. 'And it was not Bart.' His nod went to Lady Gudmund.

'Which still means the King's Investigator doesn't know who the killer is.' Lady Gudmund pointed out, quite unnecessarily, Hermitage thought.

'But we will find out,' Hermitage said. He had no confidence that this was the case, but in the past he had always found out in the end. Frequently, it had come as a bit of a surprise, but it always came. He just had to trust that it would this time. More facts, that was what he needed. Or a confession; that would be helpful.

'We still have the question of the letters C and V,' he said.

'Why do you keep going on about that?' Lady Gudmund asked in a most unfriendly manner.

'The letters were seen,' Hermitage insisted. He looked to Bart for some more information.

Bart looked as if he would rather keep quiet, probably for the rest of his life.

'You need to say,' Cwen nudged him pretty hard.

'I saw them,' he blurted out.

'I doubt that you can read,' Renweard dismissed the report.

'I can't.' Bart sounded very proud of the fact. 'But the monk showed me the shapes carved in the table.' He pointed towards the hall so that everyone would know where the table was. 'And he said they were the same as the ones on the hall in Gotham.'

'That's right,' Hermitage confirmed. 'And where else had you seen them?'

'At home.' Bart dropped his eyes, as if waiting for the response that he was wrong.

'Where, exactly?'

'The stables,' Bart said.

'The stables?' Renweard sounded thoroughly confused. 'You saw the letters C and V in the stables?'

'Not in them. On them.'

'That's not much better.'

'They were carved above the door.'

'I have never heard anything so ridiculous in my life,' Lady Gudmund was clearly nearing the end of her tether, which she probably kept quite close most of the time. 'Letters carved in the stables.'

'They were,' Bart insisted, finding some courage. 'I didn't know what they were until the monk here pointed to them on the table.'

'And you're sure they're the same?' Hermitage checked.

Bart nodded confidently. 'Just the same. Same size, shape and in the same order.'

Lady Gudmund looked to Renweard who shook his head.

'There are no letters carved in the Gudmund stables,' Lady Gudmund informed the gathering.

Hermitage got to have another go at assumption. 'Let us, for a moment, assume that there are. That Bart is correct.'

Lady Gudmund snorted at such foolishness.

'When was the last time you checked your stables for letters?' Cwen asked.

That only got an even bigger snort.

'There is some message here,' Hermitage said. 'It is simply too much of a coincidence.'

He bowed an acknowledgement to Renweard. 'Master Renweard is right that the letters could mean anything. C and V are in common usage. They crop up in all sorts of words that erm, have, er, C and V in them.' He was getting a bit lost now. He dragged himself back to the murder in hand. 'But we find C and V on Lord Stori's hall, the one where Osbern was murdered, and we find it again at Lord Roger's. For it to turn up at Lord Gudmund's as well makes no sense, unless there is some sense to it.'

'What are you babbling about?' Lady Gudmund asked.

'It must be a sign, or a message.'

'C and V?'

'Known to those who know what it means.'

'Very helpful, I'm sure.'

'What did you say it meant?' Cwen asked.

'Curriculum vitae, the course of life.'

'Could just be a motto, as Stori said.'

'It could indeed, but then why is it on Lord Gudmund's stables?'

'He has clever horses?' Wat suggested, to groans of complaint from everyone.

'Perhaps it's that they signify those who follow the same course of life,' Hermitage suggested slowly, suddenly seeing that this might be the case and getting all enthusiastic about it.

'The one where battle is strenuously avoided?' Wat offered.

Lady Gudmund's loins were being strenuously girded for some harsh criticism.

But Wat went on. 'Lord Stori goes to Hastings to take notes instead of fighting. Then he comes back and hides in his woodpile. Lord Gudmund we are told went off to battle, but he wasn't in the big book of the dead, and Osbern said there was good reason for that. It could be that he was avoiding all the battle-like bits of the battle. Finally, we have the manor of Rempstone and Lord Roger the Norman.' He left this last comment to end itself.

'Ah, yes,' Lord Roger slurred. 'About that.'

'Yes?' Wat asked and folded his arms to wait the expected revelation.

'What in the name of the devil is going on here?'

There was no mistaking the strong Norman accent of a fighting man; one probably looking for a fight and thinking that he's found one.

The whole ensemble of arguing Saxons shrank into silence as a well-armed and well-dressed Norman soldier strode into their midst.

Caput XX

Meet Norman

The secret to putting the fear of God up Saxons in these times was very straightforward; be Norman. The man in front of them was as Norman as anyone could imagine. Saxon children, doing scary drawings of Normans in the dust of the street would have produced a man like this.

To begin with, he was simply huge; always a good start when the fear of God is required. He had to be well over six feet tall and wore all the accoutrements of battle as if they were clinging to him for their own protection. The standard Norman helmet was on his head, the sword was at his side and the daggers were close to hand.

The amount of chain mail hanging from his shoulders looked sufficient to armour a small house and he was carrying it all as if he'd forgotten he had it on.

Most soldiers discarded their battle dress when there wasn't actually a battle. This one looked like he'd wear it to bed.

The Saxons did as they were bid; they adopted the fear of God and cowered where they stood.

The lone soldier was enough to subdue a reasonably sized village, but worse was to come as his friends emerged from the path behind the manor.

These half-dozen men all smiled horribly as they saw a gathering of Saxon folk, and they drew up behind the one who was obviously their leader; he could be anybody's leader if he wanted.

They carried the produce of the hunt about them, and if there was much edible wildlife left in the woods nearby, Hermitage would be quite surprised. Two deer, numerous rabbits, pigeon and a very fearsome looking boar were thrown to the floor.

Hermitage felt that the only difference between the Saxons and the animals was that one group was dead already.

'I don't like to repeat myself,' the massive soldier informed his Saxon audience.

If he didn't like to repeat himself, they would all make sure that he didn't have to.

The Saxons looked to one another, each expecting the other to take responsibility for this situation. Most of the glances headed for Lady Gudmund. After all, she was the most noble of them, and dealing with Normans was just the sort of thing nobles were invented for.

Hermitage, Wat, Cwen and Bart stood off to one side, allowing the main force of attention to go unhindered from the Normans to the Gudmunds. Wat was trying to look uninteresting while Bart was taking very subtle steps backwards. Cwen was glaring at the Normans as she did at most Normans; despite the trouble it frequently brought.

To Hermitage's surprise it was Roger who spoke.

'I'm glad you're here,' his voice wandered around a bit.

Well, that was an interesting approach. Hermitage waited to see what the response would be. A simple clip round the ear from one of those chain mail gloves would probably take Roger's head clean off.

'Are you drunk?' the soldier asked with obvious disdain.

Perhaps he had a rule about not knocking the heads off drunks.

'Again?' the soldier added with a shake of the head.

Again? Hermitage looked to Wat and Cwen for some explanation.

'For God's sake,' the soldier complained. 'We only left you this morning. How can you have got drunk?'

They left him this morning? Hermitage's reason told him that if that was the case, this must be the real Roger de Bully after all. A real Norman noble, who really had taken over the manor and had a Norman castle built close by. He wasn't a timid Saxon hiding from attack by pretending to be Norman? That's what the situation was telling him, but he still didn't believe it.

'This is Lord Roger?' It was Wat who asked the question, the disbelief clear in his voice.

'It is,' the soldier growled at Wat.

'Roger de Bully?'

'Well, it's de Busli, actually, but he thinks de Bully frightens people more.' It sounded as if the soldier wasn't convinced of this himself.

'Really?'

'Yes, really. You got a problem with that?' It was clear that if Wat did have a problem, the gigantic Norman with all the weapons was just the man to deal with it.

'Oh no.' Wat held his hands up. 'No problem at all. De Bully, it is. I am duly frightened. It's just a bit of a surprise, that's all.'

The slight roll of the soldier's eyes indicated that he shared some of Wat's incredulity.

'He has been in his cups rather,' Wat offered lightly, obviously thinking that keeping on this Norman's good side would be for the best, plus it would be quite a long walk round to the other side.

'Cups?' the Norman snorted. 'Last time it was a bucket.' He shook his head at the slowly swaying figure of Lord Roger. 'Still,' he spoke brightly. 'Any friend of King William is a friend to us all, eh?'

The Saxons all nodded and muttered that Roger was a charming fellow, and they'd love to spend more time in his company. Perhaps have a drink with him, if there was any left.

'Which doesn't explain what you lot are doing here?' The Norman gave his attention back to the Saxons in hand. 'You,' he barked at Lady Gudmund. 'You're the best dressed. Tell me what's going on.'

Tipping her head in acknowledgement of her status, the lady explained. 'We are simply travelling back to our home south of here. We were passing by the manor and Lord Roger invited us to stop.'

'Murder,' Roger called.

Lady Gudmund winced.

'Murder?' the soldier asked, looking slightly disappointed that this might have happened without him. 'What murder? Who has been murdered?'

'A Saxon servant,' Renweard spoke up. 'At the Manor of Gotham.'

'A Saxon servant?' the soldier sounded as if he didn't understand the words. 'I thought you said murder?' he asked Roger.

'That's right.' Roger confirmed. 'Shot with a bow.' He hiccoughed. 'And an arrow.'

The soldier shook his head as if shooting Saxon servants was nothing to do with him.

'And the King's Investigator is looking into it,' Roger added. He now looked around and found a convenient tree stump to go and sit on. He made it with some difficulty and looked as if he might fall off at any moment.

'The King's Investigator?' the soldier demanded, scanning the crowd to see who owned up to this nonsense.

Hermitage very cautiously raised his hand, hoping that this would not be sufficient provocation for the soldier to chop it off.

The man took two very large steps and stood in front of Hermitage. 'You're the King's Investigator?'

Hermitage shrugged that he supposed he was.

'Brother Hermitage?' the soldier asked, which worried Hermitage no end.

'Erm, yes.'

The soldier now reached up and removed his helmet, which he held under his arm. He nodded his head once. 'It's an honour,' he said.

'Oh, erm.' Hermitage couldn't help but think this was some sort of trick.

'I am Tancred.'

'Er, hello Tancred.'

'I was in King William's camp when you dealt with the matter of Lord Umair.'[10]

'Ah, I see.'

'Very impressive.' Tancred now cast a disparaging eye over the rest of the gathering. 'And now you're doing a Saxon servant?' He obviously thought that Hermitage had let himself go rather.

'He was shot,' Hermitage pointed out.

Tancred shrugged as if people got shot all the time; which in his experience, they probably did. 'Why does the king want you to find out who killed a Saxon servant?' The implication was clear that the king didn't care who killed Saxons at all,

---

[10] *The Case of the Curious Corpse* covers Umair in unnecessary detail.

servant or not.

'Oh, no,' Hermitage started, and then saw this might finish badly. 'This is just a little local difficulty. I'm just, erm, investigating this as a, ah, favour.'

'A favour?' Tancred really was having some trouble with that word. He simply gave a look that said he didn't really understand non-fighting folk and the sorts of things they got up to.

'These two are with you then? Like for Umair.' He nodded at Wat and Cwen, who returned the compliment.

'That's right.'

'Who's he?' Tancred glared at Bart.

'Oh, he's erm, helping me with my enquiries.'

'Is he?' Tancred clearly thought that was probably slightly disgusting and best not gone into. 'They're with you, Lord Roger is with me, which just leaves this lot.' Tancred turned his attention to "this lot".

Lady Gudmund tried to look as if she was still in charge, but if she was, it was of not very much anymore.

'They probably did it then,' Tancred concluded, as if this investigation business was pretty straightforward. 'I mean, the King's Investigator isn't going to go shooting people, is he? Not if he's then got to investigate it.' He gave this a quick thought. 'Probably find out who did it quite quickly if that was the case.'

'It is a complicated matter,' Hermitage said.

'Doesn't sound very complicated; shooting Saxons.'

Hermitage really didn't know how far he should go with this Norman, or how much he should say. Despite her being a difficult woman, he didn't really want to bring Lady Gudmund's family to the attention of the Normans. Mind you, when the Normans were right in front of you, it was hard to deny them anything.

'He was shot through a window,' Wat added some detail.

'Was he?' Tancred sounded quite impressed with this. 'Big window?'

'No, quite a small one.'

The Norman nodded appreciatively. 'Crossbow?'

'No, long bow.'

'Pah,' Tancred coughed his contempt. 'One of those things? Bound to have been a Saxon then.'

'Well, we found a long bow, anyway,' Wat said.

'I suppose it's possible.' Tancred accepted the information. 'Mind you, if I wanted to shoot someone through a small window, I'd choose a crossbow.'

'Really?'

'Every time.' It sounded as if shooting people through small windows was an everyday occurrence for Tancred. 'More control, you see. Those longbows are hard things to get any accuracy with.'

'Are they?'

Tancred was clearly on a favourite subject; the means of delivering death. 'Absolutely. Get a troop of archers together and they're fine. Launch a volley into the air, very effective. But for your neat, single shot?' He shook his head as if everyone should know that a neat, single shot death was best achieved with a crossbow.

'Saxons have been using them for generations though,' Wat went on, which Hermitage thought might not be very wise. Tancred might want to stage a demonstration next. 'Not that I'm any sort of bowman, but in the right hands…,?'

'You're looking for someone with experience then,' Tancred suggested.

'Just what we thought. Find someone with the signs of a

time-served archer.'

Tancred nodded to himself. 'Marks on the hands and arms, right arm stronger than the left.'

'Exactly.'

Hermitage was pleased they all agreed on this, although he wasn't sure where it was getting them.

'Trouble is, that's most Saxons,' Wat said. 'Brought up using a bow, you end up with the skill.'

'Including some of them?' Tancred nodded towards the Gudmunds.

'I expect so,' Wat said.

'Well.' Tancred considered them and gave it careful thought. 'Just pick one.'

'Pick one?'

'Yes. Just pick one. They could have done it.'

'What if they didn't?' Hermitage was aghast at this awful idea.

'Doesn't matter.' Tancred shrugged. 'Sets an example.'

'Sets an example?' Hermitage knew exactly what sort of example it set; a very bad one.

The Saxons around Lady Gudmund were starting to look as if they'd very much like not to be an example. Several of them seemed to be considering running away as a very reasonable alternative.

'Anyway,' Tancred went on as more thoughts crossed his rugged face. 'If they can shoot a bow, what are they doing still alive anyway?'

'I beg your pardon?' Hermitage didn't think things could get any worse and here they were, getting worse.

'Yes. Why aren't they dead at Hastings? All the fighting men went there, surely? Harold gathered them.'

Tancred obviously took it for granted that every man of

fighting age would follow the call of their king. He hadn't met Stori of Gotham. 'Have you checked them?'

'Checked them?' Wat asked.

Tancred pointed at the Saxons; pointedly.

'Erm,'

'Check them,' Tancred ordered his men. 'Looking for signs of a bowman.'

The contingent of Normans smiled their horrible smiles as they advanced on the Gudmunds.

The lady and her men looked as worried as they should do. Being checked for anything by Normans was not going to be a happy experience. And if they didn't find what they were looking for they might get cross, and then the experience would get worse.

There was no question of putting up any resistance. Even Lady Gudmund had to stand aside as the Normans barged their way into the small crowd.

'There is another possibility.' Hermitage spoke before the search could get too personal.

Tancred raised an eye.

'Bart here reports that there was a man with a hood about. It's possible that he was the bowman, but he has vanished.'

The Norman frowned and looked over his men, as if searching for one in particular. 'Ascolf,' he called.

The chosen Norman stood up straight.

'Possible hooded man skulking in the woods.'

Ascolf grinned. Finding people skulking in the woods was obviously a bit of a speciality. The man drew a dagger, grinned, bent down slightly and slipped off into the undergrowth.

Hermitage reminded himself not to go skulking anywhere when Ascolf was around.

'Here's one,' one of the soldiers searching the Saxons called out. He held up a hand with Renweard still attached to the other end.

'We know about him,' Wat said. 'The Lady's servant, does a bit of hunting.'

'Could be him,' Tancred suggested, sounding slightly disappointed that they'd found their killer so quickly.

'He says not.'

'Well he would, wouldn't he?'

Hermitage shared that frustration. If killers wouldn't keep saying they hadn't done it, he could get his investigations completed much quicker.

'Put him over there.' Tancred nodded to the right. 'If you find some more, we can gather them all together and then pick one.'

It did seem that Tancred's approach to investigation centred mainly on "pick one".

The examination of the Saxons continued with no more success. One of the Normans returned to present himself to his leader. 'All soft-handed servants,' the man said. 'Doubt if any of them know which end of an arrow is pointed.'

'There we are then.' Tancred seemed very satisfied with the result. 'We don't even have to pick one, it's him.' He looked at Renweard. 'Only one man with signs of a bow. Must be him.'

'Unless the killer is our skulking man?' Hermitage suggested.

'Hm.' Tancred sounded quite interested in all this devious behaviour, as if it was the sort of thing he'd do himself, if only he had the time. 'Just take this one's money and have done with it,' he huffed, obviously concluding that a killer in the hall was better than two in the bushes.

'Take his money?' Hermitage wasn't following.

'Yes. For the murder. Take his money as the fine for killing a servant and get on. Don't really know why you're making so much fuss about this anyway. If you weren't Brother Hermitage, I'd think you'd gone soft.'

This was getting awkward and Hermitage puzzled how he was going to explain anything. Perhaps it was best not to try and let Tancred and his men go about their business. Lady Gudmund could be released to continue south and they'd just have to forget about the murder of Osbern. And all the trouble of Lord Gudmund.

'It could be connected to a wider issue.'

Tancred frowned and it was clear that Hermitage was losing him.

'Concerned with the battle at Hastings.'

That brought a smile of fond reminiscence to the Norman face.

There was nothing for it, Hermitage would have to say more. 'Concerning the lady's husband. He went to Hastings and the servant who was murdered was about to tell us something about it. Just before he was shot.'

'Tell you something about Hastings?' Tancred sounded as if he had lots of things he could tell them about Hastings; all of them nicely horrible.

'That's right. Concerning the fate of Lord Gudmund.'

Tancred's face dropped. 'Did you say Gudmund?'

'Er, yes, that's right.'

The Norman's eyes now returned to the shape of Lady Gudmund. This time they actually showed some interest. 'Is that Lady Gudmund, then?'

'It is.'

'Well, well.'

'You know her?' Hermitage thought that would be a

surprise.

'Her? No. But Lord Gudmund? I know Lord Gudmund. We all know Lord Gudmund, don't we lads?'

The lads all whooped in a very bizarre manner. The name of Lord Gudmund was clearly one of some interest to the Normans, Hermitage thought it almost sounded like entertainment. Perhaps at last they would get some useful information. It seemed odd that it should come from the Normans, but anything was better than not knowing; at least it was to Hermitage.

But as he considered what could be revealed, he began to wonder if not knowing might actually be for the best.

Caput XXI

Lords at War

$\mathfrak{S}$trangely, Lady Gudmund did not rush forward demanding to hear what this Norman had to say about her husband. Hermitage could understand that she wouldn't trust him, but if there was any information, surely it was worth hearing. Unless it was very bad information, of course.

'Do tell,' Cwen asked with naked relish. She almost sounded as if she were licking her lips. 'Is it very bad?' she asked hopefully.

Tancred was looking from one party to the other, clearly thinking about exactly what he was going to say.

Hermitage couldn't bear the suspense. 'The Lady reports that one of King Harold's nobles summoned her husband to travel to the south. But we aren't clear whether this was in time for the battle or not.'

'Oh, it was in time for the battle,' Tancred said, rather mysteriously, Hermitage thought.

'So you saw him?'

'Not close up.'

'No?'

'From a distance.'

'Ah, the deeds of battle, eh?' Hermitage had a rough idea what the deeds of battle were, and he didn't want the gory details.

'Not exactly.' It was now odd that Tancred was being reticent. He didn't strike Hermitage as the reticent sort at all; even when he was striking someone he probably wasn't reticent. Was there some information that he didn't want to impart to Lady Gudmund? Had her husband's fate involved one of the messier deeds of battle?

'Perhaps we'd better go inside,' Tancred said. He nodded to Lady Gudmund and indicated that she was welcome to lead the way.

Young Lady Gudmund and Renweard followed, with Hermitage, Wat and Cwen bringing up the rear. Bart seemed quite happy not to go into the hall with his mistress and a heavily armed Norman.

The other Normans stayed by their booty, and bent to the task of preparing it for the pot or the spit.

Roger didn't look like he was capable of moving anywhere anymore, at least not without being sick again, which it was probably best he did outside.

Once inside the hall again, they all gathered chairs and sat around the fire.

Hermitage was quite intrigued by this experience. It was usually him having to explain to all the interested parties who it was who had done what to whom. It would make a nice change to be told for once. Although knowing about Lord Gudmund would only be half the problem. There was also the question of Osbern to answer, and he doubted that Tancred would have any information about that.

'Tell me what you know,' the Norman instructed.

Well, that was a bit of a disappointment. Hermitage had been looking forward to acquiring new knowledge; it was one of his favourite things, after all. He glanced around the space and saw that everyone else was looking at him. Ah, Tancred meant tell what Hermitage knew. He supposed he was the King's Investigator and so should take the lead in matters like this.

He took a breath. 'Lady Gudmund here came to Wat's workshop in Derby, looking for me.'

Tancred held a hand up. 'Wat?'

'Yes?' Hermitage nodded to Wat, who smiled at the attention.

'Wat of Derby?' Tancred checked.

'Erm, yes,' Hermitage was cautious. 'It was Wat who helped me with Umair. And Cwen,' he added following Cwen's silent instruction.

'Wat the Weaver?' Tancred was sounding slightly worried about this, which was odd for a giant Norman covered in weapons.

'That's the one.' Hermitage tried to sound bright, but it was never a good sign when people asked about Wat with worry in their voices.

'In our travels we've found out quite a bit about this wretched country,' Tancred said.

'Ah.'

'Including lots of things about Wat the Weaver.' It was clear from Tancred's tone what sorts of things these had been. 'Does the king know what he does?'

'Did,' Wat corrected. 'I don't do it anymore.'

'Good thing too. You'd better not let William find out. He has strong views on things like that.'

Wat nodded that he would take this advice to heart.

'Anyway,' Hermitage said, wanting to get back to the tale. 'Lady Gudmund and her people came asking me to find out what had happened to her husband, Lord Gudmund. She believes that he was murdered.' He paused, sincerely hoping that Tancred would say either yes, or no at this point. Then they could all go home.

'Don't know,' Tancred said.

'Don't know?' Hermitage felt this was most unfair. The Norman had said that he knew all about Lord Gudmund, yet he didn't know whether the man had been murdered or not. Had he got them all here under false pretences?

'What else?' Tancred asked, ignoring the question and nodding that Hermitage should carry on.

'What else?'

'Yes, what else did you do? How did you end up here?'

'Ah, I see. Well, it seems that Lord Gudmund was summoned from his home to head south by a fellow called Edgulf.' He looked to Tancred to see if this name brought any recognition; nothing. 'We thought it best to go to the Gudmund home and see what we could discover. Sort of follow the trail, if you like.'

Tancred nodded that he thought this sounded like a good idea.

'Our first stop was the Manor of Gotham where we met Lord Stori.'

'Ha!' Tancred's outburst at this name did surprise Hermitage.

'You know Lord Stori, then?'

'The note taker,' Tancred said with obvious disdain.

'Er, yes.'

'Along with our Ranulph de Sauveloy.' It was clear that Tancred thought little of either of these men.

'So we understand.'

'Both of them standing around writing down the names of important people as they got killed.'

Hermitage could only nod at this. He didn't like to say anything as Tancred was obviously contemptuous of such activity.

'Despite their own sides urging them to actually step

forward and help. Pick up a sword, throw a rock, anything really. But oh no,' Tancred's voice took on a rather complaining, whining tone. 'We've got to take the note. How can anyone know what's happened if we don't have the note?' he returned to normal. 'The dead are easy to count after they've been killed. No one has to stand around and watch it happen.'

'We gather that was Lord Stori's role.'

'The role he gave himself,' Tancred spat into the fire. 'No one told him he had to take a note. Certainly not King Harold who needed all the help he could get. And he didn't even do the note himself, he had some old man carrying his book around for him.'

'Osbern,' Hermitage said. 'He was the servant who was murdered.'

'Was he?' Tancred calmed a little. 'He seemed like a good man. Kept urging his master to do something useful. Without any luck.'

'We saw the book,' Hermitage said. 'The list of the dead.'

'Yes, very useful.' Tancred clearly didn't think so.

'And this Ranulph has one for the Normans?'

'Ranulph has a book for everything,' Tancred sighed. 'And he frequently reads them back to you, whether you want him to or not.'

Hermitage yearned for some more information that was actually pertinent. 'Lord Gudmund's name was not in the book, and Osbern said that there was a very good reason for that. But before he could tell us what it was, he was shot.'

Tancred simply nodded as if this made sense to him. Hermitage could only hope that he would explain that sense to everyone else; and quite soon.

'Anything else?' the Norman asked.

Hermitage shook his head slowly. He had reasoned that Tancred didn't want to reveal anything that they shouldn't know. If he could find out what information they had, he could simply fill in gaps. There might be secrets of King William that he didn't want to let out. It was very clever; he'd have to remember this method for future investigations.

'There's the C and V,' Cwen said.

'Oh yes,' Hermitage said, thinking this would be of little interest to Tancred. 'We found the letters C and V on Lord Stori's manor. A motto, we were told; curriculum vitae, the course of life. We then found the same letters on the table here.' Hermitage nodded towards the table. 'Which could be quite reasonable as Stori must have visited.'

'Who was the lord here?' Tancred asked.

'Godric,' Wat replied. 'At least he was when I passed through some time ago.'

'Ha, Godric,' Tancred's smile was broad. 'I might have known.'

Hermitage was getting pretty desperate to know himself now. 'And then there was a report that the same letters were found at Lord Gudmund's, although Lady Gudmund and Master Renweard insist that this is not the case.'

The lady and her man confirmed this insistence with a nod.

'C and V, eh.' Tancred was now smiling to himself, and Hermitage had a strong urge to shake the man and make him talk.

'All right,' Tancred leaned forward in his chair as if he was going to tell them all some charming night-time tale.

'There was a fight,' he began, 'at Hastings.'

They all knew that. Hermitage was disappointed if this was going to be the level of revelation.

'A fight while the battle was going on.'

'There were probably quite a few,' Wat suggested.

'Ah, but this one was special. First of all, it was separate, nothing to do with Normans versus Saxons, and it was personal. There was also no risk of anyone getting killed.'

Tancred was making this sound quite intriguing. 'And who was involved, I hear you ask?'

No one had asked, but he was certainly a master story-teller.

Tancred counted them off on his fingers. 'Stori of Gotham, Godric and Lord Gudmund.'

The ladies and Renweard also leaned forward at the mention of the name.

'Why were they fighting?' Hermitage asked. This sounded out of character for Lord Stori in particular.

'That is a very good question,' Tancred replied.

Hermitage hoped it was going to get a very good answer.

'In fact, it is the key question.'

A good answer and a key one, then.

'They were fighting over the book.'

'Fighting over the book?' Hermitage could imagine fighting over a book, in fact, it was one of the very few things he could imagine fighting over. But what were three Saxon nobles doing fighting over one? Particularly when there was a battle raging around them and he knew for certain that two of them couldn't read or write.

'Or rather, they were fighting over who had the book.'

Wat posed the next question. 'You mean Gudmund and Godric also thought that Stori should forget about the book and get on with the battle?'

'Far from it,' Tancred gave little chortle. 'They were fighting over which one of them got to have it.'

'After the battle was over,' Hermitage said. He could see

that the book might be of great value. 'You mean which one of them would have the honour of retaining the book for posterity.'

'No,' Tancred said blankly. 'I mean which one of them could have the book and take the note so they wouldn't have to get involved in any real fighting. Hence the fact that there was no risk any of them were going to get injured at all. I say it was a fight, but it was more like a bunch of March hares standing on their back legs slapping at one another.'

'You saw all this?' Hermitage asked. He imagined that Tancred would have been in the thick of the fighting.

'We all saw it. My troop was trying to break through the Saxon shield wall at the time, and we all stopped to have a look. Saxons and Normans alike. It was the funniest thing we'd seen all day.'

Hermitage couldn't think that there was anything funny to see in a battle anyway. 'What happened after that?'

'King Harold barked an order that they should pull themselves together and join the battle, but that wasn't why those three were there at all.'

'But Stori ended up with the book?' Hermitage checked.

'He did. But only because he had that Osbern on his side. The old boy fought the other two off. He was pretty good, as it happens. Forty years younger and he'd have been a force to be reckoned with.'

'What happened to Godric and Gudmund?'

Tancred shrugged. 'Ran off, I imagine. It's what people who don't want to be in battle tend to do.'

'Hm,' Cwen sounded thoughtful. 'Not quite such a great leader of men after all, eh?'

Hermitage cast a sideways glance at Lady Gudmund whose face was thunder. This did not seem to fit her version of events at all; or her version of Lord Gudmund. It was still possible that someone had murdered him of course; perhaps some robbers as he was on his way home.

'The C and V,' Cwen reminded Tancred. 'You seemed to know what that meant.'

'Oh yes.' Tancred had another of his knowing little laughs. They were starting to get quite annoying. 'We had a little chat with Stori once everything was over.'

In Tancred's world, "little chats" did not sound like comfortable affairs.

'There's not many people who get to be the laughing-stock of an entire battle, so we wanted to find out more. And when Norman soldiers who have just won that battle want to find out more, they generally succeed. Not that Stori put up much resistance; or any at all come to that.'

'The C and V,' Hermitage pressed, becoming increasingly impatient with the way this whole denouement was being dragged out.

'A secret sign,' Tancred said.

'I knew it!' Hermitage couldn't help but blurt it out.

Still the Gudmund side said nothing.

'Curriculum vitae?' Hermitage asked, not seeing how that was much of a secret.

'Apparently not,' Tancred shook this head. 'It wasn't just the three of them, Stori, Gudmund and Godric. It was used as a sign up and down the land to people of a like mind. Stori said it was,' Tancred screwed up his face as he tried to recall. 'Cito venesco, that was it.'

Everyone looked to Hermitage.

'Cito venesco?' he puzzled. 'What on earth does that mean?'

'It's Latin, they said.'

'It's not very good Latin. What did Stori say it meant?'

'I disappear quickly,' Tancred reported.

'I disappear quickly?' Hermitage felt a shiver of horror at the appalling use of language. 'It should be veterascet te cito, if anything. That would be V and C.'

'Don't forget Stori couldn't read or write at all,' Cwen pointed out. 'You have to forgive him for getting his Latin wrong.'

There were some things Hermitage could never forgive.

'Why were these people using C and V anyway?' Wat asked.

'They were just letting one another know who they were,' Tancred said. 'They all shared a common understanding that there was no need for war.'

Hermitage could appreciate that. He knew that these were not peaceful times, but striving for peace at all times should be in the hearts of everyone.

'No need for war,' Tancred went on, 'because it was dangerous. Far better to simply let whoever wanted to rule the land do so. They would stand back and let the warriors do their bit, and then agree wholeheartedly with whoever won. And if any soldiers turn up looking for a fight? CV; disappear quickly.'

'What a way to live,' Cwen shook her head in disappointment.

'Preferable to dying,' Wat commented.

Hermitage considered all that Tancred had told them. It made sense, apart from the awful Latin, of course. It fitted Lord Stori's tale and his general approach to fighting off the Normans, which was not to try. It still didn't explain Osbern though.

'If all this was common knowledge,' he said, 'why would anyone want to kill Osbern? He was only going to tell us what everyone who was at the battle already knew. If we hadn't heard it that day, we'd have heard eventually.'

Wat nodded his agreement to this. 'Nothing spreads faster than a tale from a soldier who's just survived a battle.'

Tancred shrugged that he couldn't add anything to explain Osbern. 'The only one who'd want to kill him would probably be Stori himself. After all, it was Osbern who had tried to persuade Stori to fight, without success. And King William has more respect for people who tried to fight him than those who didn't.'

'Stori wasn't in his log store after the shooting,' Hermitage said. 'And he could be the hooded figure Bart reported.'

Wat wasn't convinced. 'I'm not sure that a man who wouldn't even fight in the middle of a battle would shoot anyone. Or even could shoot anyone.'

'Through a window would be easier,' Cwen suggested. 'Easier than sticking a sword in someone at close range, anyway. Particularly if you're not keen on that sort of thing.'

'We have to go back and question him,' Hermitage said. He could let Cwen take the lead on that.

He looked over to the Gudmunds, unable to resolve their original question, or even why it had been a question at all. If this tale of Lord Gudmund was true, and he had no reason to disbelieve Tancred, he could understand why the lady would rather her husband had been murdered. To be widely reported as someone who ran away from battle would not be good. And she seemed constantly concerned about the status and reputation of her family.

Perhaps she just wanted Hermitage, as King's investigator, to suggest that he had been murdered to recover some of her dignity.

A loud clatter at the door disturbed his thoughts. The

Normans probably wanted to come in and start cooking their deer.

It was Ascolf, and he had something in his hand.

'One hooded man skulking in woods,' he reported to his commander. 'And not even skulking very well.' He threw his captive into the room.

As the man fell to the floor at Tancred's feet his hood slipped from his head revealing his face.

Hermitage gaped and had not the first idea what to say. Eventually it came to him. 'Who on earth is this?'

Caput XXII

Skulker in the Woods

Hermitage looked up from the new arrival to those in the room to see if anyone could offer an identification of this fellow. No one showed any recognition, and only young Lady Gudmund appeared at all put out by the presentation of an until-recently-hooded-one; but then it was a rather startling arrival.

Lady Gudmund was her usual, implacable self and Renweard just looked on with mild interest.

Hermitage thought it would be a coincidence too far for the woods to be full of hooded figures when Bart had only just reported one.

'Who are you then?' Tancred demanded of the man, who now got himself up from the floor and gave Ascolf a hard stare.

'No one.' The fellow clearly thought his treatment was most unfair.

'No one, eh? What were you doing skulking in the woods then, master no one?'

'I wasn't skulking.'

'He was skulking,' Ascolf reported.

'There you are,' Tancred said. 'Ascolf says you were skulking, and he should know.' There was no further explanation for this interesting claim.

'I was going about my business…,' the man began.

'Skulking business,' Ascolf explained.

'Going about my business,' the new arrival insisted. 'When this one grabbed me and dragged me here. It's outrageous.'

238

He now brushed down his dark cloak and leggings.

'You do know who we are?' Tancred checked.

The man considered those in the room.

'I mean us specifically, me and Ascolf.'

'Normans,' the man reluctantly admitted.

'Normans. That's right. Well done.' Tancred's voice now turned hard and threatening. 'And if we want to drag you anywhere we like we'll do it, yes?'

The man could only give a half-hearted nod at this.

'I'll ask again, who are you?' Tancred glared as only an armed Norman could. 'And these people will testify that me asking twice makes you a very lucky man.'

'Erbold.' The man cast his eyes to the ground.

'Erbold, excellent. Now, what are you doing skulking in the woods? And don't say you weren't skulking again; it'll only annoy me.'

This Erbold obviously saw his wisest course opening up before him. 'You're Normans,' he said.

'We've covered that.'

'And there's more of you outside.'

'Correct.'

'And I'm Saxon.'

'You look like one and sound like one, so I'll take your word for it.'

'And any Saxon with a head on his shoulders takes up skulking when he sees a band of Normans.' At least this Erbold still had his spirit about him. Hermitage just hoped he'd be allowed to keep it.

'It's a bit of a coincidence, isn't it?' Tancred asked.

'What is?'

'You in a hood, skulking about in the woods when someone has only just claimed that a hooded figure was about the place.'

'I could have been seen,' Erbold explained. 'I didn't know you were here until I got close. I haven't been skulking all the time.'

'What do you think?' Tancred turned to Hermitage. 'You're the King's Investigator dealing with the murder, what should we do with him?'

'Murder?' Erbold squeaked. 'What murder?'

Tancred waved him to be quiet. 'The one you probably did. Well?' he asked Hermitage directly.

Erbold was now looking to everyone in the room, imploring them to join him in his outrage at this ridiculous suggestion.

'I suppose we get Bart in here,' Hermitage said. 'Although the figure he reported was hooded, he may be able to recognize him.'

'Good plan,' Tancred rubbed his hands. 'Ascolf, be a good fellow and go and fetch us a lanky young Saxon. Goes by the name of Bart.'

Ascolf nodded once and made for the door.

'Just fetch him,' Tancred clarified. 'No need for any persuasion.'

Ascolf looked disappointed at this, and Hermitage was about to offer to go himself, but Ascolf had already vanished.

'Master Erbold, eh?' Tancred mused. 'And what brings you to the manor of Lord Roger, just when a troop of Saxons happen to be passing by?'

Erbold was still looking very put out by the implied murder accusation; and seemed to be realising that there was more in the way of accusation than implication. 'As I said, just going about my business.'

'And what is that business?' At this question, Tancred languorously rose from his chair and wandered over to Erbold.

The Saxon quite naturally started to back off. He discovered that he was not quite far enough away when the Norman reached out and grabbed his arms.

'Oy!'

'Just checking,' Tancred drew the Saxon's sleeves up his arms. 'Everyone gets checked, it's nothing to worry about.' He examined the arms and the hands. 'Except in your case it is something to worry about.'

Erbold looked appropriately worried.

'Been a bowman for long?' Tancred asked.

Erbold wasn't put out by the question. 'All my life,' he said. 'Like most Saxons.'

'Most well to do Saxons,' Tancred corrected.

'Don't think there are any of those anymore,' Erbold mumbled miserably.

'Ha, you'd be right there. Which begs the question: what's a well to do Saxon with skill at the bow doing skulking around in the woods?'

Erbold looked as if he was getting bored with denying the skulking and wasn't going to bother anymore.

'Skulking around in the woods where someone has just been murdered with a bow.'

'What murder?' Erbold repeated, sounding suitably desperate.

Tancred looked to Hermitage.

'A fellow called Osbern was shot,' Hermitage explained as gently as he could. He thought that this Erbold may well be an innocent passer-by and was being treated most unfairly. He then tried to tell himself that he could be a killer, lying in order to get away with murder.

'And because this man was shot, you think I did it?' Erbold tried to make it sound as if this was the most unreasonable idea.

'Why not?' Tancred said. 'It could have been you, and quite frankly, we haven't got all day.'

The door opened once more, and Bart was thrust into the room by Ascolf who followed.

'I said I'd come,' Bart protested. 'There's no need to push.'

'I like pushing,' Ascolf replied. 'And shoving.'

Bart scowled at the Norman but then looked around the room at the people gathered there; all of whom seemed to be looking at him.

'What?' he protested.

'Bart.' Hermitage stood from his chair and stepped over to the young man. 'We found this fellow out in the woods.' He gestured towards Erbold. 'Well, the Normans did. Do you think it could be the hooded one who told you you killed Osbern?'

'He killed Osbern?' Erbold protested. 'Then what are you saying it's me for?'

'He says he was told he had killed the old man.'

'Seems reasonable to assume he did then,' Erbold offered.

Bart was looking confused. 'I suppose it could be him. Can you ask him to put his hood up?'

'Ask me yourself,' Erbold retorted. 'Ow,' he said as Ascolf clipped him round the back of the head and pulled his hood up.

Bart was still not sure. 'Can you ask him to say "Bart, you've done something awful", in a growly sort of voice.'

'This is ridiculous…,' Erbold began. 'Ow. Stop hitting me. Bart, you've done something awful,' he growled with very little commitment.

'Could be, I suppose,' Bart said hesitantly.

Hermitage thought that this was hardly conclusive. They

were really no farther forward.

'Near enough,' Tancred said.

'Near enough?' Hermitage didn't understand. 'What do you mean, near enough?'

'It's got to be one of them,' Tancred said, pointing first at Renweard then at Erbold. 'This one's been doing more skulking so it's more likely him.'

'That's not how it works,' Hermitage protested. 'We have to know who did it. For certain.'

'Really?' Tancred sounded rather bored with the idea. 'You can't know for certain every time. Sometimes you must come up with the most likely person and pick them.'

'Absolutely not.'

'Good Lord, how do you ever figure out who did what? It must take forever. Talk about dragging things out.'

'It takes as long as it takes.'

Tancred sighed. 'Get on with it then, we've got things to do.'

'Somewhere to be?' Cwen asked rather impudently.

'Oh, you know, country to conquer, Saxons to kill, that sort of thing.' Tancred gave her the sort of smile that advised her to be out of sight when he got back to his routine.

Hermitage considered the situation. 'Even if we identify Erbold as the man who spoke to Bart, we still don't know that he actually did the shooting.'

'What?' Tancred's frustration was evident.

'It becomes more likely, but we still don't know for certain.'

Tancred considered the room as if he were doing so for the last time. 'I've had enough of this.' He strode over to Erbold and took him by the scruff of the neck. 'This one did it. Let's take him outside and deal with him, then we can get on.' He headed for the door. 'Honestly,' he muttered as he went, 'if a

Norman had shot this wretched man, we wouldn't be having all this trouble in the first place.'

'I beg your pardon,' Hermitage said as his head started to swim. 'Could you say that again?' An idea had either popped into his head or had sprung out from where it had been hiding, prompted by Tancred's words. He wasn't yet sure how it fitted with all the other things that were in his head with it, but it seemed to be going around introducing itself.

'I said if a Norman had shot this man, we wouldn't be bothering with all this. Don't need a King's Investigator when Normans kill people; we're allowed.'

'Ooh,' Hermitage said as the ideas started to move like leaves caught in a whirlpool.

'Ooh?' Tancred repeated.

'I think he means "aha",' Cwen explained. 'Or he will do in a moment.'

Hermitage couldn't say anything else now. He didn't want to disturb the thoughts that were making their own progress towards some sort of order. He felt that if he so much as breathed, they might scatter, never to be seen again.

When he was confident that they had got themselves into a bare structure he risked a walk around the room. He needed to look at the people involved in all this to see where they fitted. The ideas were fine, but he needed faces to go with them.

He considered Lady Gudmund first and was oblivious to the pointed look she returned; probably the pointed look she gave everyone who stared at her.

Next, he moved on to Renweard and frowned deeply. He even put his tongue between his teeth as he struggled to fit the man into the picture.

Young Lady Gudmund came next and she got a short and

simple nod; he moved quickly on.

Bart and Erbold were next, followed by the Normans. Finally, he came to Wat and Cwen and the sight of them recovered some of his senses.

'Aha?' Cwen suggested.

Just one more thing. Hermitage squeezed his eyes to make it drop into place. 'Aha,' he said.

'There you are,' Cwen informed the room. 'Told you so.'

'Aha, what?' Tancred asked.

'Hermitage knows who did it.'

'I know who did it,' Tancred insisted. 'Near enough.'

'Yes, but Hermitage knows for certain. Don't you Hermitage?'

'Well..,' Hermitage could never be quite that confident, but everything seemed to fit now. And what a tale it was. Of course, he could still be wrong. There must be alternatives, but he couldn't think of one that would cover all the facts that he had.

'And?' Tancred asked, sounding increasingly impatient with all this mucking about over one dead Saxon. 'It was Erbold, right?'

Hermitage took a breath. It wasn't a deliberate action to generate anxiety or tension, he just needed to breathe, but as he did so, he noticed that everyone else in the room seemed to be saving their breath for the moment of revelation.

'Yes,' he said.

The room breathed again.

'What?' Erbold protested loudly.

'See,' Tancred repeated Cwen's words back at her. 'I told you so, and I didn't need this waste of time.'

'Or rather, no,' Hermitage added.

This did not make Tancred happy. 'What are you talking

about, yes, or rather no? Talk straight.'

'I mean, yes and no.'

'That's not much better. Did this man shoot the Saxon?' Tancred held an arm out towards Erbold.

'Yes,' Hermitage said definitively.

'Good. Erbold it is then,'

'No,' Hermitage said,

'Stop it!' Tancred ordered.

'Sorry,' Hermitage could see that he might be confusing people. He wished there was a better way of imparting his thinking than having to talk about it. Words were so inadequate, sometimes. 'This man did it..,'

'Good.'

'But he is not Erbold.'

Tancred looked as if his head was spinning and he wished it would stop. 'Who is then?'

That wasn't the question Hermitage was ready for.

'Erm, I don't know.'

Tancred now put his head in his hands and rubbed it vigorously. 'Argh,' he said.

'Who is he, Hermitage?' Cwen asked.

Ah, that was the question.

'It's Edgulf.'

Erbold was now looking as confused as Tancred. 'What did you say this monk was, King's Investigator? I assume that comes from the Latin, *vestigare,* to track? He doesn't seem very good at it.'

'Why is it Edgulf?' Wat asked this, sounding not much less puzzled than the others.

'Why?' Hermitage didn't really understand the question. 'Because he is.'

'I mean how do you know it's Edgulf?'

'I don't, directly. But Lady Gudmund does.'

Lady Gudmund's face was as blank as ever.

'I mean young Lady Gudmund. She recognised him.'

Young Lady Gudmund didn't respond to this.

Hermitage had another thought. 'I think they're betrothed.'

'Oh,' Wat's disappointment escaped his lips. 'Ow,' he said as Cwen kicked him once again.

Caput XXIII

Aha!

'She recognised him?' Cwen asked. She came over to Hermitage and seemed to take on the role of translator, helping him get his thoughts into words the others would understand.

'When he first came in, she was the only one who reacted. I noticed it at the time but thought it was just the shock of having some rough fellow thrust into the room. But the Gudmunds are excellent at not giving anything away. Lady Gudmund and Renweard didn't move an inch. It would obviously be part of the young lady's upbringing to show no reactions. But when she saw Edgulf, she could not stop herself.'

'So she recognised him. Why does that make him Edgulf? He could be anyone.'

'I thought that as well, to begin with. But why would she react to just anyone? This would have to be someone close to her. A brother, a close relative? But we know that she has none. Who else would prompt such a reaction? A betrothed.'

'It's a bit of a long shot,' Cwen didn't sound convinced.

'It is, but when you put it together with everything else, you see that it fits.'

'If we could have the everything else then?' Tancred asked. 'Quick as you like.'

'We have to go back to the beginning,' Hermitage said.

'Do we really?' Tancred didn't sound keen.

'Of course. And it starts with Lord Gudmund. He was the

one who was summoned to attend his king's battle. But when he got there, he did his best to avoid any fighting and Tancred suspects that he ran away.'

The Norman nodded his agreement.

'But then, when Tancred said that if a Norman had shot Osbern we wouldn't be investigating at all, it got me thinking.'

'That's a good thing,' Cwen explained to the room.

'Lady Gudmund knew her husband had gone off to battle, why else would Edgulf have summoned him, and the chances were that he would be killed by a Norman. Yet she came all the way to Derby to get me to look into his murder.'

'How did she know?' Cwen asked.

'Exactly. How did Lady Gudmund even suspect he'd been murdered, when all she knew was that he had left for the battle.'

'His reputation?' Wat suggested, hobbling up to the fire, rubbing his leg.

'His reputation is key,' Hermitage said. 'The C and V, albeit they were the wrong way round. And the fact that he is not well thought of by Renweard, or anyone else it seems. He must have been a dashing young man who captured the heart of a youthful Lady Gudmund, but he soon turned out to be all dash and not much else.'

'Hence an only child,' Wat said with a smirk.

Not one of the Gudmunds offered anything to that comment.

'We have Lady Gudmund, who we know was the one with the estate and the title, and Lord Gudmund, who was perhaps a wastrel and almost certainly a man of little honour. He was bringing shame upon her family and the sooner he died, the better. But there was no certainty that he would die in battle, not with a reputation for avoiding danger at all costs.'

'Being forced to go would help,' Cwen said.

'It would. The chances of being killed in battle were pretty high.'

'Unless you're not that keen on battle in the first place,' Wat suggested. 'We heard earlier about Edling and Lord Gudmund's propensity for a good plot or two. In this case it was a plot to avoid being killed, followed by running away.'

'Precisely,' Hermitage confirmed. 'So perhaps a little assistance in going to his death would be in order.'

'Edgulf,' Cwen said with breath of revelation.

'I suspect so. Renweard has already told us that he was a good man and a friend of the family. That must mean that he was a friend of Lady Gudmund's side, not her husband's.'

Renweard's mouth had dropped open and he was considering his mistress with new eyes. Hermitage was pleased to see this, it meant that her own man believed she was quite capable of organising her husband's early demise.

'We've further been told that it was Edgulf who brought news of Gudmund's death, yet we have Tancred's report that he was seen alive; probably leaving the battle as quickly as he could, along with Godric and Edling, no doubt.'

'Have to be a very good friend of the family,' Wat suggested. 'What does Lady Gudmund say, "do me a favour Edgulf, dear boy, would you mind awfully killing my husband for me"?'

Hermitage shook his head sadly. 'It could be that Edgulf thought Lord Gudmund deserved death as well. It could be that he wanted to marry young Lady Gudmund and this was his trial.'

'What?' Wat coughed. 'I have a task to prove yourself worthy of my daughter's hand; murder her father?'

Hermitage had already concluded that the whole family was pretty appalling. He wouldn't put anything past them.

Cwen was frowning now. 'Her husband's dead, just as she likes him. Her friend Edgulf did it for her, why does Lady Gudmund involve the King's Investigator?'

'That is just as we thought. She wants his death confirmed as murder, rather than death in battle, so that she can retain her estates. The position of her family seems to be the most important thing in her life. All she needed was the murder confirmed.

'Then she could plead with William that her husband did not fight and so should not have the estates confiscated. She wouldn't want Edgulf or her part in it all discovered, and as the death took place in the middle of a battle, it would be hard to accuse anyone in particular.'

'Then how could you be expected to show it was murder at all?'

'I don't know,' Hermitage said. He cast his mind back over the short period since they had met the Gudmunds. Although it was short, it was starting to feel quite long.

He looked at young Lady Gudmund and a feeling of disappointment wandered through him. 'Mistress Gudmund told me that her father was horrible and that anyone would want to kill him.'

'Charming,' Cwen gave the young woman a nasty stare.

'And I now suspect that was part of the ruse to make me look for a murderer.'

Young Lady Gudmund looked as if that had been another young Lady Gudmund altogether.

Hermitage tried to put that deception from his mind and carry on. 'We now have Tancred's word that Gudmund was leaving the battle. Perhaps we would have found the body miles away; or killed in some manner that could not possibly have happened in battle. Poison?' Hermitage liked that idea. 'I can't imagine there are many deaths in battle from poison, it would take too long.'

'So why kill Osbern?' Wat asked.

'Because he knew,' Hermitage said. 'He was at the battle. We know that he even fought Gudmund and Godric away from the book. He could have seen what happened to Lord Gudmund and was about to tell us. It wasn't just that the man was running away, it was that Edgulf had killed him.'

Wat completed the picture. 'If Edgulf was identified as the killer and was well known as a friend of the Gudmunds, it would suggest that the lady had something to do with the death of her husband. Even King William probably doesn't care for that sort of thing.'

'The sad fact is that Osbern would likely not have had a bad word about Edgulf. We know that he thought little of Stori, his own master and doubtless even less of Gudmund and Godric. He could well have wished them to their deaths. He was probably going to tell us that Gudmund was a coward who ran away, and that the good man Edgulf dealt with him. That was why he wasn't in the book. But Edgulf couldn't take that risk.'

'Has he been following us all this time then?' Cwen asked.

'That I don't know. He could have been close to the Gudmunds all along, or only just arrived in time to kill Osbern. He would have to keep himself hidden in case the Normans found him. He probably did take an active part in the battle, and it's all very well Tancred saying that King William respects those who fight against him..,'

The Norman nodded at this.

'But it doesn't stop the king executing them respectfully as well.'

Tancred seemed to accept that this could well be the case.

'But trying to say Bart did it,' Cwen sounded very disappointed at this devious behaviour.

'Edgulf had to make sure he wasn't found,' Hermitage said. 'And Bart was told to run away, rather than held for punishment.'

Cwen snorted that this was not much of an excuse.

'What now?' she said, casting a disappointed eye over the gathered Gudmunds.

Lady Gudmund gave a short snort. 'A very interesting story,' she said. 'For story it is. I can repeat it by the fireside, along with other nonsense tales.'

Hermitage was saddened by her denial. The more he had explained the possibilities, the more he had believed them. He still had to admit that they were only possibilities.

'Could it be, Brother Investigator, that this is not Edgulf but some passing unfortunate called Erbold? Is it possible that Edgulf really did bring word of my husband's death and that I came to you in all humility to search out his killer? And is there no chance that the servant Osbern was shot by some passing ne'er-do-well?'

'No,' it was Cwen who spoke. 'It could be that this is Erbold and not Edgulf,' she acknowledged. 'But it is impossible that you went anywhere with humility. You don't know the meaning of the word. And Osbern was not murdered by a stranger. He really was a humble servant who deserved better than to have his life taken from him just to protect your reputation. Which, I have to tell you, is now very poor indeed.'

Lady Gudmund gazed at Cwen with shock at such an impudent outburst.

'And the Normans are in charge now,' Cwen tipped her head towards Tancred. 'Whatever you have to say, they'll decide what to do with you.'

Tancred released a great sigh. 'I really don't care anymore.'

'Don't care?' Cwen was horrified.

'Bloody Saxons,' the Norman complained. 'If you want to wander the country killing one another it saves us the trouble.'

'What about Edgulf?'

'Is it him or is it Erbold. Your names all sound the same to me anyway.'

'You're not going to do anything?'

'Look, young lady, I've got a castle half built, I've got a Lord who spends his days drinking until he can't stand up and I've got land to distribute. That's more than enough without having to deal with squabbling locals.'

'Murdering locals,' Cwen corrected.

'Yes, them too.'

'But..,'

'What I will say is this.' Tancred looked very serious and addressed the Gudmunds directly. 'I suggest you go back to your estate, wherever it is, as quickly as possible.'

Lady Gudmund accepted this with a condescending nod.

'That will give you time to prepare to hand it over to its new Norman lord.'

Lady Gudmund looked a lot less condescending now. Somehow, Hermitage could tell that she was bursting to say something like "do you know who I am?".

'If you're in an out-of-the way spot you might be lucky and have a few weeks. More likely it will be days. King William is carving the country up pretty damn quick. If you're in the way when his liege man arrives, things will not go well.'

He smiled at the worry that was now clear in the Gudmund household.

'And,' Tancred went on, 'if this turns out to be Erbygulf, or whatever his name is, and he did fight at Hastings, he better find another country to live in altogether. Am I clear?'

There were reluctant nods that the big Norman was clear.

'Come Ascolf,' he called as he strode from the hall. 'Let's get away from these ridiculous Saxons. How they ever managed to run a country is beyond me.' He waved his man to follow. 'With any luck, Lord Roger is still conscious.'

'I don't believe it,' Cwen complained when the Normans were gone. She pointed a rude finger at Erbold/Edgulf. 'You are Edgulf, and you murdered Gudmund.'

'Oh yes?' Edgulf replied casually. 'Prove it.'

'I don't have to prove it. Hermitage knows it. He's never wrong.'

Edgulf now shrugged that it didn't really matter what was proved. 'Unfortunately, the Normans, who I think you said are in charge now, have told us to leave. We'd better do as we're told.' He moved over to young Lady Gudmund, who slipped her hand through his arm.

'You lot are rotten to the core,' Cwen said, which didn't seem to bother the Gudmunds in the slightest.

'And we seem to have the Normans permission to go on disposing of our enemies,' Edgulf said with some menace.

Wat gave a wry smile to this discussion. 'But the whole business of trying to prove that Lord Gudmund was murdered has turned out to be a complete waste of time, hasn't it? The Normans are going to come and take your land whether he died in battle, was murdered or flew away with the pixies.'

The stiffness of Lady Gudmund's features had now spread to the rest of her body.

'And you know what else I think?' Wat asked.

The Gudmunds showed no sign of having any interest in

what Wat was thinking. He told them anyway. 'I don't think Tancred has all the information.'

'I don't think he's interested in any more,' Edgulf sneered.

'There is one piece he might find enticing.'

'Oh yes, and what's that?' Edgulf was sounding supremely confident.

'The Lady Gudmund's name before she was married.'

That did bring an icy calm to the room.

'You don't know it,' Edgulf didn't sound so confident now.

'But I can have a guess.' Wat nodded mainly to himself, but Hermitage and Cwen gave him their attention. 'Based on the family pride, the importance you give yourselves and the callousness of the way murder is committed to protect that name.'

'Really?' Edgulf sounded contemptuous now, as if whatever Wat said would be wrong.

'Godwin.'

Hermitage coughed and Cwen whistled.

'Godwin?' Edgulf was trying to appear as if he had never heard the name before, but it was obvious that he had.

'As in Harold, the king. Erm, ex-king?' Cwen asked.

'That's the one. Godwin, Godwinsons, Godwyne, it'll be one of them. They're all related, and Lady Gudmund here appears to think her good name is more important than anything. Certainly more important than her own husband's life. And why else would Harold have had anything to say about Lady Gudmund's wedding plans? Unless he was a relative?'

'If Tancred thought we had some Godwin relations in here, I'd bet he'd come back like a shot,' Cwen suggested.

'Probably with a shot,' Wat said.

'And even if we were wrong, and you're not Godwins, it

probably wouldn't worry him much. Best be rid of you, just to be on the safe side.' Wat smiled at the Gudmunds. 'Don't forget, Hermitage is King William's favourite investigator; who is Tancred likely to believe?'

Edgulf's face now said that his head was thinking very hard and very quickly. He stepped over to Lady Gudmund and whispered in her ear. The lady did not look happy but gave him short nod of acquiescence.

'This is all nonsense,' Edgulf said. 'You may think what you like, but we will leave now. Hopefully never to meet again.'

'Unlikely, I'd have thought.' Wat gave the Gudmunds a light bow heavy with contempt.

With a nod of instruction, Lady Gudmund led her party towards the door.

'Oh, Lady Gudmund,' Wat called, as if he had just remembered something.

The lady did turn and grace him with a withering glance.

'Sorry, I meant young Lady Gudmund.'

The daughter of the house was just as capable of withering.

'Just a piece of advice really, although I know you probably won't take it from us.'

Hermitage could hear that Cwen was growling quietly.

The young Lady Gudmund looked as if she wouldn't take advice from Wat on how to avoid being eaten by a bear.

'It's about betrothal.'

Cwen's growl was starting to sound like a hungry bear.

'Being betrothed to a Saxon warrior probably isn't the wisest idea these days. You need to look for a Norman. Tancred might be free. Seems like a nice chap.'

Young Lady Gudmund glared at Wat with the force of the sun but did give Edgulf a sideways look that was horribly calculating.

As the family left the hall and were out of earshot, Edgulf turned back and pointed a finger at Wat.

'I did deal with Gudmund at Hastings,' he snarled. 'And I'd have done the traitor Waltheof if I'd seen him. And I can do the same to anyone.'

'Not from exile, you can't,' Wat replied with a grin.

'The way I despatched the coward Gudmund even impressed the Normans,' Edgulf went on with angry pride. 'Their Ranulph fellow said he would take a note and make sure it was reported in the histories. So watch out.' He clenched his finger into a fist now and made sure it was pointing at Wat.

'Oh, yes,' Cwen asked lightly. 'What did you do, bore him to death?'

'No. I shot him. From a very long way off.' The implication was clear that he could probably hit Wat from Spain.

Hermitage shivered as Edgulf described the result of his action.

'And I got him right in the eye.'

𝔉𝔦𝔫𝔦𝔰… 𝔦𝔰𝔥

Brother Hermitage will return in;

The **1066** via Derby

Read the opening exposition below:

The **1066** via Derby

by
Howard of Warwick

(The Superfluous Chronicles of
Brother Hermitage)

Caput I

Norman is as Norman Does

𝔄 swarm of Normans; Brother Hermitage was not at all happy with the term. He couldn't actually point to an authority on how many constituted a swarm, but he felt confident that it was more than six.

Six bees would be a nuisance, not a swarm, but six Normans were definitely more than a nuisance.

His own experience as the very reluctant King's Investigator had convinced him that even one Norman could be a nuisance, particularly if it was King William. But then he was the country's nuisance-in-chief.

When old Jeb complained to Hermitage that the Normans were swarming all over Derby these days, and gestured towards the one who was prowling along the street, the investigator exercised admirable restraint in not correcting the description. Trying to explain anything to old Jeb was considered a waste of time by almost everyone in town.

Anyway, explaining things to old Jeb was now the least of anyone's worries; the Normans had arrived. Of course, they'd been heard and seen - and felt, for some time now as they made their presence known. There was no getting away from the fact that they had conquered the country, well, the bits of it they'd got to so far.

Word from the south was that the Normans were in complete charge. King Harold was long gone, Norman nobles were springing up everywhere and if anyone had any objections, they could make them from the other side of the grave.

Word from the North was that the Normans were welcome to have a go but they'd soon be sent packing when they came up against some real opposition instead of a bunch of soft southerners. This neatly ignored the fact that most of the northern nobility had gone south with Harold and ended up quite soft themselves.

The general Norman approach, north or south, appeared to be simply taking it for granted that the whole place was theirs now, and they could do what they liked with it.

What they liked seemed to be building castles, or rather getting other people to build them. Piling up a huge mound of soil and then sticking a wooden stockade on top was all it took, but it was pretty effective in suppressing the local population. And now it was Derby's turn.

It was pretty obvious that six Normans on their own couldn't build a castle, but six fully armed and armoured Normans could get the locals to do exactly what they were told. At least the new arrivals hadn't started the building process yet, they appeared to be scouting out the land to select the most suitable spot. And the town was grateful that they were doing it from their own camp, and were not imposing themselves on the hospitality of the locals; which was not very hospitable anyway.

The town tried to carry on normally but it was hard when a Norman would suddenly appear from nowhere and just stare at you. It was clear they were assessing soil-piling up ability, so everyone did their best to look weak and infirm most of the time.

Naturally, no one had actually spoken to the Normans or asked what they were doing; that way lay doom. Even the head man had thought it best to wait until they were approached; but then that was his chosen strategy for most situations. As he often said, "never put off till tomorrow, what you can do today, ignore it altogether and it might go away." Ignoring Normans was the only sensible response, but everyone knew that it wouldn't last long.

And it was at that point that someone in the town came up with a marvellous idea; Brother Hermitage.

It had happened after mass one day, when the town gathered chatting once they'd got out of the priest's clutches. Of course, the topic of the day was the Normans and what could be done about them. With no contact between the two sides, the folk were just waiting for the horrible day when the instruction would come; start digging.

A very brief discussion on the role of the head man in all this took place. Shouldn't he be the one going to the Normans and making sure that the townsfolk were treated right? The head man seemed to think that this would only provoke more trouble and it was far better to keep their heads down.

The trail to the voicing of the marvellous idea was complex, and Hermitage was still trying to work out how it had come about several hours later.

Someone had suggested that the head man would be more use to the town if he didn't keep his head down quite so often. In fact, they were surprised that he hadn't hurt his back as he kept his head so far down most of the time.

Another had said that if the head man wouldn't do it, they needed someone who could talk to Normans.

A third pointed out that Brother Hermitage was the King's Investigator and so would be well used to dealing with them.

The final conclusion was that he could go and talk to these Normans and perhaps persuade them that the best spot for a castle was Nottingham.

Then they all agreed that this was indeed a marvellous idea.

It was even more marvellous because Hermitage was so clever. He'd run rings round the Normans and have them on their way before they knew what they were doing.

'Brother Hermitage is so smart he can turn his eyes right around and look inside his own head,' one of them said with authority.

Hermitage was about to correct this nonsense when another one raised a shout. 'Of course, that's how he does it.'

'Does what?' the first one asked, ignoring the fact that Hermitage was standing right in front of them.

'Finds out about all them murders.'

'Oh ar?'

'Yes.' The man paused for a moment to get his complex theory in order before its exposition. 'We all think things, right?'

There was nodded agreement to this proposal, although someone at the back muttered that they had their doubts about old Jeb.

'But we only think the thoughts when we have them.'

He'd lost some of the audience with this step.

'But Brother Hermitage here,' he pointed at Hermitage, more specifically at his head, 'he can turn his eyes around and look at his thoughts before he thinks them.'

Ah, now they saw the truth of it.

'That way, he can see what he's going to think before he thinks it.' The man stuck his chest out in pride at this great feat of reasoning. 'There you are.'

The others all nodded that this could well be an explanation for Hermitage's investigatory skills.

'You and I,' the man went on, seeing that his fellows were enthralled, 'we might see something and then only think

266

about it later when we get a jug of ale at the end of the day. We have to sit down and have a think and then it all comes back. Brother Hermitage can have a peek any time he wants.'

The others were all nodding now and gazing with some wonder at Hermitage's head. Perhaps if they looked in through his eyes they'd be able to see his thoughts as well.

'Seeing the thoughts of half-a-dozen Norman soldiers will be a piece of pie.'

Hermitage breathed a short-lived sigh of relief when it was pointed out that it was quite risky sending a poor monk into the Norman camp on his own.

Further arguments were that this wouldn't be a problem as Hermitage must know these Normans personally. After all, there couldn't be that many in the world, could there? And if Hermitage had met their king, the others would all recognise him, surely?

When Wat the Weaver, standing with Cwen at Hermitage's side, pointed out quite plainly that there were thousands upon thousands of Normans, the locals had another idea; he and Cwen could go along as well. The three of them did all this investigating business together, they could deal with six Normans, no problem.

Wat and Cwen just looked on blankly at this. Mass was the only time the townsfolk would have anything to do with Wat; well, anything to do with him in public. In private, quite a few of them wanted a lot to do with him, but he didn't make those old tapestries anymore, the ones that had got him his reputation for making extremely rude tapestries, so they were frequently disappointed.

And some of them blamed Hermitage for this. The influence of a monk on Wat the Weaver's subject matter was not a good thing; unless you had any shred of decency about you, which they all did, of course, but still it was a shame. Several men of the town liked to gaze upon the old works of Wat for hours at time, frequently muttering how disgusting they were.

The idea that any of them could persuade Cwen to do anything she didn't want to do was plainly ridiculous. These days, simply calling her Cwen instead of Cwen the Weaver was enough to be on the receiving end of some sharp correction. Their only hope was that she might see the sense of this plan. From the look on her face, she didn't.

The best Hermitage could do was offer to think about it.

One of the fit young men of the town, who was clearly bright enough to see himself as excellent castle-building material, said that the thinking had better be pretty rapid; the first time he was handed a spade, he would tell the Norman concerned to check with the King's Investigator, who lived just down the road.

Back at Wat's workshop once more, Hermitage fretted over the options before him. His preferred path was to have a very good think about it, preferably accompanied by appropriate research of a number of suitable texts. This research would then firmly conclude that the answer was some more research. By the time that had been completed, the original problem would be long forgotten.

Unfortunately, it was very hard to forget Normans when they were in your neighbourhood.

'It might be for the best, Hermitage,' Cwen suggested mildly.

He looked at her in some alarm.

They had taken seats in Wat's upper chamber, the one in which he conducted his business. Hermitage felt that it was also becoming the one in which murders were announced.

Too many times they had sat here before setting out to resolve some deed of evil. Talking to a few Normans couldn't be as bad as dealing with murder, but it didn't feel like it at the moment. The murders were always distant, somehow. The Normans were virtually on the doorstep.

'If they happen to find out that the King's Investigator is here, they might be disappointed that you didn't make yourself known.'

Hermitage had enough experience of disappointed Normans to know that they were best avoided.

'What if they come here to take the apprentices away for castle building?' she asked.

Wat looked quite horrified at that prospect. 'They wouldn't.'

'A room full of fit young men just sitting around all day? Who better?'

'What about my business?'

'I hate to break it to you like this,' Cwen laid a sympathetic hand on his arm, 'but the Normans don't care about your business.'

Wat shook his head at this appalling state of affairs.

'But if they do come knocking and find that King William's investigator is here, they may tread more gently.' Cwen pointed her glance at Hermitage.

Hermitage felt as if were being backed into a corner, a corner that was already full of Normans.

'And you are bound to bump into them sometime or other,' Cwen went on. 'They do keep appearing here and there. What are you going to say when they ask you who you are?'

Hermitage had thought that "just a monk" would suffice. He could see that it wouldn't, really. 'I suppose there is nothing for it,' he sighed.

'That's the spirit.' Wat was encouraging. 'And while you're there tell them all my apprentices have bad backs and can't dig. I can give you a note if you like.'

'Oh, we're going with him,' Cwen said.

Wat had an objection to this on the tip of his tongue but wisely kept it there.

'That would be marvellous,' Hermitage gave a weak smile.

'After all, the three of us are the king's investigation service, when you think about it.'

An investigation service? Hermitage thought that sounded like the most revolting idea. It was bad enough that they had to investigate murders, heaven forfend that anyone else should be made to do it.

'And there's the next murder to think about,' Wat said nonchalantly.

'Next murder?' Hermitage gave a little shriek.

'Of course. A band of Normans in a town like this? They're bound to get a bit carried away once work on the castle starts. I wouldn't be surprised to find someone turns up dead.'

'I can't investigate Normans.' Hermitage thought this would be obvious. He couldn't immediately think why it was obvious, it just was.

'You can if they kill someone.'

'But, but, they're allowed.'

'Allowed?'

Hermitage knew it wasn't quite the right word, but it was the one that sprang to mind. 'What's going to happen if I find out one of them has killed someone? King William is hardly going to punish them, is he?'

'You might be able to make them feel bad about it,' Cwen offered.

'Or simply the presence of the King's Investigator will put

them on their best behaviour,' Wat said. 'Which is another good reason for letting them know that you're here. If they think the king's man is watching them they may be less trouble.'

'Or more,' Cwen suggested. 'If they want the king to hear about what awful men they are, so that he can reward them.'

'Enough, enough.' Hermitage put his face in his hands. 'I'll go, I'll go.'

'We'll go,' Cwen stated. 'Come on Wat.'

'Do we even know where they are?' Wat sounded as if locating the Normans would be an insurmountable problem.

'Spot six Normans in a town full of Saxons?' Cwen snorted. 'I think it will be easier than you think.' She tipped her head to indicate that they would go straight away.

'Now?' Wat whined. 'It's nearly noon. Time to eat.'

'It'll go down easier if we've got the Normans out of the way.'

The reluctant party trod the rickety wooden stairs down to the front door and each took a deep breath before Cwen opened it and revealed the path before them; a path that had three men on it.

'Oh, hello,' Cwen said.

These men were not Normans, which was a great relief to Hermitage. The head man was there though, which did not bode well. And he was accompanied by two others Hermitage recognised, although he didn't know their names.

'All right, all right,' Wat said, 'we're going. We're going now. Off to the see the Normans. Satisfied?'

'Very good,' the headman acknowledge. 'But we haven't come about that. We need Brother Hermitage.' He gave a little bow.

'Me?' Hermitage asked. 'What do you want me for?' Even

as he said these words he knew perfectly well what they wanted him for. He knew perfectly well what everyone wanted him for; what people only ever wanted him for.

'Who's dead?' he asked, the resignation causing his shoulders to drop.

'See,' one of the men said. 'I told you he was clever.'

Hermitage now saw that this was the fellow with the ludicrous ideas about eyes and thoughts.

The head man was looking quite stunned at Hermitage's foresight. 'Old mother Agnes,' he said. 'How did you know?'

'Have you any idea how many people have come here asking for me without a death to report?' Hermitage asked.

The head man shook his head man head.

'None,' Hermitage sighed. 'If you've come to find me, someone is dead.' As he said this, he realised that he should have gone to the Normans as soon as he was asked. Now it was too late. This old mother Agnes, whoever she was, was dead, and it must be partly his fault. Largely his fault, actually.

'You'd better come in,' Wat said.

The three men glanced rather nervously at the workshop of Wat the Weaver, then looked around to make sure no one was watching them as they crossed the threshold.

As Hermitage followed back up the stairs to the fatal chamber, the thought did cross his mind as to why the Normans would want to kill anyone called old mother Agnes; she didn't sound like much of a threat.

Printed in Great Britain
by Amazon